SKY OF WIND

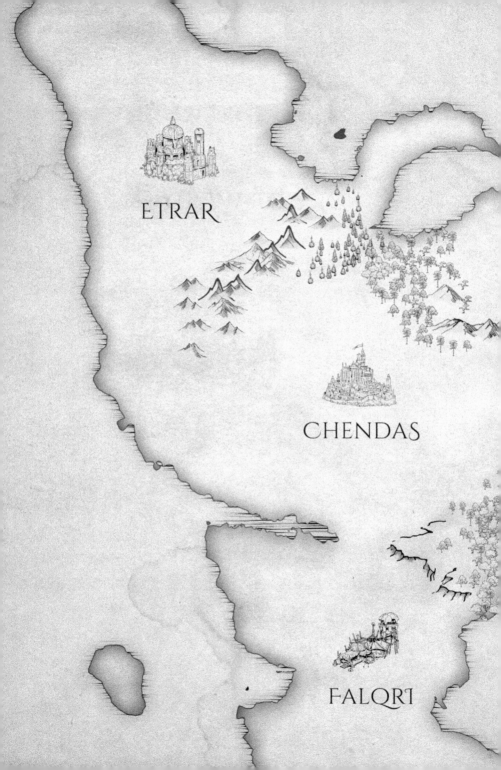

ETRAR

CHENDAS

FALQRI

ALLYS

ISELDIS

Isle of Exile

SKY OF WIND

AN EAST OF THE SUN WEST OF THE MOON ROMANCE

EMILY DEADY

Editor: Allison Erin Wright

Cover Design: Covers by Combs

ISBN: 978-1-7349865-7-0

❀ Created with Vellum

To Future Me:
(Cheekily)

*Every book might feel more difficult, but that's just because you are
striving to improve.*

Keep Going.
It's worth it.

CHAPTER 1

*P*rincess Meena snaked through the small tunnel of underbrush. Her stomach twisted with the uncomfortable feeling that had become too familiar since Erich's return. She skillfully managed to keep her purple skirt wrapped around one arm as she shuffled through the mossy dirt on her knees and elbows. Fresh leaves tugged at her hair, pulling it free from her loose braid. She didn't mind the physical discomforts, but it was harder to ignore the swirling thoughts that threatened to cloud her mind.

This was supposed to be a lighthearted distraction.

The bushes around Meena gave way to a small hollow. Sitting up on her knees, she made room for her companion to join her.

A much younger girl emerged from the tunnel and took in their surroundings as she too sat up on her knees. Celesta's eyes sparkled conspiratorially when they met Meena's.

Holding a finger to her lips, Meena gestured ahead to an opening in the leaves at the front of the hollow.

Celesta lifted her small shoulders to her ears and awkwardly tiptoed forward as quietly as she could while hunched over.

Meena quickly covered the smile that flitted to her lips. As Celesta was exceptionally good at picking up on facial expressions, Meena did not want her young friend to think she was laughing at her.

As the only girl in her family, Meena had spent many hours crawling through these same tunnels to keep up with her four older brothers. Her fondest memories included sneaking across the Iseldis castle grounds and wandering through the nearby forests and hills in search of adventures.

Huddling forward, she looked over Celesta's shoulder at the meadow down the hill below them. A short distance away, her brother Erich sat on a blanket with a basket of food.

Celesta shifted her weight. A stick cracked below her feet.

Meena jumped with a small start, glancing back at Erich. Fortunately, her brother hadn't noticed the sound, as his attention was entirely focused on the woman sitting next to him. Her red hair sparkled like fire in the dappled sunlight that broke through the leafy tree branches above them.

With a bright smile, Celesta looked up at Meena, excitement clearly painted on her face. She adored her older sister, Aizel. Meena had only known Aizel for a few days, and she was fairly certain she adored the brave magic-wielder as well.

But they were not here to admire the newly married couple. Meena reached inside a pocket tied to her waist and pulled out a small drawstring bag.

Celesta watched with wide eyes, her shoulders shaking with glee.

Meena quietly opened the bag, slipping a handful of acorns onto the mossy ground.

Celesta reached out a finger to touch them, then suddenly pulled it back. She looked up at Meena with concern on her face.

Meena's heart melted. The young girl was both precocious and timid. With a reassuring smile, Meena guided Celesta's hand back to the acorns and encouraged her to pick one up.

Meena did the same and pinched the small kernel between two fingers, holding it out between them as she wordlessly communicated the next part of their plan. Opening her hand flat, she set the acorn in the center of her palm.

Celesta copied her movements exactly, pinching her lips. Meena couldn't tell if it was in concentration or excitement.

Looking back to her own palm, Meena positioned the pointer finger and thumb of her other hand.

She carefully took aim, then flicked the acorn out of her palm. It flew with deadly precision out of the opening in the bushes and down the hill toward Erich and Aizel. Meena smirked in satisfaction as it hit the tree behind Erich with a satisfying thud.

Erich literally jumped in fright, propelling himself away from the tree and nearly landing on top of Aizel.

Meena and Celesta covered their faces as they silently snickered in laughter.

"What was that?" Erich straightened up, trying to regain his composure. "I mean, it was probably just a squirrel or woodfox—you know, not the dangerous type."

Aizel tilted her head. "I thought squirrels chatter and throw things when they are angry." Her eyes darted around the secluded clearing, looking up into the branches as though trying to find the offending woodland animal. "I didn't hear any chattering."

Meena nudged Celesta with her shoulder.

Rounding her small fingers, Celesta tried to gauge the aim of her projectile before she flicked it off her waiting hand.

The acorn flew out of the bush but landed a short distance ahead of them in the soft grass.

"I could provide some chattering, if that's what you are looking for." Erich was talking to Aizel and had not seemed to notice Celesta's acorn at all.

With a mock frown of disappointment, Meena glanced down at Celesta.

The younger girl had placed her finger in her mouth. Her eyes opened wide, and she blinked rapidly.

"Oh, no. Did that hurt?" Meena asked, gently touching Celesta's cheek. She hoped her empathetic face would convey her question.

Celesta nodded.

"I'll do the next one," Meena whispered, pointing to herself to communicate with her hands as well as her whispered words. With another careful flick, the third acorn flew into the clearing, bouncing smartly off the tree.

This time, Erich was so surprised he flipped completely around, landing in a defensive prowl with his knees on the ground.

Meena looked down to see Celesta's reaction. She seemed to have forgotten the pain in her finger and was shaking with laughter. Meena smiled. They both had needed a distraction today.

Nodding her head vigorously, Celesta pointed to the pile

of remaining acorns.

Meena raised her eyebrows in a smirk and proceeded to comply with her friend's wish.

Another acorn bounced against the tree trunk in the meadow below them.

This time, however, Erich was already alert—and other than whipping his head around, he was disappointingly stationary.

"I'll find you." His voice menacingly low, he advanced toward the offending tree, moving in the opposite direction from where Meena and Celesta remained safely hidden from view. "No one disturbs my lady!" he yelled at the imaginary squirrel.

Aizel remained seated on the blanket, her eyes scanning the meadow around her.

Meena and Celesta froze as she examined the very bushes they hid in. She must have sensed something, for her eyes remained glued in their direction.

"Begone, ruffian!" Erich called heroically up into the tree.

Celesta tapped Meena's shoulder, then quietly crawled out of hiding. As soon as she was visible, she made a motion with her hands, talking to Aizel in their voiceless language.

Meena crawled out into the open after Celesta, watching Aizel's carefully schooled reaction. Fortunately, Celesta's older sister did not make a sound or alert Erich to their presence.

Instead, Aizel nodded in response to whatever Celesta had said with her hands.

Meena could not follow what they said to each other. She had been learning the hand motions so she could communicate with Celesta, but she'd only known the girl for a few days.

Celesta reached back, motioning for Meena to take her hand.

Completely willing to follow this new direction, Meena nodded and dropped her hand into Celesta's.

Aizel was already heading up the hill toward them, quietly sprinting.

Celesta dragged Meena down to the blanket while Aizel disappeared into their previous hiding spot.

Realizing they had switched places, Meena opened her mouth in jubilant surprise and nodded gleefully at Celesta.

However, Celesta didn't catch the gleeful nod because she was busy helping herself to the small feast laid out on the blanket in front of her.

"I return to you, victorious!" Erich called as he came back from the canopy of trees. He was holding up a stick as though it were a trophy, but he drew up short and dropped his hand when his eyes registered Meena and Celesta sitting on the blanket.

"What have you done with my wife?" he cried, brandishing the stick like a sword in front of him. "Release her at once!"

Celesta, popping a handful of berries into her mouth, stood and squared her shoulders, her face fierce and smiling. Waving her arms, she rushed at Erich. The small girl attacked the grown man who was twice as tall as she was, but Erich—good-natured as always—fell to the ground under the weight of her assault.

"Tell Aizel that her name was on my dying breath." He sighed dramatically and flopped his head to the side.

Celesta spun around to Meena, gleeful victory written all over her face. Meena stood, throwing her arms in the air.

"We are victorious!" she shouted, sharing her own jubilation through her movement.

Celesta ran toward her, giggling, and they grasped hands as they danced through the grass.

Aizel rushed out of the bushes, feigning shock. "Oh, no!" she cried. "Whatever happened to my dear Erich?" She rushed to his side, but her hands were moving through the air, translating her words to Celesta. Dropping down on one knee, she briefly examined Erich's face. "Only the greatest warrior could have felled such a knight so strong as this."

Erich tried to remain playfully dead, but Meena didn't miss the grin that flickered across his face.

Watching their lighthearted interaction brought an intense joy to Meena's chest. Outside the castle's walls, her world might be falling apart, but inside, her family was still the most important thing she had ever known. Between Celesta's gleeful dancing and the adoring look that Aizel and Erich openly shared, Meena thought she might burst with joy. She could face anything because she would always have this to return home to.

Celesta clapped sharply, bringing all eyes back to her as she spoke with her hands to Aizel.

"True love's kiss?" Aizel responded, both vocally and non-vocally. "You want me to try true love's kiss on this brave knight and see if he comes back to us?"

Celesta nodded eagerly.

"How do you even know about true love's kiss?" Aizel asked, eyes narrowing. "Never mind," she quickly added, turning back to Erich. "Only one thing is more powerful than the strength of a knight," Aizel said, somehow both dramatically and softly at the same time. "And that is me!"

Meena knew the entire thing was a jest, but she found

herself watching the playful exchange with as much rapture and attention as Celesta.

"Come back to me, brave warrior!" Aizel leaned down and placed a light kiss on Erich's nose.

Celesta stilled.

Nothing happened.

Aizel tapped her chin. "I thought that would work." She leaned down and placed another kiss on his forehead. This time, she held the kiss for a few seconds. "That one ought to be powerful enough."

Celesta narrowed her eyes, and Meena found herself doing the same.

Nothing happened.

Clapping again to gain Aizel's attention, Celesta shook her head. She pointed to her own mouth.

"I do not think that will work," Aizel responded, placing her hands on her hips.

Celesta copied her actions, placing her hands on her own hips and stomping her foot in addition.

"Very well. I'll try it. But don't blame me if it fails. You were the one to attack him, after all." Leaning down, Aizel gently brought her lips to touch Erich's.

For a moment, Meena felt as though the playacting were real. These two were only a few seasons older than she, but they seemed to have found a solid rock in each other despite the storms they had already endured.

Then, just as Aizel started to stiffen so she could sit back up, Erich threw his arms around her and pulled her on top of him.

"I'm cured!" he cried, tickling her as he rolled her onto the grass so he could stand up. "I found the one more powerful than I!"

Aizel was naturally translating his words with her hands.

Celesta jumped up and down again, pointing to herself.

"Exactly," Erich replied, leaning forward and scooping her off the ground. "You are the strongest of them all." He spun Celesta through the air.

Meena felt her chest fill with happiness. Her brother had always been her most mischievous friend, and she loved to see him so happy.

When he dropped Celesta safely back onto the mossy grass, the young girl reached down into the moss at her feet and grabbed something. Placing her hand behind her back, she tiptoed to Meena with a grin on her face.

The girl didn't need to be secretive now that Erich had turned his focus back to Aizel, but Meena didn't need to point that out to her fellow conspirator.

Angling her body away from the kissing couple, Celesta slowly opened her tight fist, holding out its contents to Meena. It was a tiny acorn, likely the same one they had bounced off the tree moments before.

Meena crouched so her face was level with the shorter girl's and took Celesta's outstretched hand in her own. With a grin, she wrapped Celesta's fingers back around the acorn and guided her hand to place the small kernel in the pocket of her dress.

Letting the happiness inside her flow out, Meena leaned forward and dropped a light kiss on Celesta's upturned nose. The girl was probably too old for that kind of endearment, but Meena could think of no other way to easily communicate her affection and joy at practically having a younger sister. Celesta was family now, and Meena would never let anyone say otherwise.

The younger girl scrunched up her nose and threw her

arms around Meena's neck. For someone so small and scrawny, Celesta had an impressive grip.

Meena gladly returned the wholehearted hug. "You are the best partner in crime I've ever had." The words poured from her lips before she remembered Celesta would not be able to hear them.

She must have sensed Meena's movement, for Celesta leaned back out of the hug, training her eyes to Meena's lips.

Meena repeated the words, using her hands to emphasize as much of the sentiment as she could think to do quickly.

Celesta appeared to have understood. She patted the acorn in her pocket and attempted to wink—which resulted in both her eyes quickly squeezing shut.

Meena winked back.

"What are you two cyphers conspiring about?" Erich called, bringing Meena's attention back to the small castle glade. "Want to enjoy this feast with us?"

Grabbing Celesta's hand, Meena shook her head. Erich and Aizel had only been married for a handful of days and had not had much time alone yet. She'd only meant to jest with them for a moment before leaving them in peace. "We have more important things to do. Secrets and adventures and such."

Erich waved them away with a laugh.

Not quite ready to leave, Meena narrowed her eyes and pointed to the basket of food. "But we will demand a tax of your very finest feast to sustain us on our adventures."

"Of course," Aizel responded.

Moments later, Meena and Celesta crawled back into the bushy tunnel, happily munching on two small meat pies.

CHAPTER 2

*S*ol tilted his head back, gulping down the refreshing liquid from the soft waterskin. He hadn't slaked his thirst since midday. The merciless sun had been a constant companion as he'd traveled on foot.

Though the waterskin was barely half full, Sol resisted his desire to empty its contents. The older man standing next to him was also thirsty, and the soldier standing over them did not look patient.

Five other Quotidian soldiers were setting up camp for the night in the small glade they'd found off the main road. The soldiers were dressed like woodsmen to hide their true purpose from passing travelers. Standing under the guard's grim stare, Sol thought the cruelty in his eyes was a far cry from the man's disguise. Perhaps all Quotidian men had the same shallow look.

Sol, too, was dressed as a woodsman, but he was no soldier. The cowl around his neck not only increased the effects of the sun, it also hid the small gemstone tied snuggly around his throat. The soldiers knew it was there, of course. They had placed it on him, and they wanted it to remain out of sight.

What the soldiers didn't know was that the gemstone around his neck was a counterfeit.

With a strength of will he prided himself on, Sol swallowed and passed the remaining water to his fellow prisoner.

Neven took the waterskin and quickly raised it to his lips. Just as the first drops of water spilled from the spout, however, the soldier standing guard over them snatched it from his hands.

Sol curled his hands into fists as his clenched jaw pressed forward. Literally biting back his tongue, he forced himself to hold in the curses he wished to spew. Six weeks of self-control had made his tongue rather raw, but the pain reminded him to stay still despite his tense body.

Tipping the waterskin upside down, the soldier let the remaining liquid pour onto the mossy ground at their feet. "Just thought you might want a taste of what's to come." His face held a smile, but it was not one of happiness.

"A parched throat?" Neven spat.

Sol tilted his face forward to hide his hatred and disdain from the soldier. Their captors enjoyed tormenting them, especially when Neven or Sol responded with emotion. At the moment, Neven was giving the man exactly what he wanted.

The soldier twisted the waterskin, wringing the last few drops of water from it. "Squeezed. Drained. Depleted." He forced another drop out. "The mages in Chendas will eke out every drop of magic in your carcass, day after day." The soldier dropped the empty waterskin at his feet.

Neven made the motion of spitting at the soldier's feet, but his mouth was too dry to complete his defiant action.

A light breeze fluttered through the forest around Sol, and he bristled his shoulders as it tickled his neck. A strong desire spiraled through his core. He breathed in deeply, smelling the fresh scent of the wind as he inhaled it. His throat longed to open, to release the soothing vibration of a powerful song. He could bend the wind to his submission and use it to distract the soldiers while he and Neven escaped into the forest.

He was a hated stranger in an unknown land. His time was near. He forced his body to remain still despite the pulsing rage that pounded from his feet to his fists.

The other soldiers laughed at the guard's cleverness. Neven's tormenter turned to join them, shoulders lifted in pride.

Sol turned away from their glee in disgust, refocusing his attention on the older man beside him.

Neven looked drained already, and they hadn't even arrived at their destination.

Sol wanted to kick himself. The water had eased the burning in his throat, but he would have survived the night without it. He should have passed the waterskin to his elder immediately, before their Quotidian captors had thought up another way to demonstrate their power.

Neven dropped to the ground.

Sol sat down as well, easing the tension in his legs. He had no words of comfort for the older man, and even if he had, he would not have been able to utter them. The gem tied at his throat was designed to silence him, cutting off his ability to speak and thereby rendering his magic inaccessible.

He'd never met Neven before they'd both been taken

from the island of Istroya. Their shared plight had brought them together, but the shame of their situation also kept them apart. Not that Sol had tried particularly hard to connect with his fellow Majis.

Friends were a risk Sol couldn't afford.

One of the other soldiers left the fireside, carrying a long length of thin chain. The man's pale skin and trimmed hair looked out of place with his ragged woodcutter's disguise. He dropped one end of the chain to the ground and began to walk in a loop around Sol and Neven while intoning a high chant. The melody was deceptively pleasant, each note rising and falling only a few steps apart from the next, keeping the song in a high register.

Sol braced himself. He had become well acquainted with this ritual. At any moment, the mage would unpredictably drop his cadence to a dissonant set of notes.

The mage kept his melody pleasant as he finished circling the two prisoners. He reconnected the ends of the chain to create an unbroken loop around them.

Sol braced himself.

The mage's song dropped from his higher-pitched head voice to a dissonant note deep in his chest.

As the melody became unpredictable and sporadic, Sol felt his mind slip into panic. A burning emptiness seeped into his lungs, and he struggled to draw in a breath.

The mage continued to sing, his voice slipping effortlessly between melody and dissonance as though he was replying to his own song, intent on tearing it apart.

Sol tried to breathe. He tried to ignore the sounds that washed over his body and seeped into his mind. No matter how hard he fought, the burning in his lungs only increased.

The mage began to move his hands, pinching the air in front of Sol and pulling it away from him.

Sol felt the air drain from his lungs as though the mage had literally pulled it out of him. His body froze, immobile under an unseen weight. His mind panicked further as his body refused to respond to his directives. His chest began to tremble from the lack of air, and he reminded himself that he would not actually die. This was a magical assault, not a physical one.

The mage continued, his quiet voice softly humming.

The burning inside Sol's chest spread out toward his frozen arms and legs. He tried to imagine himself breathing, tried to ignore the pain. This would be over soon. As the burning continued, he felt the energy leave his body. That small reserve of self-control and hope disappeared as the mage drew it out of him.

Sol tightened his throat. His body screamed at him to sob in despair and shout his pain. Sol refused to give them the satisfaction of hearing him crumble to their torment.

More importantly, he could not let them know the gem around his neck was a fake.

Though it felt like hours, Sol knew that only a few moments had passed. Using the only bit of remaining strength he had left, he lowered his eyes to the chain at his feet. The gems embedded in the metal strand had begun to glow. That was a good sign. It would be over soon.

After a few more moments, the mage dropped his hands and abruptly stopped the song.

Released from the spell, Sol felt his whole body sag toward the ground. He tried to fight the instinct, but his muscles were too sore to hold him up. He fell to his knees, gasping in air as bright flashes of light seemed to pop in the corner of his vision.

While his lungs were once again filled with air, Sol still felt empty inside.

Drained.

Squeezed.

The mage examined the chain. "Fully charged in record time," he muttered to himself. "They will be pleased with this one."

"They'll never know me." Sol spoke the words soundlessly, still treasuring every breath.

The mage had already returned to the fire with the other soldiers.

Sol stretched his hand forward, moving it slowly to reach over the chain on the ground. Just as his fingertips hovered over the chain, an intense burning sensation spread up his arm and into his chest. It was the same pain he had felt moments earlier as the mage drained his magic, only now it was attacking him from the outside rather than emanating from his core. Barely containing the yelp that formed in his throat, he yanked his hand back to the relative safety of his prison.

The chain had created an invisible barrier around him, using his own magic to imprison him.

Sol clenched his fist, gritting his teeth as the burning pain slowly dissipated.

He was not broken.

He would not fall to their games.

His body felt weak and empty, but he clung to each breath he took. They were playing *his* game.

Tonight was the last night.

Letting his muscles relax in his seated position, Sol closed his eyes. If he blocked the light of the small campfire, his vision would better adjust to the growing darkness in the forest behind him. He pretended to relax into sleep, but his ears remained alert, listening to every crackle of flame and rustle of leaves.

An owl hooted in the distance. Once. Twice.

Sol held his breath, waiting for the agreed-upon signal.

Only silence.

He exhaled through his nose. It was just an owl.

A cool wind wrapped around his face, soothing his over-heated body. Sol breathed in the scent of the fresh forest around him, willing his body to rest but refusing to let his mind relax into sleep.

Eventually, the harsh sound of the boasting voices around the campfire faded as the soldiers drifted off to sleep.

The soft crunch of coals and light crackle of new flames told Sol that a fresh log had been thrown onto the fire. At least one Quotidian remained awake and on guard.

An owl hooted again. Once. Twice.

Sol inhaled.

A scream sounded from the main road, a small distance from the other side of the fire.

It was time.

Sol kept his face trained on the ground even though every muscle in his body was ready to spring into action.

From beneath his half-closed eyelids, he watched the silhouette of the soldier guarding the fire. The Quotidian man straightened his back and swiveled his head, peering out into the darkness around him.

"Lox," the soldier whispered, kicking a sleeping soldier on the ground at his feet. "Did you hear that?"

The sleeping soldier grunted.

Another scream sounded from the direction of the road, out of sight. "Give that back!" This time, the voice was very human, very feminine, and very distressed.

The guarding soldier kicked his sleeping comrade loud enough that Sol could hear the impact. "Something's happening on the main road!"

The sounds of movement told Sol that most of the party had been awakened from slumber.

Sol immediately used the auditory distraction to start a slight hum in his throat. Slowly, he released the large breath he'd been holding, stringing together a low melody that was as familiar to him as his childhood.

A soft wind ruffled the loose curls behind his ear, tickling his neck. It wrapped around his body, cooling the heat of his muscles, and spiraled down toward the ground. The leaves around the chain rustled lightly as the wind circled around it.

A third scream sounded.

"Let's go see what's happening," one of the soldiers said. Sol heard the crisp sound of metal sliding from a sheath.

Sol slowed the pace of his song. He did not want the sound of the leaves to attract attention. Using a small motion of his hands, he directed the wind back into the forest behind him.

He tried to focus on the calming presence of the lightly dancing air, but his ears could not ignore the conversation still taking place at the fireside.

"It could be a trap." That was the voice of the mage.

"Or it could be an opportunity to see that the king's justice is done."

Sol wasn't sure what the speaking soldier meant by

justice, but he had a feeling they would disagree on the topic if they ever discussed it together.

As if a Quotidian soldier could have any concept of justice. Sol could not even jest about having such a conversation. The Quotidian taskers he'd known on Istroya would not even be capable of entering into a dialogue. It was better to remain silent.

As his thoughts swirled in growing anger, the wind he controlled with his magic increased its pace, spinning around him with a greater intensity. Sol pushed back against the resentment filling his chest. He needed to slow the pace of the wind before it grew out of his control and someone noticed. But the more he fought against the growing rage, the more it pushed back against him.

"Go do your justice. I'll remain with the prisoners." That was the mage again.

Sol stopped humming, forcing himself to take a few deep breaths. This moment wasn't about revenge. It was about getting free. It was about breaking away so he could re-establish justice. Keeping his mind focused on the active thoughts, he waited for the sound of the soldiers tramping away from the fire to cover his next few moments of humming.

The light glow of the gem at his feet flickered and went out.

Sol smiled in the darkness. The plan was working exactly as intended. He'd hoped a simple soldier would have remained with them instead of the mage, but at least they had argued long enough for him to drain the binding chain of its chaos magic.

Reaching out with his hand, he crossed the invisible barrier immediately above the chain. He flinched as a small spark crackled against his fingertip. No pain crawled up his arm, and the tingling sensation disappeared immediately. The small crackle sounded deafening in the quiet glade.

The mage remained focused on the departing soldiers.

Sol repositioned his feet so he was crouching over them instead of sitting on top of them, ready to spring up and move.

He'd done it. He'd freed himself. Almost.

The mage glanced back at the prisoners.

Sol froze in place, slumping his shoulders to appear as sullen as possible. He dropped closer to the ground so his active position would not be noticed.

The sound of a scuffle from the road drew the mage's attention away from Sol. He turned back toward the fire and stared toward the road.

Sol heard the dull thud of metal striking a wooden implement, perhaps a shield or staff.

Another scream sounded, this time significantly lower in pitch, but not in desperation. "Lox!"

"How many are there?" another soldier called.

"I can't tell—it's too dark."

"Where is the woman?"

Sol's grim smile returned as he noted the panic in their gruff voices.

"Curses," the mage muttered. He immediately released a low hum in his throat. A small orb of light appeared between his outstretched hands. With a gentle motion, he sent it into the forest toward the road. It shed light on everything it passed.

Taking advantage of their captors' distraction, Sol turned toward Neven.

The older man had awoken at some point during the

quickly escalating events, and his wide eyes reflected the flickering flames of the fire.

Sol didn't have time to explain. He gave the man a quick nod before dropping to his side and painlessly rolling over the chain barrier. Without waiting to see if Neven had followed him, Sol dove into the undergrowth of the dark forest as quietly as he could.

Once he was safely behind a thick tree trunk, he rolled back up to a standing position, leveraging his weight so that his feet sank into the soft forest floor. Istroya had been mainly covered in sand, making soundless movement an easy feat. The mossy ground on the forest floor, however, was lush with new silverreign growth, and Sol had been learning how to move silently over the new terrain during their trip through the mainland.

A branch cracked behind him. Neven had followed him, not having known to practice his stealth prior to this escape.

Sol's body momentarily tensed. Neven had been one of the unfortunate ones chosen by the Quotidian. Sol, too, had been chosen—but he had carefully concocted a plan to *be* chosen.

While he and Neven had never shared a word, Sol knew that Neven could be trusted. What he didn't know was whether he could trust Neven's already exhausted body to make the escape.

"Return!" the mage yelled. "It was a trap."

They'd been found out.

Released from the necessity for silence, Sol dashed into the forest. His eyes could make out the black shadow of the tree trunks against the hazy gray of the bushes and undergrowth. Hopefully, that would give him an advantage over the mage.

A small orb of light shot over his shoulder, momentarily blinding his vision as it pushed into the forest around him. It might have revealed his location to the mage, but it also gave him a clearer view of the forest in front of him.

With the benefit of light, he quickened his pace. He didn't have the luxury of glancing behind him, but the sound of heavy footfalls told him Neven was right behind him.

"Assemble!" The voice of the mage sounded distant over the pounding in Sol's ears. With any luck, they'd gotten enough of a start to stay ahead.

He followed the glowing orb for a few more moments before it dissipated. The mage must not have created it to last long.

Suddenly, a familiar burn blossomed in his lungs, and his chest began to tighten. Sol skidded to a halt. Before his lungs emptied of air, he forced a small vibration through his throat. The motion immediately began to ease the grip on his lungs and poured more voice into his own song to combat the mage's magic.

Now that he had stopped running, he could hear the mage once again singing in dissonant tones.

This time, however, Sol didn't have to hide his voice. He could fight back.

He intoned a melody that flowed through him, tingling out to his toes and fingertips and releasing his body from the mage's painful hold. Closing his eyes for a moment, he focused as much of his own magic as he could into his protective spell.

He felt empty. The mage had already drained him of his magic store so recently.

His throat, tickling from the vibration of his song,

clenched involuntarily. He stopped to cough, his magic reserve empty.

Hoping his protective spell would last for a few minutes, Sol pressed off from his back foot to continue his escape.

A strangled inhale from behind stopped him.

Neven.

The older man was standing some steps behind Sol, his head thrown back and his hands clenched. The mage was draining his power as well.

For a fraction of a second, Sol considered leaving the other Majis to his fate. The mage was occupied and the soldiers not yet returned. With a few more moments, he could escape deep enough into the forest to evade detection. She was supposed to meet him and show him an ideal hiding spot.

This plan was too important to risk.

The lives of his people were at stake.

Neven was his people.

Ignoring the muscles in his body that begged to carry him to safety, Sol dashed back to Neven.

He didn't have any more magic to release the man with. He would have to defeat the mage without it.

"Resist, Neven," he called, keeping his voice low. "Don't let them take what little you have left."

A soothing breeze rustled across Sol's overheated face.

The wind.

Grabbing his friend by the shoulders, Sol closed his eyes, remembering the feeling moments prior when he'd asked the wind to wrap around him and softly carry away the magic embedded in the stones.

With the wind around his face once more, he exhaled, letting the air run out of him in the smallest, faintest sigh.

The wind had dissipated his magic earlier—perhaps it could bring some of it back?

His barely perceptible sigh disappeared in the air around him. He could feel the slightest energy vibrate from his throat down his underarm and through his hands, which still rested on Neven's shoulder.

Neven's muscles were tight as his body tensed under the onslaught of the mage's chaos magic.

The wind gently wrapped around Sol's ear again, tickling his cheek, then disappeared.

He could hear the mage intoning his dissonant chant from the edge of the forest a short distance away. Frantic footsteps from the road told him the other soldiers were heading back toward the camp.

"What's going on?" a soldier yelled.

The mage, still intoning his dissonant chaos magic, did not stop to respond.

Sol hoped his unseen allies would be able to distract the rest of the soldiers for a few moments longer.

Inhaling against the panic rising in his chest, Sol reached inside himself for any remaining thread of magic. Each moment and each breath restored his reserve, but not quickly.

Gripping Neven's shoulders, he tried to stop hearing the noises outside of himself and listened instead for the sounds of leaves rustling around him. Sol exhaled as slowly as he could, relaxing his throat so the air moving through it caused a low, deep note.

Again, the pitch of the vibration traveled down from his throat, reverberating through his chest and tingling along his arms to his fingertips. He relaxed his grip on Neven's shoulders as the breath continued to leave his body.

His fellow prisoner was in pain, and Sol focused his entire being into wishing his friend to be well.

Finally, the breath in his lungs wavered. He squeezed his chest, forcing out every last drop of air he could muster. The vibration in his chest turned into a tremor as his lungs emptied. The final wave of energy tingled down his arms to his fingertips.

He was spent. His magic was gone. He could do nothing to help his immobile friend.

The sound of the mage's voice grew louder. He was walking toward them. Other footsteps followed.

Sol had to leave. Immediately. It was likely too late.

As the final tremor of energy flickered through his fingertips, Sol felt a heavy wind whip through his hair, stinging his cheek.

The power of the wind increased, pressing against Sol's entire body.

He increased his grip on Neven's shoulders to keep himself from doubling over.

A new strength returned to his arms, flowing through him and wrapping around him, seeping into Neven.

Bolstered, Sol stood back up. The wind was still moving fiercely, but it no longer pushed against him—rather it seemed to be supporting him.

Neven slumped forward, gasping for air. He was released from the mage's grip.

Relieved, Sol supported his friend with an arm, but his ears and eyes immediately returned to the situation outside him.

The wind had picked up everything in its path, creating a wash of moving shadows in the leaves and dust it had gathered. Sol could see nothing.

But he could hear the curses of the soldiers barely a few steps away.

"After them," the mage yelled.

"I can't see," a soldier yelled.

Sol grabbed Neven's arm and moved fearlessly into the spinning wind, away from the voices chasing them.

"Try opening your eyes, you fool," the mage said. "I'm lighting your way."

"I can't," a soldier replied.

"This dust is worse than a sandstorm." That was another soldier.

The torrent of wind parted for Sol and Neven, opening in front of them and gently pushing them from behind, guiding them through the dark forest.

The last thing Sol heard from their pursuers was the angry voice of the mage. "This dust storm is not natural, fools—they've unlocked their magic."

Sol felt a glow of accomplishment in his chest, though it wasn't big enough to bring a full smile to his face. If his plan worked out, he would never let his magic be locked again.

CHAPTER 3

"*P*rincess Philomena."

"Just Meena." Meena's mouth spoke the words before her mind fully recognized her older brother's teasing voice. She crossed her arms, squinting her eyes into a glare at Onric's approach.

"Sorry, *Phil.*" Onric lightly punched her shoulder as he strode by her without stopping.

"At least that's better than Phil-o-mena," Meena muttered, lurching forward as she attempted to punch her brother in return. Since he was already out of her reach, she stumbled forward and her arm swung wide. "Ornery."

Her brother's confident swagger faltered for a moment.

Meena felt her frustration bend into a wry grin. Running forward a few steps, she threw her arm over her brother's shoulders. "You've been so good-natured since you met Ashlin, I haven't had a reason to call you 'Ornery Onric' in far too long. Maybe I should tell Ashlin about that one. She'd probably find a better use for it than me."

Onric shrugged her arm from his shoulder. "Don't you dare mention that old name to her," he hissed.

Meena batted her eyelashes and flipped her long braid over her shoulder. "Too late. Already did." Dancing forward quickly, she skillfully moved herself out of Onric's reach.

Fortunately, he was too frozen in shock to give her another good-natured punch.

Laughing at the look on his face, Meena decided to keep the upper hand by ending the conversation and continuing down the hall toward her destination.

"You didn't? Right?" Onric called after her as she dashed away. "You're jesting with me?"

Meena danced with her feet as she ran, swinging her hips just enough to flair out the edge of her skirt. Maybe she was too old to be acting like—well, like such a little girl—but she didn't care. Teasing her brothers was more than worth it.

Another brother, the eldest, walked toward her. Ian's stride held a speed and purpose that reminded Meena of their father. His face was tense, and his eyes hardly seemed to register her existence as he walked around her.

Meena knew her older brother had plenty of things to be legitimately worried about, such as the fact that the neighboring king had tried to murder Erich, or the fact that everything they knew about the exiled Majis had been wrong.

"Beware of Onric!" Meena called after Ian, ensuring her voice carried down the stone halls. She knew she was being cheeky, but even Ian deserved a reason to smile despite the current situation. "He's feeling ornery today!"

Ian stopped, turning on his heel to face her. His frown had deepened.

Meena rolled her eyes. She should have known Ian would miss the silly tone of her voice.

"I was jesting," she explained, feeling as though all the fun had been stolen out of the moment. "Ornery Onric?"

Ian nodded once in recognition. The confusion on his face melted slightly as he seemed to realize her words were not noteworthy enough to stop whatever important activity he was headed toward.

When his back was turned, Meena rolled her eyes again. He didn't have to be so serious all the time. She was worried about all the same things, but at least she was keeping a cheerful face.

Meena squeezed her own eyes shut for a moment, missing a beat of the easy pace she was sounding on the stone floor. A small hollow feeling bloomed in her chest as she exhaled. Ian was the crown prince. Onric was the captain of the castle guard. They were both skilled tacticians and swordsmen.

Meena corrected the motion of her hips, adjusting her stride to mimic Ian's purposeful movements. She was . . . just the youngest. The only daughter after four sons.

As she rounded the corner, Meena barely had time to recognize another body racing toward her. She quickly jumped out of the way as Erich tripped over his own feet, trying to slow down enough to round the corner.

Meena embraced the smile that naturally relaxed her face. It was typical of Erich to be making a mad dash through the castle halls. He knew how to enjoy himself despite the copious amount of worry that was probably running through his mind as well.

"If you quicken your pace, you'll fall flat on your face!" Meena raised her voice, hoping it sounded as commanding as her mother's had all those times the queen had reprimanded her for running inside the palace.

Erich waved his hand dismissively without turning back to face her. "I'm late."

"For what?" Meena called after him.

"Don't tell Mum!" Erich disappeared down the hall.

Meena felt her eyes start to roll again, and she blinked away the instinct. Her mother had once told her that her eyes would get permanently stuck in the wrong position if she kept rolling them so frequently. Meena was fairly certain her mother had been jesting, but she didn't want to find out.

Continuing down the now empty hall, Meena shook the worry from her mind. Perhaps she would show Celesta some of her favorite secret tunnels today. They could pretend they were spies and sneak around the castle, gathering information. She could even hide a treasure in the tunnel below the old ruins . . .

Meena stopped.

She slowly turned around, staring in the direction that Ian, Onric, and Erich had all been heading. Was Erich late for a meeting that involved all three of her brothers?

He had to be.

And of course, she hadn't been invited. They were probably trying to protect her from something as though she were still in her twelfth greenreign and not her eighteenth.

Or had they not invited her because she talked too much?

Meena blinked rapidly, inhaling sharply through her nose. They didn't say it often, but Meena knew Ian and Aden found her constant chatter annoying. She'd seen the restrained impatience in their eyes when she tried to join important discussions. Her father probably felt the same way, though his expression would never betray it.

Meena retraced her steps. Her stride was as purposeful as Ian's now, and she wasn't even forcing it.

As expected this late in the afternoon, the council room was empty.

She entered it regardless and made her way around the long table that ran the length of the hall. The far side of the room split into a low hallway. Her father often worked in a small study near the council room. It was the perfect place for a moment of peace between important meetings—or for holding more private conversations.

Feeling like a cypher, she quietly made her way down the hall. The door to her father's study was closed.

Meena reached for the handle, but her hand stopped just short of opening it. She had never before hesitated to bother her father while he worked. For all his stern facial expressions, King Frederich always welcomed her presence. If he was having an important conversation, he would merely ask her to leave and return at a better time—which was exactly what he would do if she burst into a private meeting between him and her brothers that she had not been invited to.

Stealthily hunching her shoulders, Meena sidled past the door and crouched low against the wall on the other side. A real cypher would have done a better job of hiding than sitting on the floor of a hallway, but no one came through this hall except to speak to her father. And no one would dare do that when he was in a private meeting. At least, Meena hoped they wouldn't. But she wasn't sure if anyone else knew about the private meeting because then it wouldn't be quite so private. The hallway was empty with nothing else to hide behind, so she didn't have many options.

Breathing soundlessly through her nose, Meena strained her ears to hear what was being said on the other side of the door.

"They would never believe us." King Frederich's voice

was quiet and measured, but Meena could still hear her father's frustration through the wall that separated them.

"We have to try." That was Onric, ever valiant and straightforward.

"What further proof do you need?" Erich's voice was loud. Meena could imagine her enthusiastic brother throwing his hand to the side as he asked the question. "My wife can personally confirm everything. Gareth's treachery, the lies about the Majis, the truth about the harmony magic, and how the Quotidian is using chaos magic in secret."

"It's not that simple," King Frederich responded. "We need more . . ." His voice trailed off.

"You don't believe her." Erich's voice had dropped to a lower pitch. "This isn't about them—it's about you. You don't believe us."

"No." King Frederich's voice was so loud, Meena startled in surprise. "No." He dropped his tone back down. "You have my full trust and support—"

"And my wife?" Erich cut in. "Does she have your full trust and support?"

"Yes. I was referring to both of you."

"And her people?" Erich continued to push. "The Majis. Are they still your enemy?"

Meena bit her lips closed so the sound of her breath would not pierce the silence that followed Erich's question. *She* believed the Majis were no longer their enemy. Aizel's revelation about the Isle of Exile and the way her people had been enslaved appalled and angered Meena.

"No. They are not." King Frederich paused again. "You are fixated on the wrong problem. It is not my trust you need to earn. I cannot approach the other kingdoms without more proof."

Meena stood. She wanted to burst through the door and tell her father to see reason. He was a kind and just king—Meena truly believed there had never been a better one. It made sense to her that the other kingdoms would not immediately accept Aizel's statements, but surely they could still do something?

"They would believe us if we attacked Gareth first." Onric's direct approach made Meena nod.

"And if they still don't believe us?" King Frederich's voice was growing brittle. "If they side with Chendas and turn on us? We do not have the power to attack even Chendas alone, much less defend ourselves against three other kingdoms."

"Allys would side with us," Erich responded.

"Allys barely has half our fighting power. Their support would be appreciated, but it would not turn the tide of this war." Ian's practical voice entered the conversation for the first time.

Meena's stomach bent into the familiar uncomfortable twist. The ideal solution wouldn't involve going to war.

"So what do you plan to do?" Erich no longer sounded like her carefree older brother. "Sit back and wait for the battle to come to us? Just like we've always done? The attack is still coming. And it's not the one we prepared for."

"We don't know what Gareth wants. His lack of communication is disconcerting. No threat, no attempt to reconcile —" King Frederich started to respond.

"He wants me dead," Erich said, cutting him off. "Did you forget that part?"

"Enough." A hand slammed down on a wooden surface.

Meena jumped backward, the sound of the slap reverberating through the door and tickling her ear. She held in a sigh and rolled her eyes. They were too focused on disagreeing with each other to ask the right questions.

"It's been three days and we don't know who has the power here," her father continued. "Our first priority is to the people of Iseldis."

"My wife needs to know her family is safe!" Erich continued to raise his voice, speaking louder than the king.

"Are they talking about me?"

Meena's whole body started in surprise. Her new sister, Aizel, was crouching next to her in the hall. Meena had been so engaged in the conversation happening in the next room that she had completely missed Aizel's quiet approach.

"Sorry!" Aizel whispered, placing a calming hand on Meena's shoulder.

"No, it's fine." Meena smiled a quick welcome. "I was just . . ." She gestured toward the closed door. "And yes, they are." Meena looked away, embarrassed by her family's actions. She didn't want Aizel to be offended by her father's median stance, but she also was not ready to defend her father's position to her new sister.

"Do you do this often?" Aizel's eyes darted around the small hall, taking in the situation. Meena admired her presence of mind. Aizel wouldn't let anyone approach her by surprise.

"Only when they don't invite me and I know something is going on," Meena answered.

King Frederich's voice cut through the door, stopping further conversation between Meena and Aizel. "We will do everything in our power to help whom we can. But we cannot instantaneously turn our enemies into our allies and our previous allies into our new enemies. We do not even have a representative from the Majis to create an alliance with."

Meena rolled her eyes again, pinching her lips in exasperation. She turned back toward Aizel to fill her in on what they had been discussing, but Aizel's hand was on the door.

"They'll only kick us out," Meena hissed, grabbing Aizel's shoulder.

"I won't let them," Aizel responded, throwing the door wide open. "Did you ever consider speaking about it with this particular Majis?" She stepped into the room, her eyes scanning each of its occupants.

Meena followed Aizel into the room, avoiding her father's gaze. "You don't have to invite *me* to every meeting," Meena said. "But at least consider whether you are leaving out someone important." Meena knew her words were more bitter than they needed to be, but it was too late to take them back. She was hurt they hadn't included her in this family discussion, but it felt even more ridiculous that they hadn't included Aizel—someone who would have knowledge and an important opinion on the matters at hand.

"I didn't want to worry you," Erich soothed.

Aizel spun to face him. "This won't happen again." Her voice was firm, but not angry. "I didn't wed you to be coddled and spoiled. I will not rest until my people see justice, and I will participate in this conversation." Her eyes went from Erich's to King Frederich's.

Meena pumped her fist in victory.

One day, she would command a room as Aizel did, with confidence, calm, and clarity.

CHAPTER 4

*L*eaning into the swirling wind, Sol kept his arm on the stumbling Neven as they pushed through the dark forest. He couldn't tell if the wind was creating their path or the protective bubble of air was following his lead. Either way, they were moving as quickly away from their pursuers as they could.

Sol kept his ears alert for any sound of danger from those behind them or aid from those ahead.

The low rumble of an owl's hoot came through under the higher pitch of the wind's whistle.

Sol veered toward the sound, adjusting the angle of their path.

He hoped it was a signal from his correspondent, but perhaps he was blindly following the call of a forest owl.

The owl hooted again.

Sol continued toward it with confidence. The forest was alive with activity, and no wild bird would reveal its location in such chaos.

"An eagle's talon," a voice hissed through the wind.

Sol stopped, glancing in every direction for signs of the speaker. "Cannot stop the flow of the river," he responded into the shadows.

"Sol—here." The voice sounded above him.

Sol looked up to see a hooded figure sitting in the branches of a tree. "Lady Robin?" he asked. It was too dark to make out any features.

"You're not alone?" The voice sounded like a woman's, but she did not answer his question. As she spoke, she threw a soft object from the tree.

"A fellow prisoner," Sol explained, deftly catching the object despite the darkness. It was a bundled rope ladder, still attached somewhere above his head.

"Quickly," she urged. "Quietly."

Sol shook out the ladder and gestured to Neven to climb it first.

Once they stopped moving, the wind continued to circle them, slowly losing its power. Sol breathed his thanks to the quieting gust. He had never seen magic respond in such a way, but his mind was too worried about their pursuers to examine the anomaly.

Sol followed his companion up the ladder and helped Robin draw it quickly back up into the tree. From what he could see in the darkness, they were crouching on a small platform that had been built into the branches of the tree.

As soon as he had taken in his surroundings, he reached behind Neven's head and fumbled to quickly unclasp the gem tied around his neck.

Neven exhaled audibly.

Sol tucked the gem into his pocket, knowing exactly how it felt to be freed of the hated device. The chaos magic in the gem was physically painless, but it separated a person from their magic, muting more than their voice.

"We'll wait here until it's safe," Robin whispered.

"Hopefully that won't be hours," Neven breathed.

"Or days," Sol added.

"I have so many questions, young man—but tell me, are we going somewhere better than our previous destination?" Neven said.

Sol could feel Neven's gaze on him in the darkness. "In good time," Sol responded, his voice barely a whisper. "We are still in danger."

Neven nodded, leaning back against the thick branch behind him.

Sol remained alert, crouching over his toes. Scanning the forest around them, he approximated where their pursuers would come from and calculated which directions appeared best to use as escape routes.

The sounds of the forest slowly played out around him, occasionally interrupted by a shuffle from Neven or a breath from Robin.

Exhaustion gnawed at Sol's mind—as did the myriad of questions he wished to ask Robin—but he could not relax even if he tried.

A short time later, the sound of footsteps broke through the forest.

Two Quotidian soldiers walked toward them, carrying a torch that lit the forest around them.

Sol stopped breathing completely, muscles tensing in readiness.

The soldiers walked warily, even gazing up into the trees as they searched.

The distant sounds of a scuffle attracted their attention,

and the soldiers immediately broke into a sprint toward the sound.

Sol caught a hint of a smile on Robin's face as the torch-light faded away. He leaned his head back against a tree branch behind him, allowing only his neck to relax. His eyes remained open throughout the night, watching for any sign of danger and catching every shade of dawn until morning came.

"We should be safe to move to a more secure spot," Robin said, finally breaking the hours of silence.

Sol nodded, dropping nimbly out of the tree after her. His joints and muscles complained when he landed on the firm ground. He stood tall to stretch out the aches and numbness.

As Neven followed them out of the tree, Sol took a moment to look up at their hiding place in the light. The small platform was skillfully hidden between the twisting trunk and draping leaves. He subconsciously nodded his head in approval as he realized why the soldiers had not seen them in the tree hours before.

Robin led them further into the forest. Though she followed no set path, she navigated her way with confidence and ease.

Sol appreciated the thick cover of the trees overhead, which blocked the rising sun and its heat. His mouth was dry and his stomach rumbled, but he ignored the discomfort.

Sooner than he expected, Robin led them into an open glade.

Sol stopped at the edge of it, carefully noticing his surroundings with a quick glance. The first thing to catch his attention, however, was the enticing smell of freshly roasted meat. Two men sat near an open fire, tending to food that sizzled temptingly on a spit. Behind them, a woodman's hut nestled under the trees at the far side of the open area. Beneath a large, low tree in the center of the glade, a woman sat fletching an arrow.

Robin had walked confidently into the open area, approaching the two men at the fire.

"Lane and Fletcher?" she asked.

"Sleeping." One of the men gestured toward the cabin behind him.

"Willa?" Robin continued.

"She made it back just after dawn. Took a small sleep then set out to do a round," the second man answered.

"A success?" The first one spoke again.

Robin nodded, her shoulders relaxing in a smooth motion as she slipped off her cape. "We did it." She turned to Sol, her smile triumphant. "Not that I had any doubts, of course," she hurried to add.

Sol stiffly returned her smile. This was indeed a success, but so much more remained to be done. "Thank you, Lady Robin." He dipped his head in a quick bow. "It is an honor to finally see you with my own eyes."

"Please—I no longer accept the title of lady," Robin replied. "Call me Robin."

"This would not have been possible without you," Sol insisted.

"You would have found a way," Robin replied. "It was my honor and duty to assist you. Please, you must be hungry. Sit and eat."

"I, too, would like to thank you," Neven interjected, following her direction and seating himself by the fire. "But I still do not know what is happening here."

Robin looked at Sol, a question in her eyes.

Sol broke the contact, appreciating that she would let him

choose what secrets to share. He turned to his companion. "Neven?" He extended his hand. "I'm Sol."

Neven leaned forward to shake his hand. The older man's grip was firm despite the exhaustion in his eyes.

"I am sorry that our meeting takes place under such unfortunate circumstances," Sol continued. "I hail from the western side of Istroya. I gathered you are from the northern port?"

Neven nodded. "Unfortunate circumstances. That's putting it lightly. No one wants to be chosen."

"I was not chosen," Sol responded slowly. "I chose to be chosen."

"You must be mad," Neven said. "Though that much has been made clear, of course. Attempting an escape?"

"Our fate was already worse than death. What more could they have done if we'd been recaptured?" Sol responded.

"But you didn't have to be chosen at all. Why volunteer for such a position?" Neven turned to Robin. "Not that I am ungrateful to be included in the escape, of course. No offense, my lady."

"It's Robin. None taken."

"I am not so naïve as to think this escape was planned around me," Neven said, turning his attention back to Sol.

"Your assumption would be correct," Sol responded. "But I am glad that my plan could benefit you nonetheless."

Neven nodded.

"Come, let us eat," Robin said, seating herself around the fire.

Sol instinctively walked to the other side of the fire so he could keep an eye on the area behind his companion's backs.

"Ulli, Nele," Robin said, indicating the two men already seated. "Sol. Neven."

Sol nodded a greeting as Ulli handed him a sharp stick loaded with crispy chunks of roasted meat. His stomach grumbled in anticipation, and he breathed gently on the steaming food.

"And you are?" Neven directed his question to Robin.

"A member of River's Talon," she replied casually.

Sol noted that she did not introduce herself as the leader of River's Talon, but he did not press the matter. She could present herself as she pleased.

Neven's eyes went wide, and he blinked rapidly, dipping awkwardly into a bow from his seated position. "My life is at your service. And not just because I owe it to you."

Robin shook her head. "Sol is the one who risked his life to save you. My team merely created a distraction."

Neven turned back to Sol. "How did you access your magic?"

Sol tugged the counterfeit gem from his neck. "It was a fake."

"This entire time?" Neven asked in disbelief.

Sol nodded. He wanted to toss the gem deep into the forest, never to be seen again. But life had taught him to waste not. He shoved it into his pocket, out of sight.

Neven smiled, relaxing back onto his wooden stool as though he felt safe for the first time. "What is next? Can I aid you?" Neven turned back to Sol.

"Perhaps," Sol replied, looking at his companion more closely than he ever had. Only four people in the world knew his plan, and one of them was Robin. It wasn't that he didn't trust Neven; he just wasn't about to share every detail with a near stranger. Even if he and that stranger had endured a grueling six weeks of captivity together. "My plan is to strike Gareth at the root of his power, creating a drawback that might give someone else a chance to win against him."

Neven looked up. His mouth was full, but he had stopped chewing. After a lengthy pause, he swallowed heavily. "I would say you were mad, but I've already said that. And I would say it's impossible, but somehow I'm here and not on my way to Chendas. So I suppose I shall say nothing at all." He took another bite from his skewer.

Sol turned back to Robin. "You wrote that you could provide weapons and food for the next length of my journey?"

"Of course," Robin said. "But we have time for all that. Eat."

"I intend to leave before the night has set," Sol replied. He took a large bite of meat. He needed to eat so he could finish preparing for the next part of the journey.

"You are exhausted. Surely you can rest for a few days," Robin said.

"We are already short on time," Sol said over the food in his mouth, "and I cannot endanger you by staying any longer. They will be searching this place."

Robin raised her eyebrows. "No one can find this place."

Sol pursed his lips. His eyes darted around the peaceful glade, but he held back any words of criticism. Robin had aided him at a peril to herself, and it was not his responsibility to tell her how to manage her home and people.

She smiled at him condescendingly, as though she could read the thoughts in his mind.

"I would say one thing more," Neven interjected, drawing Sol's attention. "I wish you luck, Sol. And if I may aid you, tell me and I will do so."

"My thanks," Sol replied. He had no grand illusion of even surviving his quest. "Stay here with the River's Talon and regain your strength."

Neven tilted his head slightly back, observing Sol. "You have given me a new life. I cannot return to my family in Istroya. At least allow me to help you defeat Gareth."

Sol returned the man's gaze, thinking through his next words. He had no desire to risk another's life, nor would he let in someone who might be a risk to his goal. "I must travel to Chendas and watch . . . the activity of our enemy, among other things. I will alert River's Talon should I need aid in the final action." Sol looked down, stuffing his mouth with the remainder of his meal.

"Sol." Robin's voice was somber. "Come, let us look at the weaponry we might give to you."

Sol stood, concern knotting his forehead. He was eager to avoid more questions but certain he was about to hear bad news.

"Some things have changed since our last communication," Robin said, her voice low as she led him away from the fire.

"You were unable to discover the location?" Sol guessed.

Robin shook her head. "My weeks in Chendas were not fruitful"—she held up her hand, stopping Sol from speaking —"because I discovered our target is not in Chendas."

"That's impossible," Sol responded, his voice calm and quiet despite the consternation he felt. "Every report said the chosen Majis are transported to Chendas."

"Were," Robin corrected him. "They *were* transported to Chendas. Gareth recently moved operations to Falqri and, as far as we know, the receptacles as well."

"Then we go to Falqri. It should be easier to search a fort than a capital kingdom."

"It's not that simple." Robin sighed. "We've been building up our allies in Chendas for years. We have no stable contacts in Falqri yet because it is so remote. I might have a full recruit there soon, but it's too soon to risk your identity by alerting him."

"I thought you had a hold in all five of the kingdoms?" Sol said. He'd made it this far—he wasn't about to give up.

"We had a cypher there." Robin sighed. "She was ratted out in the aftermath of Aizel's escape."

Sol felt his body deflate. Surely it was merely the exhaustion. His plan was fruitless if he could not get inside the fort. "I'm sorry," he said, not sure if his words were for himself or for the loss of Robin's comrade.

"It not only affects access to the fort; it deters entry into Falqri as well."

"Aizel?" Sol's head shot back up as Robin's earlier words finally registered in his mind. "You know Aizel? She's alive? And she's here?" He looked around, half expecting his childhood friend to walk out of the hut they were whispering in front of.

Robin nodded. "Not *here* here." She pointed to the ground at her feet. "But here in Iseldis, at the palace." She pointed behind her, toward the forest.

"And what of Celesta?" Sol asked, feeling relief and concern at the same time. "They came for her soon after Aizel disappeared."

"Celesta is alive and well. She spent a nasty few weeks in Gareth's dungeon—"

Sol clenched his fists, anger rushing from his head to his tensed feet.

Robin immediately placed a calming hand on his arm. "But she's recovering now, and happy. I saw her with my own eyes. She's resilient."

"She's a child. She shouldn't have to *be* resilient." Sol was not placated. "Surely Iseldis is treating them no better? Can we not find a way to release them? Would that give us time to find a new cypher in Falqri?"

"That's not all about Falqri," Robin responded slowly. She stepped inside the hut, holding the door open.

Appreciating the additional privacy, Sol followed her inside.

"The northern border is surrounded by steep cliffs," Robin continued. "And the only passes through are guarded by Gareth's men. It would be certain death to cross over the cliffs and desert in the heat of greenreign. The faster way to the fort is by sea. Which brings us back to Iseldis."

Sol crossed his arms. "Aizel and Celesta." His voice was close to breaking. He'd thought he had mastered the art of not getting too close to anyone. Then Aizel and Celesta had been taken. They were as dear to him as his own younger sisters and brothers.

"Sol, they're safe," Robin said. "Safe and well. They are guests at the palace, not prisoners."

Sol felt relief, but his body was no less tense. directed the conversation back to something less personal. "We can access Falqri by sea, then."

"Yes," Robin responded, her voice crisp and high. "If we can get you on a ship sailing from Iseldis, which is possible but will take some preparation."

Sol nodded. He would do whatever was necessary to get to his destination, and he trusted Robin to know the ideal means of doing so. His mind was having trouble grasping the particulars of the new plan so quickly, so he distracted himself for a moment by glancing at the multiple longbows lining the wall of the humble cabin.

Following his eyeline, Robin stepped to his side. She looked between him and the various bows, then grabbed two from the wall. "You could save a considerable length of time —and see that Aizel and Celesta are safe—if you went straight to the palace and asked for their aid."

Sol accepted the bow she held out to him. It was nearly as tall as he was, though it was unstrung. "You said I could ask for their aid—not *we* could ask?"

Robin took the bow from his hands and swung one end of it behind her foot, leaning into its curve as she harnessed its power and deftly slid the string into its proper notch. "I am not welcome in the palace." Her voice was unconcerned, but Sol did not miss the way she avoided his eyes as she said it.

"I am not afraid to enter the enemy's house," Sol responded. "But would it not be less risk to find a local shipping merchant?"

Robin handed the strung bow back to him. "Iseldis is not dangerous for you. Their son, Erich, was recently attacked by Gareth, so I have good reason to believe they are no longer allies with Chendas."

"That alone does not make them allies of mine." Sol lifted the bow, testing the weight of its pull. It was heavy, but years spent working in the sea had given him considerable strength as well. He drew the string back to his chin, holding it there for a moment.

"The Sirilian family appear to have allied themselves to you, however," Robin replied. "That same son, Erich, wed Aizel a sennight prior."

Sol quickly released the tension in the bowstring—he knew better than to let it fire without an arrow—and guided the string back into place with his hand despite the biting pain in his fingertips. "You said she was not a prisoner. Aizel would never stoop so low as to marry a Quotidian prince. What kind of chaos did he weave over her?"

"The magic of love?" Robin's mouth curved into a small smile.

Sol did not try to hide his scoff. From everything he knew of Robin, she was not one to rely on sentiment.

"Your best option is to ally with Iseldis. It will be the swiftest route to Falqri and offers the most effective means of support."

"I have you," Sol responded.

"And I will be here to support you, but the strength of an entire kingdom is far more powerful than that of a handful of outlawed men and women."

Sol handed the bow back to Robin. "It is very powerful, but I have no skill with an arrow. A dagger or spear would suit me better."

Robin returned the bow to the wall and opened a chest on the floor below it.

"I thank you for your thoughts," Sol said, returning to their more important conversation. "But I have no wish to be reliant on Quotidian men."

Robin handed him a sheathed dagger. "I am Quotidian, and you seem to have no issue with my support."

Sol accepted the dagger, happy for the excuse to drop his eyes from her face. He would go to Iseldis if it truly was the best option. "But only to ensure that Aizel is not being held there against her will."

CHAPTER 5

"This isn't about proving anything," Aizel said to King Frederich, her voice quiet and firm. "My people have no intention of attacking your shores. We don't want retaliation for what your ancestors did, but we do want justice for what the Quotidian is doing now."

"What power do your people have?" King Frederich asked. "My first responsibility is for the safety of my people. Would you not be the perfect tool for the Quotidian to control if they wished to move against us? If they can control your magic by controlling you—"

"You have magic," Aizel interjected. "We are not so different."

"I don't have armies of soldiers trained in how to use magic," King Frederich was quick to respond. "Gareth and the Chendas Examiners promised to unlock and teach us a magical form of defense, but they never unlocked . . . or they never shared what they uncovered."

Meena struggled to follow the quick implications of the

conversation happening in front of her, but she was relieved to see her father sink his head into his hands with a sigh. For him to show any sign of physical or emotional weakness was rare and never happened with anyone other than very close family members and advisors. Though Aizel had only been introduced to the family a few days prior, her father's open stance meant he trusted her to some extent.

"I mean no harm or disrespect to you or your people, but you must see how I am crushed between two forces with more power than I can comprehend. What is Gareth plotting, and why did he hide the magic and his knowledge of the Isle of Exile—"

"Istroya," Aizel corrected.

"Istroya," King Frederich repeated. "He's been hiding this from me."

Meena began squeezing each finger against her palm one at a time, working her way across one hand and then the other. This conversation was important, but even with Aizel present, it felt like it was going in circles. Surely her father was right? He was a good and kind king. But the flash in Aizel's eye and the curtness of her tone made Meena uncomfortable. If the Majis were truly innocent, her father was sitting on a stolen throne.

Meena bit her tongue. Her father had not personally committed any of the horrors Aizel had shared with them against the Majis in Istroya—he had not even known they were happening!

Erich stepped forward to Aizel's side, placing his hand on her back in silent support. Together, they stepped closer to Frederich's desk and continued their conversation.

Meena turned to Onric. "Has Ashlin left yet?" she asked.

"No, she's still sewing."

"This late?" Meena asked, slightly jealous that her new friend and almost-sister had an active role in this turmoil.

"Time is precious. She wants to finish as many panels as she can to see if Aizel knows any of the stories or the meaning behind them."

"She'll work herself to death." Meena could hear the childish whine in her own voice. She was concerned about Ashlin overworking herself, but she was mostly jealous that both Ashlin and Aizel had a meaningful way to help combat this intangible problem.

"I'm aware of that," Onric growled.

Meena smiled. At least Onric was also frustrated, even if it was for a different reason.

"I'll go check on her," Meena replied, thankful for a reason to seek out her friend.

"Convince her to stay here tonight," Onric said before she could leave. "The castle is safer than being in town . . . especially right now."

"Tell her yourself."

"I don't want to pressure her."

"I'll do my best," Meena said to make her escape.

"Tell her I'll sleep on Mistress Cedrice's doorstep if she insists on going home tonight!"

"That won't pressure her at all!" Meena responded, slipping out of the room before Onric could give her any more directives. Ashlin was her friend, too.

Meena hurried through the back courtyard. The shadowless dusk made her feel eerie, as did the quiet guard who moved through the space lighting torches along the wall.

"Good evening, Drirsi," she called with a small smile.

The young guard dipped his head respectfully. "Princess."

He moved on to light the next torch, not indulging in the usual banter they shared.

Meena shivered, though the evening air was still warm. Everyone was too somber. Even Drirsi had a responsibility to keep him focused.

On the other side of the courtyard, she pressed open a small wooden door that led to the ruins of the ancient Iseldis castle. The old hall instantly darkened as the door closed behind her. Meena rushed up a winding staircase to her left as quickly as she could. Normally, she wasn't afraid of the dark, but her stomach was already tied up in knots and she didn't want to be alone.

The upper room of the eastern tower was softly lit with a few candles, and Ashlin hovered over a large makeshift table. She immediately glanced up, welcoming Meena with a smile.

Meena exhaled. Here, the candles emitted a soft warmth —or maybe that was Ashlin. Either way, the tension in her stomach eased.

"Hello, Great Wielder of the Needle," Meena said.

"Bringer of Sunny Skies," Ashlin responded.

Meena approached the opposite end of the table, her smile growing. "I do that?"

"You always make my day more bright," Ashlin replied. Her voice was light with a touch of jest, but Meena could still hear the sincerity behind her words.

"How is the latest panel coming?" Meena asked, changing the subject.

"It appears to be the simplest yet most puzzling." Ashlin's voice had returned to a serious tone, matching Meena's.

"How so?" Meena examined the panel on the table in front of her. It was nearly as wide as her arms could reach, but only half as tall.

"See this black thread, here?" Ashlin pointed to the swooping tail of a large embroidered letter.

Meena leaned closer to the tapestry so her eyes could make out each individual, deliberate stitch. "It looks more like a dark blue than a black," she said. The thought left her mouth as she was thinking it. "I mean," she quickly corrected herself, "it's probably just the light . . ."

"You are exactly right." Ashlin stopped her kindly. "It is blue. I'm so glad you see it, too."

Meena felt her face relax into a smile again. She loved that even when Ashlin was discussing difficult matters, she did it in a way that did not cause an uncomfortable pit to form in Meena's stomach.

"See," Ashlin continued, "this next panel appears to be significant. If these panels were destroyed with intention—which we still believe is the case—this panel might be the exception. It's only a single word."

Meena looked back down at the partially restored image. Unlike the other more colorful panels, this one was a simple woven background of warm cream with tall, flowing letters embroidered to fill the entire space. It appeared that Ashlin had finished outlining the letters but was still stitching in the fill color, so the word itself was visible, although the way she was facing made it appear upside down.

Meena tilted her head to the side as she read the fanciful old-fashioned script. "Mmmhh," she whispered, trying to make it out.

"It's written out in two different colors of thread," Ashlin said. "See, these black letters have small areas done in a dark blue, like this letter here. The shape making up the simple symbol is in black, but if you look closely, it's rounded out into a different symbol with the dark blue. At first I thought the needle was guiding me incorrectly when it wanted me to switch the color. The difference is barely perceptible."

"Perhaps the original weavers left a message in the panel!" Meena rushed around the table to look at the word from the right direction.

"That would be quite an adventure."

Meena barely registered Ashlin's positive, if doubt-filled, words. "Imagine actually finding a secret message. We could learn what really happened one thousand seasons ago. Aizel's story makes so much sense." As she was speaking, Meena reached out, touching each of the areas she could identify that had been stitched in the dark blue instead of black. "I do not see a pattern yet, though. Maybe we should try to redraw it on some parchment with a greater contrast in the colors. Then we could see the difference between the blue and black more clearly. I'll go get some." Meena looked up.

Ashlin was staring blankly ahead, her raised hand holding the needle, poised in the air as though she were frozen in time. Her eyes blinked, moving from the needle to the tapestry.

"Or not . . . if you think it's a bad idea," Meena said, confused at Ashlin's reaction.

"Oh, no." Ashlin quickly smiled. Her tense pose relaxed as her eyes moved back to Meena. "You'll go get some parchment," she repeated, "to see the contrast in the colors." She nodded slowly, as though she were hearing Meena's words for the first time. "That is a wonderful idea."

"Are you feeling unwell?" Meena asked.

Ashlin shook her head, blinking a few times. "I'm only tired. Don't worry about me."

"You should sleep here tonight. It is already late."

"Did Onric tell you to tell me that?"

Meena smiled and shrugged. "I will be back immediately with some parchment."

Ashlin shook her head, returning her gaze to the iron needle in her hand.

Meena practically flew down the spiral stairs. She felt so much better now that she had something to offer. Her thoughts tumbled with ideas as she ran. She should find multiple colors of ink to make the writing more visible than the stitching. Or perhaps chalk, like she'd used when she was a child. That would be faster to use and less of a mess to work with up in the tower. When she was a child, she had loved to use the ink on her mother's desk to draw out treasure maps for her adventures. Most of the time, she'd ended up staining something she shouldn't have.

The thought of the old treasure maps made her smile. She found a few pieces of parchment and chalk in separate colors. Celesta would probably love following a treasure map.

"Meena!" Onric called her name as she ran back toward the courtyard.

"Thank you for using my proper name!" she called, not stopping her sprint as she dashed by him.

"Did she agree to stay?" Onric asked, picking up his pace to match her slapping sandals.

"Ask her yourself," Meena responded. "I thought you said your favorite pastime in the whole kingdom was just talking to her?"

"I did. It is."

The back courtyard was lit only by the torchlight as night had completely fallen. Meena threw open the door of the old ruins.

"That is beside the point!" Onric continued yelling after her.

Meena stepped into the old castle. The ancient hall was completely steeped in darkness. Meena turned around at the door, searching for a lantern to carry through the darkness. "Can you go find Aizel?" she called to Onric. "We think we may have found a clue in the tapestry."

Onric handed her an oil lantern. "Why didn't you lead with that?" His head shot up, his voice deeper.

"I was answering your question." Meena held the open end of the lantern up to one of the lit torches on the courtyard wall.

"What did you find?" Onric asked, taking the lantern back from her hand and lifting it higher to catch the flame faster.

"We don't know yet." Meena took the now-lit lantern back from his hands. "Go find Aizel and mayhap we'll find some more answers to all your questions."

"Yes, Captain." Onric's voice was filled with gentle mockery, but he turned and walked quickly back into the castle.

With the help of the lantern, Meena made her way safely back up into the old ruins. Erich used to scare her with stories of the monsters created by the Majis who came out in the hall after dark. They lived in the old tunnels that ran under the hall as an escape route.

Meena shook away the old fears. If there were any monsters, they'd been created by Erich. But the old tunnels might be the perfect place to hide a treasure for Celesta.

She dashed up the staircase, bursting into the upper room of the tower. "I found parchment and chalk!" she declared. "I'm ready to find the coded message!"

Ashlin stood still, bent over the tapestry while holding the needle at eye level. Her eyes were tense, scrunched together tightly under her eyebrows. "Just a moment," she whispered, her eyes not leaving the needle.

Meena stopped at the door, approaching the table cautiously. "What's wrong?"

Ashlin closed her eyes and dropped the needle into the tapestry, gently running the dull point of the clumsy iron implement across the section she had been restoring.

Meena watched, her concern growing by the second.

Ashlin directed the needle to an empty section of fabric and cautiously poked it through. The needle slid between the close weave of the fabric, naturally stretching the threads apart. Rather than force the needle completely through the fabric, Ashlin pulled it back out in reverse. The small hole that had formed in the fabric remained pressed out of shape, leaving a tiny gap in the perfectly interwoven threads.

"It no longer works." Ashlin's voice was barely a whisper.

"The needle?" Meena asked, even though she knew the answer was obvious. The small hole in the otherwise flawless fabric gaped at Meena, mocking her.

"It's not guiding me," Ashlin replied. "It just feels like a regular needle now, and a rather clumsy one at that." Her fingers worked over the hole, massaging the threads back into place.

"Are you sure?" Meena asked, the words coming out louder and faster than she intended. "Perhaps you are just overtired?" Meena made her way around the table to reach her distraught friend. "Or maybe the needle is."

"The needle is?" Ashlin asked.

"Tired. Perhaps the needle is tired."

Ashlin shook her head, turning sorrowful eyes to meet Meena. "It is a spelled needle. Perhaps someone removed the spell?"

"We can ask . . ."

As if summoned, Aizel pushed through the door, followed closely by Onric and Erich.

"What did you find?" Onric asked, rushing forward to reach Ashlin first.

Meena looked from Ashlin to Onric. "It's something else—"

"What's wrong?" Onric asked, cutting her off as he reached Ashlin's side.

"The needle stopped working. It feels . . . dead, somehow. Hollow." Ashlin leaned into Onric's supportive hug, but her eyes sought out Aizel. "Can you sense when an object has magic in it?"

Aizel nodded. "Usually."

Meena handed her the needle. "It's no longer pulsing with magic. Can you feel anything?"

"No." Aizel twisted the needle in her hand. "It's empty."

Ashlin's shoulders fell. "Did I break it?"

"What? No. It's not broken. It's empty. It ran out of magic."

"Items can do that?" Meena replied.

"Of course." Aizel handed the needle back to Ashlin. "A spelled item holds no particular power in and of itself. It only has the power that you give it."

"Can you give it more power?" Ashlin asked.

Aizel's mouth spread into a firm line.

Meena did not think they were going to like the answer.

Aizel kept her eyes on the tapestry as she answered the question. "Only someone who knew what the original tapestry looked like could imbue the needle with the magic to share that knowledge with someone else. I could fill its reserve with magic, but it would only be the kind of power that increased the needle's ability to be a better needle."

"Like not leaving behind a gaping hole every time it is pressed through the fabric?" Meena asked, trying to figure out how a needle could be better at its own function.

"Precisely." Aizel nodded at Meena, but her gaze quickly returned to Ashlin.

The seamstress set the needle on the table in front of her. "We failed."

Meena looked around the room. The somber faces, lit from below by the flickering candlelight, made her want to flee from the room. "No." She stepped closer to Ashlin, throwing her arms around her and Onric. "You did not fail. You and Onric were the first to question that the magic might be different from what we believed. You were willing to restore this tapestry even though using the needle itself was outlawed. And, you sabotaged King Gareth's first attempt to attack Ian."

"That is not the failure she was referring to." Aizel's soft voice broke the silence. "Those feats you mentioned are noteworthy, but the loss of this . . ." She spread her hands delicately over the tapestry in front of her, focusing on a particularly destroyed section. "We failed to recover this. This was part of my story."

"I'm so sorry." Ashlin turned her face away from the table, as though too pained to look at the tapestry any longer.

Aizel opened her mouth but then closed it, swallowing audibly.

"But you saved nearly six panels before the needle was drained," Meena said, her eyes looking from Ashlin to Aizel. "Surely this is not a complete loss. And there are so many panels that were undamaged, at least twenty."

"Sixteen." Ashlin threw Meena a sad smile, pushing herself out of Onric's embrace. She picked up a length of dark blue thread and deftly wrapped it around her fingers, securing it in a skein for storage. "I know you want to make this better. You're just like Onric. But there are four more panels that are permanently destroyed. It doesn't sound like much, but we think they were destroyed because they contained important information about magic and its history."

"How much of my story will I never know?" Aizel asked.

Meena felt her own shoulders deflate. She couldn't fix this. Every problem seemed more tangled than the ruined sections of the tapestry itself.

CHAPTER 6

"This is the back door you referred to?" Sol asked, looking down at the iron grate Robin had uncovered on the forest floor. Sol kept his tone light but still managed to convey his doubt.

"Would you prefer to walk up to the front gate and announce your presence?" Robin replied, throwing her weight against the rusted latch.

"I would prefer not to be immediately murdered upon entry," Sol mumbled, gripping the dagger that now hung from his belt. "If you truly trust these *allies*, why are you sending me through a secret escape route no one but the royal family is supposed to be aware of?"

Robin stood. "I do trust the Sirilians. Mostly. I am not going to ask you to blindly trust them based on my word. They would not kill you on sight if you approached the front gate. But if you've never been up close and personal with a king before, you can't just walk up to their home and demand to speak with them."

Sol exhaled. "I don't have time for jesting."

Robin dropped her voice into a lower register. "This way gives you control over your entrance. The passage comes up in an old, unused portion of the castle. You can do what you do best—enter the enemy's lair, scope out his strengths and weaknesses, then act on your plan."

Sol nodded. He appreciated the straightforward honesty.

"You can also find Aizel first. She will have more timely knowledge of where the kingdoms currently stand, and she can walk you into the king's home."

"Thank you, Lady Robin." Sol dipped his head in a small token of his respect.

Robin threw her arms around his neck. "It was good to meet you in person after all these seasons of working together." Her voice was thick and full of emotion in his ear.

"This will not be our last meeting." He slowly put his arms around the Quotidian woman who had helped countless people escape Istroya. It felt nice to hold her, but he was not used to such blatant displays of affection. His body tensed at her closeness. It was nice. But it was unexpected and not a comfort he'd ever had consistently.

"I will aid you as I can in Falqri." Robin stepped back.

"You have done enough," Sol responded, adjusting the satchel of food and clothing Robin had given him. "I will not ask you to endanger more than you already have."

"And you have not done enough?" Robin raised her eyebrows, challenging his statement.

Sol dropped halfway into the tunnel, which was surprisingly larger and more stable than he'd anticipated. "Thank you, Robin," he said, ignoring her words.

"Do you need a torch?" she asked him, gesturing to the

dusty pile of wooden implements just inside the cave door. "I don't know if they still keep the oil fresh on this side."

Sol inhaled, letting the scent of clean dirt tickle his nose. "Mhhhhhh," he intoned. He lifted his hands in front of him, and a small orb began to glow between his palms. "I think I can do without."

Robin's pursed lips relaxed into a smile. "Of course. Sorry, I forget."

Sol pulled the small grate shut behind him and stood to his full height in the tunnel. It was broad enough for three people to stand side by side, with enough clearance above his head to be comfortable. Rafters and stonework lined the ceilings and walls.

With a final nod to Robin, who was already covering the grate with greenery, Sol turned and made his way down the tunnel.

As the darkness settled around him, his other senses heightened and he felt his mind slip into a state of focused concentration, which relaxed him. He liked the darkness. He felt safe and in control.

But he would not be able to find his way through the unknown tunnel blindly. Drawing on the calming atmosphere around him, he moved his hands together and reformed the orb of light between them. Keeping it as dim as possible so as not to blind himself with brightness, he silently made his way down the smoothly carved corridor.

$\mathcal{M}$eena placed a protective hand over the small wooden chest under her arm. She peered into the courtyard, keeping the chest hidden behind the door. Celesta was nowhere in sight.

A small crowd, however, had gathered around the outer gate. Standing next to King Frederich, Onric addressed four of the regular guards.

Aizel stood at one side of the group, but she was watching a carpenter reinforce the gate.

Meena waited behind the door. This gathering looked serious, and she wanted to avoid it. It wasn't the seriousness of it that she wanted to avoid, of course, but she did not want anyone to judge her because her own plan was frivolous.

"Yes." Onric appeared to be answering a guard's question. "Her magic will only be applied to items that bolster the castle's defense. It will have no effect on you or any other person at all."

Two of the men shuffled their feet uncomfortably.

Meena hid a little further behind the door. She was glad her father had accepted Aizel's help, but she couldn't blame the men for being wary.

Aizel looked small, standing a step away from the rest of the group with her arms crossed.

"How can a nail be a better nail?" one of the guards asked, directing his question over Aizel to Onric and the king.

Onric appeared to have no answer to that question and looked to his father.

"A nail only has one function. It's just got to go into the wood," another guard said over the silence. "How do we know it won't be dangerous?"

"Yeah," a third one spoke up, emboldened by his peers. His glance strayed to Aizel, animosity in his eyes.

Aizel leaned her shoulders back but kept her feet in place.

Meena straightened her neck. Discomfort could be tolerated; stupidity could not.

Dropping the wooden chest to the floor, she walked into the courtyard and strode confidently toward the group. Onric stepped aside, catching her eye as she joined the circle. She did not stop walking, however, and the guards separated so she could approach the gate behind them.

"A nail has two functions," she said loudly. "To go into the wood and *not come out*." She emphasized the final few words as she tugged at a particularly loose nail on the gate. It slid out of its place into her hand. She turned around to face the quiet group of men behind her. "A nail can always be a better nail."

"Thank you, Philomena," King Frederich said. His voice carried neither censure nor praise.

Onric smirked at her before addressing the rest of the

men. "Aizel's harmony magic does not pose a threat to any of us here. We are grateful for her aid."

"Yes, Captain," one of the soldiers replied.

They seemed somewhat subdued.

Though the air had previously been calm, a strong gust of wind blew forcefully through the courtyard, whipping Meena's hair around her face.

Meena spun around to shake her face free of the tangles of hair that blocked her vision.

The wind calmed.

Feeling that her input was no longer necessary, Meena walked back through the group of men, giving Aizel a quick smile as she passed. She entered the door to the old ruins and closed it behind her.

Meena knew nearly everyone who lived or worked at the palace. They were good, trustworthy people. People she enjoyed conversing with and being surrounded by. The only reason the soldiers were confident enough to question Onric was because King Frederich tolerated it and encouraged them to be equals, not underlings.

She hated to see the distrust growing into an uneasy tension and driving a wedge between her community.

She breathed in deeply, stretching her arms to ease the uncomfortable feeling in her chest. The motion made her arm feel empty.

She'd left the chest on the other side of the courtyard.

Stepping back outside, she noticed that the group had dispersed, leaving only the usual gate guard. She gave him a light nod and moved firmly toward the door opposite her. She had no desire to stop and chat with the likely still-disgruntled guard.

But she had barely taken a few steps into the courtyard

when the wind picked up once again. One moment, the air was calm. The next moment, Meena could hardly breathe as wind sped around her, whipping her already-tousled hair into another frenzy.

She spun in a circle, trying to wrangle her hair back into place so she could see again.

The wind calmed. She was facing the door to the ruins again. She'd never experienced wind quite like that before. Any other time, she would have taken a moment to play in it. But now it did not feel right.

With the air calm once again, she turned back to the palace to continue on her original errand. But as soon as her feet began to move, the wind picked up again.

"I knew I should have taken the time to braid my hair this morning," Meena grumbled to herself as she swung her head upside down and twisted the flying curls into a tight knot around her hand.

But the wind didn't let up as she walked. She blinked her eyes. They were beginning to water from the air snapping swiftly across her face. She dropped her head again, this time to protect her eyes.

Hunched over in the wind, blinded by tears, and with her hand still holding her long hair to her scalp, she couldn't help but laugh at herself. "This is so not worth it." She ran against the wind as best she could, grabbed the wooden chest behind the door to the palace, and dashed back into the frenzied greenreign weather.

At least on her return trip, the wind pushed at her back, speeding her along.

Back inside the relative safety of the old stone ruins, she managed to shoulder the door closed behind her.

Setting the chest down once again, she used both hands to attempt to untwist her tangled hair and shake it free.

The strong wind shook the wooden door behind her, but the walls of the hall around her kept her safe from its capricious whims. The old hall she stood in had a rounded ceiling, which had likely been very sophisticated for its time but felt ominously low as Meena picked her way across the room.

Random piles of wood and broken furniture lined the walls. Meena skirted around them, remembering how she used to dig through them for treasure. At the moment, she was slightly more worried about disturbing the rodents or snakes that had decided to inhabit the old furniture. Fortunately, she'd never been concerned about that as a child.

Lifting her chin a little higher, she clenched her skirt in her hands. "I'm not afraid of snakes," she murmured, aware that she was attempting to convince herself.

The back of the large hall spread out into various passageways and smaller rooms. Meena's favorite was a trapdoor that led from the main hall to an underground tunnel, which led to a secluded place in the forest. It had likely been created to allow the inhabitants of the castle to escape during a siege. It felt a little riskier than the other places she had taken Celesta, but her father had frequently had the tunnel maintained and checked so that his own children would be safe playing in it.

And it was the perfect spot to hide a treasure. She'd already drawn out a simple map that led from the palace bedrooms to the tunnel.

As she opened the hidden door along one wall, a gentle breeze once again began teasing her hair. Perhaps the walls were not as wind safe as she'd assumed. At least this time, it wasn't impeding her vision. Brushing her hair over her shoulder out of habit, she looked down into the darkness of the tunnel. Her fingers and toes tingled with excitement.

She might be afraid of snakes, but she was not afraid of tunnels or treasure hunts.

Picking up an oil lamp and flint from a small alcove near the door, she struck a flame and descended into the familiar old tunnel. After a short staircase, the tunnel took a sharp turn, blocking the light from the door at the top of the stairs behind her.

The flame of the lamp shed a soft light on the walls around her, though it flickered softly as though someone were blowing on it. Meena cupped her hand around the flame to protect it. Turning a knob on the lamp, she increased the length of the wick to strengthen the flame.

She lightly ran the fingers of her left hand on the dusty wall to her side as she lowered the lantern so as not to blind her eyes. Currents of air continued to rustle through her hair, whispering her along. The air pushing at her back was warm, replacing the chill in the tunnel with its fresh scent.

The tunnel itself was wide enough for multiple people to walk in comfortably at once. Likely another feature designed specifically to make it a safe escape route. Despite how long it had been since she had last visited, Meena was proud that she still remembered every twist and turn. Even without the lantern, she could have made it safely through, though she was glad to have the light.

Meena kept her eyes on the floor, looking for a place to hide the treasure chest. Perhaps leaving it closer to the door would be the best plan, especially if Celesta found the tunnel frightening. Meena had a feeling her young friend was as adventurous as she was.

Holding the chest tucked under her arm, she continued down the tunnel rather than turn back immediately. There was one more staircase carved into the stone ground under the castle cellars that led to the deepest part of the tunnel itself, and she wanted to see it before she hid the treasure. If Onric and Erich were with her, they could go all the way to the end of the tunnel and pry open the far door into the forest. But it was likely overgrown and would be too difficult to force open on her own. Since her brothers were consumed with preparing the castle defenses, she did not think they would approve of opening tunnel leading directly into the heart of the castle. That didn't sound like an upgrade in defense.

Surprisingly, the rustling breeze grew stronger as she descended the lower staircase. In fact, she had never felt air flow this far into the tunnel. She distinctly remembered how stagnant the deepest area used to feel, as though this place were frozen in time forever. The tingling in her hands and feet wormed its way into her stomach. Perhaps it was not a good idea to come down here alone. Especially without telling anyone she was doing so.

Meena turned around, deciding she had gone far enough. She had hardly taken two steps back up before the wind suddenly picked up, howling through the tunnel. It whipped around her hair and blew out the small flame of the lamp. With a gasp, Meena threw her back against the wall, holding up the dead lamp as though its power could still ward off the darkness.

As her heart pounded in her ears, Meena reminded herself that she knew this tunnel inside and out—she could find her way to the top very quickly and easily. She would do so in just a moment, after she had caught her breath. Her feet seemed quite unwilling to move. Her heart sounded loudly in her ears.

With a brave inhale, she pushed herself off the wall and leaned forward to move back up the tunnel. She nodded reassuringly as her foot lightly crunched across the soft dirt below her. But her bravery disappeared as her knees threatened to crumble beneath her.

Her feet were still glued to the floor, and she hadn't moved them.

Someone else had made the footstep.

Someone else was here with her.

Meena froze, listening as the footsteps grew closer. They were firm but wary, their owner moving very slowly to the tunnel. Toward her.

Meena didn't dare to breathe. She was deep enough in that there was no light at all. It was completely black. Perhaps this was just a servant and they would walk right past her. She closed her eyes, trying not to remind herself that a servant would be carrying a lamp. Except maybe their lamp had gotten blown out in the wind as well. She inhaled shakily. Should she call out?

Of course she should call out. No one knew this tunnel existed. King Gareth wouldn't know to send a surprise attack at them this way.

The footsteps stopped. The intruder—or servant—was standing right next to her. And if they had stopped exactly at that spot, they clearly knew she was there. As silently as possible, Meena reached into her pocket, searching for anything she could use as a weapon.

"Aizel?" a deep voice whispered as a small flash of light suddenly formed in front of her.

Meena's heart stopped in her throat. The stranger was doing magic. The last time Meena had seen someone holding a ball of light, her brother Aden had been cursed and turned into a beast. Through sheer strength of will, Meena refused to give in to her weakened knees. Whatever was about to happen, she would take it standing. At least that was what her mind was saying. Her eyes blinked against the new light source, her mouth already open. "Aizel?" she asked. "How do you know Aizel?"

The stranger leapt backward, holding his glowing orb in front of him as though it were a weapon as well as a light source. He was young. Much younger than the councilor who'd cursed Aden. He could be as young as one of Meena's brothers. But his dark eyes, lit from below by the orb between them, looked tired and wary.

"Who are you?" he asked, his voice low and rough.

Her mind told her to scream for help, or to hide her identity, or to refuse to answer him at all. But apparently, her mouth still wasn't listening. "Who am I? Who are you and what are you doing in my castle?"

"How did you find me here?" he said, stepping forward. He was considerably taller than she was, and she had to tilt her head up to meet his eyes.

"How did I find you here? Again, this is *my* castle." Meena said, straightening her spine to stand as tall as she could. Her mind screamed at her to stop aggravating the angry Majis.

"Where's Aizel?" He leaned toward her, still holding his orb of light between them menacingly.

"Will you stop answering questions with questions?" Meena spat back.

"This was not part of the plan." The man leaned back,

removing himself from Meena's immediate space. His eyes darted quickly to the left and right of the dark tunnel.

Meena took a moment to take him in from head to toe as well. His brown hair was lighter than hers, and it was glowing a bit in the soft light. His face was hard, wary, and defensive. He was tall like her brothers, but his broad shoulders and wide stance definitely made him larger. He was tense, every muscle in his body prepared for action.

Her heart thudded in her chest. She was frightened, but not scared. She knew it didn't make sense, so she focused on things she could understand.

Things like the color of his eyes, which was somewhere between gray and green. She thought she even saw some flecks of gold in his irises, but that was probably her imagination in the flickering light.

She did not have time to imagine things. She had to get herself safely out of here.

If it was still dark, she was sure she could beat him out of the tunnel. He was clearly new here, and she had the advantage of knowing the space. Unfortunately, he controlled the source of light, and she didn't know how to extinguish it.

"I can't leave you down here," he muttered to himself. "You've already seen me. But I don't suppose killing you would help further the plan either."

"That definitely would not further the plan." Meena's voice was high, and she shook her head. "I would prefer not to be killed."

"I would prefer not to kill anyone." His eyes scanned her from head to toe. It seemed that his eyes never stopped moving, as though he was always in full awareness of his surroundings. "But it's a little too late for that."

Meena continued shaking her head. "It doesn't have to be too late."

"No." The man used his orb to gesture toward Meena.

Her instincts wanted her to flinch, but she inhaled sharply to cover her own movement, hoping he hadn't seen her fear.

"I didn't mean right here in this situation," he continued. "I was talking about the state of things as a whole." His hands, still holding the orb, made a small arc at eye level to emphasize his words.

The arcing motion reminded Meena of the way Celesta said her name with her hands. And that reminded her that this man was looking for Aizel. "Are you from Istroya? Your green eyes remind me of . . ." Meena snapped her mouth shut.

This Majis had likely been sent by Gareth to assassinate Aizel, so Meena knew she shouldn't reveal anything about her friend to the intruder. It seemed most everyone wanted to kill Aizel simply because she was a Majis. Except this man here was a magic-wielder as well. Shouldn't that mean he would be Aizel's ally instead of enemy? Meena reined in her racing thoughts, knowing she had said too much already.

"You do know too much already," he said, his eyes narrowing. "What do my green eyes remind you of?"

"They'll be looking for me in a moment," Meena replied as confidently as she could. "They sent me to grab some items, which shouldn't have taken long, so they'll miss me." Her confidence wavered as she realized she was trying to convince herself more than him.

"They sent you to grab items from this tunnel?" His eyes darted up and down the empty tunnel again, which was completely bare of anything except dirt and dust.

Meena almost rolled her eyes. If it was one of her brothers, they would tease her mercilessly about such a useless excuse. The stranger seemed to have actually believed her.

"It was less to grab and more to put," she said. The longer she talked, the more time she would have to come up with an escape plan. She lifted her shoulder, showing off the small chest under her arm. "I was going to place this back up the tunnel, but the wind called me further in . . . I mean, they *are* looking for me."

"The wind?" He was peering at her again, quite intently.

"Forget it." Why had she mentioned the stupid wind?

"The wind called to you?"

"Do you ever stop asking questions?" Meena asked.

"What did it say?" he asked—another question.

If it weren't for the serious tone of his voice, Meena would have thought he was making fun of her. Before she could respond, she heard another set of footsteps. This time they were coming from the entrance on her side. She exhaled in relief. Whoever it was would be from the castle. Maybe someone had seen her descend into the tunnel, or they'd happened upon the open door in the hall and had come down to investigate.

Pushing herself off the wall, she repositioned her weight so she could break into a sprint—away from the intruder. "I told you they were looking for me."

But the stranger was no longer paying attention to her. He immediately extinguished the light in his hand.

More than willing to take her chance in the dark, Meena dashed forward. Before she had taken a single step, a firm hand caught her wrist, holding her in place.

"I need you." His quiet whisper sounded like barely more than a scratch in the dark.

"I doubt that," Meena whispered back. Then, realizing she was not the one in hiding, she opened her mouth. "I'm here!" she yelled.

The hand on her wrists tightened, pulling her backward. "You said they knew you were here." His voice sounded both confused and mocking.

"And there's a strange Majis with me!" she yelled.

A light glowed in the far distance, and Meena twisted her wrist, straining forward.

The footsteps increased in pace, and Aizel dashed around the corner. A magical orb of light glowed between her two hands.

As soon as he saw her, the stranger stepped forward, keeping his grip on Meena's wrist and pushing her to his side.

"Watch out!" Meena yelled to her friend. "I don't know if he's dangerous." She stopped trying to escape and instead leaned against the stranger, trying to use her weight as a shield for her friend.

"Sol?" Aizel slid to a stop, looking between Meena and the intruder.

"Aizel?" Sol pushed forward, easily sidestepping Meena's attempt to hold him back.

"Let her go," Aizel commanded. "And what are you doing here? How did you get here?"

"I don't know her," Sol responded, his grip still tight on Meena's wrist.

"I do. She's a friend. Let her go."

Sol's grip loosened slightly. "She's Quotidian."

"She's a princess." Aizel stepped forward.

Meena shrank back from the power in her friend's voice.

Sol's grip tightened again, and he twisted Meena around to face him.

She yanked at her wrist, using her other hand to try and pry his fingers from her.

"Is her family holding you here against your will?"

"No." Aizel stepped forward, releasing the orb into the air where it floated on its own in the tunnel. She threw her arm around Meena's shoulder and pushed Sol away. "But you are holding her against her will. And mine."

"Alright." Sol dropped Meena's wrist and stepped back.

Meena rubbed her wrist and leaned into Aizel's comforting hug. "Do you know him?" she asked.

"He's from my village in Istroya," Aizel explained. "He's not as good at pearl diving as I am."

"You're alive," Sol said to Aizel. "We thought they'd taken you."

"No. I escaped. On my own. To save Celesta. It kind of backfired, but she's safe now." Aizel loosened her hold on Meena and threw her arms around Sol's chest. "It's so good to see someone from home."

Sol returned her hug, leaning his head over hers protectively.

Meena crossed her arms as she watched their reunion. She was not mad at Aizel for leaving her side and embracing the intruder. Not at all.

"Why are you here?" Aizel stood back, looking up at Sol's face. "And how?"

"I got myself chosen. And then escaped once we'd crossed the sea."

"Did you come for me?" Aizel asked. "But you thought I was dead?"

Sol put his hands on Aizel's shoulders. "I would have if I'd known you were alive, but it appears you've done fine without me." His eyes flicked to Meena.

"You got yourself *chosen*?" Aizel's voice was louder than Meena had ever heard it. "Intentionally?"

"Chosen?" Meena asked, trying to follow along and not feel left out.

"Chosen by the Quotidian to fuel their magic reserves," Aizel explained, still looking at Sol.

"That doesn't sound good . . ." Meena replied.

"It's not," Aizel said. "What was your plan if you hadn't escaped?" Aizel directed this question to Sol. "You would be stuck in some castle dungeon in Chendas, living a life worse than death? Powering gems through your pain?"

"That wasn't going to happen," Sol replied. "I knew what I was doing. It was a risk I needed to take."

Aizel stepped back, crossing her arms as she looked up at Sol. She remained silent, but her fixed attention on Sol seemed to indicate she still expected an answer.

Sol glanced at Meena again.

"She can be trusted," Aizel said in answer to his unspoken question.

"How much does she know?"

"Everything," Aizel said. "Except for what you haven't told me."

Sol returned his gaze to Aizel, breathing slowly before he finally answered, "I'm on a mission for the Thorn."

Aizel finally turned away from Sol. "His father led a rebellion group called River's Thorn," she explained. "But he was found out and taken when I was Celesta's age. River's Thorn disbanded after he was sent to the shipyard . . ." Aizel paused, staring at Sol.

He said nothing, but he dropped his eyes to the ground.

"It never disbanded. You've been leading the resistance this entire time?" Aizel's arms were crossed.

Meena shrank back, glad she was not the recipient of Aizel's glare.

"And you *never* thought to tell me? I aided you. I frequently gave you pearls so you wouldn't have to work extra shifts even if it meant coming below count on *mine* so I had to sacrifice my break day. You didn't think you could trust me after all that?"

Sol looked down, some remorse seeming to have gotten through to him. "He wasn't sent to the shipyard." His words were low, and Meena had to lean forward to catch them.

Aizel opened her eyes a little wider. She said nothing as she waited for him to elaborate.

"He was taken." Sol looked back up at Aizel, his face clearly pained, but not in a look of remorse. "It was too dangerous to involve anyone else."

"I'm so sorry." Aizel stepped forward to place a hand on Sol's arm for a moment. Then her hands went back to her hips. "I still don't forgive you for keeping this to yourself and not trusting me."

"Thanks for the pearls over all the years," Sol responded, talking over her. "I wasn't a bad diver, I just often spent my time under communicating with other members of the Thorn, or with Lady Robin."

A small jabbing pain under her arm reminded Meena she was still holding the wooden chest. "Shall we take him up to the palace?" she offered.

Sol looked over at her again. "Will your king stand in the way of my mission?"

Though she was surprised by his bluntness, Meena

responded as honestly as she could. "I cannot promise he will aid you, but I can promise he will not stand in your way."

Sol dipped his head once in acknowledgment.

Deciding to hide the chest somewhere else, Meena carried it with her out of the tunnel. Not that she was scared of returning. She'd just had enough adventure in closed, dark spaces.

CHAPTER 8

*S*ol met the gaze of the Iseldan ruler without bowing. This man was not his king.

The sharp edge of the wooden crate poked into his thighs, and he shifted his weight so he was partially sitting back and partially standing.

The king himself sat on a wooden chest across from Sol. The princess had arranged for this meeting to take place in an old tower room for the sake of privacy, but Sol instantly appreciated its lack of decorum as well. He was far more comfortable discussing plans in an unused storeroom than a throne room.

He'd been introduced to the other faces in the room—all members of the king's family—but he kept his attention focused on the man who held the power in the room.

"You have information on King Gareth of Chendas?" the king asked him.

Sol nodded.

"In exchange for what?"

"Swift passage to the Falqri Fort." Sol did not hesitate to share what he needed. He was already in enemy territory with little time to spare.

"And?" the king pressed further.

"And," Sol responded, still not breaking the man's shrewd gaze, "access to someone who could get me inside the Fort would be appreciated." No harm in asking if the man was offering.

The king exhaled slowly. "My standing in Falqri has somewhat lessened recently. I take no pride in admitting this pain. I know not whether I can offer this to you, as I know not whether they would welcome me and mine in a place that Chendas favors greatly."

The door squeaked open, and another prince stepped in. "Sorry, I'm late." He was breathing heavily.

Aizel, who had been standing supportively at Sol's side, approached the man and took his hand. "Erich, this is Sol."

Sol stood fully as she led the newcomer toward him.

Erich extended his hand in welcome.

Sol took in the man's loud purple doublet, welcoming smile, and guileless eyes. He did not immediately accept the prince's hand.

"The master diver who taught you how to swim before your skill grew greater than his?" Erich's words were spoken to Aizel, but he still held his hand out in welcome.

Sol felt the ghost of a smile play across his lips. The prince managed to convey admiration for Aizel, humor for a welcome, and a knowledge of who Sol was in such a simple greeting.

Sol kept his face solemn but extended his own hand to the prince. "That's the way we are telling the story now?" he said, glancing quickly to Aizel, who shrugged.

"Welcome to Iseldis," Erich responded. "I look forward to learning much from you."

Sol nodded, unsure how to respond to such a greeting.

Erich had already turned back toward his father. "Where's Mum?" he asked.

"Steward Daniel requested her presence quite urgently. She assured me she would join us as soon as she could."

Spinning fully around, Erich took in the room and leaned back against the chest next to Sol, where Aizel had been a few moments before. She settled in next to him.

"Meena." King Frederich turned to the daughter at his side. "Would you mind going to look for her?"

The princess crossed her arms. "Yes, in fact. I would mind."

Shocked at her response, Sol glanced at the king.

"It was worth an attempt," King Frederich muttered under his breath, seemingly unsurprised.

"You'll have to try harder than that." Meena pushed herself from her makeshift chair and came to stand on the other side of Sol.

Sol followed her movement, confused at the interaction he had just been witness to.

Glancing up at him as she settled herself beside him, Meena must have seen something in his face. "He was trying to get me out of the room before the discussion got too serious," she whispered, but her voice was loud enough to be heard by everyone in the room.

Sol quickly forced his face back into a neutral expression. He did not have the luxury of showing his thoughts. He flexed his ankle, lightly nudging the chest behind him with the bottom of his foot. He should not have let his guard down. It would not happen again.

His eyes quickly scanned the rest of the room, ensuring no one else had seen his earlier expression. It crossed his mind that the two other women in the room—Aizel and a dark-haired seamstress whose name he could not recall—had not been asked to leave. It was none of his concern, though. He could not blame the king for wanting to shield his daughter from the horrors of the world. Sol only wished he could shield every child on Istroya from the darkness they had faced at the hands of the Quotidian.

"I do not believe you are my enemy," King Frederich said, bringing Sol's attention back to him. "Nor do I clearly understand whom or what I am fighting against. Should you share the information you have knowledge of, I will do my best to aid you in service of the safety of . . ." The king paused for a barely perceptible moment. "Our people."

Sol glanced to his side, looking past Erich to Aizel. She was the only person in the room he trusted, but even that was shaky ground now that so many things about their circumstances had changed.

"We stand no chance, and neither do they," she said quietly. "There is no secret you can share that would worsen our situation."

Sol inhaled. She'd verbalized his thoughts. Before he looked back at the king, however, he found himself glancing to the other side, at the princess.

She looked back at him. Despite the tense turn of her lips, she looked so young, so untouched by the worries and pains that plagued every other person of his small community. He did not want to be the one who shattered her understanding of the world, but another small part of him reveled in the words he was about to say. Something angry tightened inside him. Anger that his sisters and his mother had never been offered the same opportunity for a carefree childhood. That his father had been sentenced to seasons of torment for trying to give them a better chance.

Sol finally turned his gaze back to the king. The thoughts swirled through his mind for barely a moment, though he felt them deeply. He inhaled, preparing to speak. If he'd had the ability to shield someone he loved from unnecessary pain, he would do anything to make that possible. Though he might shatter this girl's world, he would not take pleasure in doing so.

"My people are skilled craftsmen. Under the cruel eye of the Quotidian taskers on Istroya, we have constructed several warships complete with magical additions and properties."

King Frederich's face remained passive, but Sol could see the way his eyelids rose slightly and his nostrils flared. "To what end?" he asked.

"Gareth intends to sail the fleet to destroy the shores of Iseldis, and I doubt he means to stop there."

"My cyphers have heard no tale of this fleet?"

"It is on the eastern shore of the island, hidden from the main port, which Gareth tightly controls."

"Who will be manning this fleet?"

"His own soldiers. He has been amassing an army there for several decades."

"What of your own people?" King Frederich asked, leaning forward. Sol could see that his forehead was pale, but his cheeks burned red beneath his beard. "They have been forced to build this fleet, and they will be offered the chance to remain on their island home while Gareth sails out to conquer the world?"

Sol bit back the tip of his tongue. He'd hoped to avoid this fact, but King Frederich was too shrewd. "My brothers and sisters will be sent to the front of the attack, to fuel the magic and take the worst of the initial damage." Sol's voice was hoarse. He had not spoken so many words all at once in a very long time.

The king leaned back, stabilizing himself with his hands pressing on the chest below him. "And you cannot sway them by turning on these taskers? Would it not be easier to end this fight before it began? Surely there are enough of them to turn the tide."

Sol scoffed through his nose, pressing a finger into his forehead, which had begun to ache. "Do not humiliate me, king. I am not here begging to be rescued by the distant descendant of the Quotidian who stole this kingdom from my ancestors."

"It is not my intention to humiliate," the king responded, his voice deflated. "But I must know what I am facing if I am to lend you my aid."

The king's words still stung with condescension, but Sol pushed the man's ignorance aside.

The princess at Sol's side made a sniffing sound that sounded suspiciously like the scoff Sol had recently made.

He glanced at her quickly. Her brow furrowed in confusion, but she did not seem to notice his gaze as she frowned at her father.

"They hold our families hostage," Sol responded. "They take our fathers and uncles and even mothers and sisters as well. They send them to work in the eastern port and demand certain requirements from either side of the family under threat of death."

Sol found himself glancing toward the princess out of the corner of his eye.

Her eyes blinked rapidly, and she shook her head as if disbelieving what she'd heard.

She was not his problem. He returned his attention to her father.

"All that withstanding, my people would sacrifice everything to turn on those who have harmed us. But even if those forced into fighting miraculously turned the tide on the trained Quotidian soldiers, sailors, and mages who will accompany the fleet, Gareth has devised a tool that keeps the magical power in his own hands." Sol inhaled.

Before he could continue speaking to the deathly silent room, the door once again squeaked open.

An older woman entered the room. Her dark hair and eyes were so similar to those of the princess at his side, Sol assumed she must be the queen. She wore a small smile on her face, which contrasted greatly with the shocked expressions of everyone else in the room.

"Aden's returned," she said immediately.

Behind her, a tall man with similar features pushed his way into the room, a boyish grin on his face.

"A day early!" The princess jumped up, running forward and throwing herself into her brother's arms. She was not the first to do so, however; the eldest prince was already embracing him. Within moments, the other brothers joined in the jovial welcome.

Sol stood. He had no desire to witness or participate in the family's apparent reunion. He could skirt around the family and let them have this moment in privacy.

The king opposite him stood at the same time. "Stay," he commanded, lifting a hand. "Please." He dropped the hand to his side. "This discussion cannot wait."

Sol nodded and leaned back against the chest, arms crossed.

While the occupants of the room focused on their returning family member, Sol was the only one who noticed a small woman enter the doorway behind him. She stood back from the crowd of hugs, glancing around the rest of the room. She took in Aizel, who was still standing by Sol, and the seamstress woman who had remained behind the large table covered in woven fabric and threads. Finally, her eyes also moved to Sol.

Sol looked away first. He was in no position to welcome the stranger to this family.

Extricating herself from the center of her enthusiastic brothers, Meena approached the stranger. Apparently, Sol was not the only person in the room to have noticed her presence.

"Thank you," the princess said, eyes blinking rapidly as she threw her arms around the woman's shoulders. "Thank you for a way to reverse the curse. It must have taken courage to dare to mess with the magic, but there is no way we can ever repay you!"

"Curse?" Sol whispered to Aizel.

"Aden was cursed by a Quotidian mage and was turned into the form of a beast."

"Robin could have mentioned that," Sol muttered. This family had more grief from Gareth than he'd realized.

"Robin?" Aizel asked. "You know Robin?"

"She's been my correspondent here for several seasons," Sol replied as his eyes continued to watch the activity in the room. He was uncomfortable with the uninhibited exuberance of so many people at once. "She met me briefly last night to aid in escaping the soldiers."

"She played a part in rescuing Erich and Celesta as well."

"She also could have mentioned that," Sol muttered. He thought it odd that she had rescued one of the princes but remained unwelcome in Iseldis. Something was not right.

"She's far too modest about her work," Aizel said, responding to Sol's unspoken thought. "Rather similar to someone else I know." Aizel poked his arm.

"More skilled than the master who taught her how to swim?" Sol risked a wry smile at Aizel. "Perhaps you could learn something from the leaders of the River's Talon and River's Thorn."

"Not so humble anymore, are we?" Aizel responded.

Sol turned away. He needed to focus on getting out of here and getting to Falqri instead of letting this family's infectious joy get to him.

"I'm Meena, by the way. If Aden told you my name was Philomena, don't listen to him. Let me introduce you to the others." The princess led the stranger into the room, stopping first at the seamstress's table. "Ashlin, this is Isa. Isa, this is Ashlin."

Ashlin. That was her name.

"Now that I finally have sisters instead of just brothers," the princess continued, pulling Isa toward Sol and Aizel, "I've decided that sisters are my favorite. Technically, Aizel is the only one who is really my sister, since she and Erich got married before the family had even met her, but I've decided Ashlin will always be my sister now, too. And Celesta, even though she's Aizel's younger sister. This is Aizel." The princess finally stopped talking long enough to catch her breath.

Isa smiled at Aizel. Her eyes moved to Sol, waiting for the introduction.

"Oh, no. You and Aden didn't get married before you arrived, did you? Not that it would be a problem, because I can tell we are going to be great friends and hopefully sisters, too, but I was just poking fun at Erich and Aizel—I didn't mean to offend you if you'd already done the same thing."

Isa turned back to the princess. "No, Aden and I have not yet chosen to wed one another."

"I certainly hope you do decide to do so," Meena responded, raising her eyebrows.

Isa laughed at that. Her laugh was clear but not derisive. "I certainly hope we do, too." She turned back to Sol.

"This is Sol," the princess said. She paused, and Sol noticed her face was slightly flushed. Meena looked at him with an awkward smile, then dropped her eyes to the floor.

Sol appreciated that she did not reveal his identity as a magic-wielder, though her awkward expression surely gave something away.

"You broke a curse?" he asked Isa.

"I did," she responded slowly.

"You are Majis?" he asked.

"I am not," she responded. She turned to look toward the door, her eyes scanning the group that still surrounded the man she had entered with.

"But you understand how to wield magic?" Sol asked.

"I do not." She turned to Meena. "Who is this?"

"He is . . ." Meena looked to Sol.

"I am a friend of Aizel's," he started vaguely. "A Majis from Istroya." This entire family knew his identity now; it was better to claim it with pride while he had the rare chance.

Isa's face transformed from aloof to excited. "Can you explain how I cured the curse, then? Am I Majis?" she asked.

"Yes," Sol responded. "And no. Anyone can harness the magic of harmony—or chaos—but that does not make them a Majis."

Only when the room fell completely silent did Sol realize everyone had heard his final statement.

"Anyone can harness the magic of harmony and chaos?" Meena repeated.

"Yes," Sol confirmed. These people truly were ignorant.

"Is everything I ever knew an untruth?" The princess sank down onto a small box, her eyes wide with shock.

"What did you think the Quotidian soldiers were?" Sol asked, looking around the room.

"Majis who hated other Majis?" Onric proffered.

"Erich?" Aizel spoke to her husband across the room. "Did you not understand what the Quotidian meant?"

Erich shook his head, biting his lower lip and tensing his neck in a way that made the veins visible. "I thought they were magic abusers who used chaos." He walked toward her. "At least that is what I inferred from the explanations you've given."

Aizel's face relaxed. "No, that is true," she said. "But you didn't know that magic is accessible to everyone?"

Erich shook his head again, this time less embarrassed. "I did not realize that."

"What does the word 'Majis' mean, then?" Aden asked. "We've always associated it with magic-wielders."

"The Majis are descendants of the Kerev, the tenders of Iseldis who were driven out one thousand seasons ago by wielders of chaos magic."

"Can you teach us to wield magic?" Ian asked. "So we can defend ourselves?"

Sol leaned back. "Can Aizel share a skill that has been

perfected over centuries to hundreds of your people in a few weeks' time?" He crossed his arms. "No. She cannot. This harmony with magic is not a shield one can throw up at the last second."

"What are you going to be doing?" Aizel asked.

"I'm going to destroy it," Sol responded.

Aizel's eyes opened wide. "No, Sol. No. It's impossible."

"It's our only chance," Sol replied.

"It's not even a chance." Aizel raised her voice. "It's a fool's errand."

Sol felt the king's gaze resting heavily on him. The older man was quietly, yet firmly, waiting for an explanation. "Even if the Majis find a way to outwit Gareth's soldiers and fight them with magic, the scale has already been tipped. Since the beginning of the exile, Quotidian taskers have chosen certain Majis to fuel a battery of reserve magic. We cannot begin to fathom the store of power it has reserved."

"Fuel a battery?" The seamstress spoke for the first time. "With chaos magic? Through tormenting innocent Majis?" Her face twisted in horror.

Sol nodded. "This battery could likely fuel any attack Gareth wished to make several times over."

"And you will destroy it?" King Frederich asked. "How?"

"With whatever it takes."

CHAPTER 9

*M*eena's eyes flew open the moment she heard her bedroom door creak. She was usually a deep sleeper, but her dreams kept her fitfully awake throughout the night, imagining warships and separated families and unfathomable magical power.

She heard someone slip into her room, but the bright morning light assaulted her sleepy eyes, blinding her until she scrunched them closed. Squinting more carefully, she gazed at the intruder who danced across her floor with light footsteps.

It was Celesta.

Meena closed her eyes again, holding back a groan as she felt the young girl jump onto her bed. She pulled the covers up to her chin and then relaxed into a smile, deciding to enjoy the intrusion. She could think of worse ways to wake up.

"Someone got a full night of sleep," Meena said, blinking her eyes open to adjust to the sunlight. Her body attempted to snuggle further into the bed in protest, but Celesta's smiling face quickly drove away any remnants of sleep.

Grinning down at Meena, Celesta held up a rolled piece of parchment.

Meena grinned in return. She'd managed to hide the treasure in a better location before the conversation with Sol. Then she'd promptly forgotten about it. "You found a treasure map?"

Celesta nodded. She pointed to herself, to Meena, and to the door.

"You want to go treasure hunting with me? Right now?" Meena clarified.

Celesta nodded again, her large eyes wide and sparkling.

Meena clutched the blankets a little tighter, slowly pulling them over her face to jest with the younger girl.

Celesta placed her palm flat on her chest and made small circular motions. Her eyes opened even wider.

Meena instantly recognized the hand motion as a polite way to make a request. "Yes!" She nodded enthusiastically in response. "Let's go find the treasure!"

Lifting her covers, Meena threw them over Celesta's head and jumped out of the bed.

Celesta scrambled out of the tangled blankets, smiling and brushing the tousled hair from her face. She slid off the bed and grabbed Meena's hand, pulling her toward the door.

Meena dug her heels into the ground. "Wait." She gently tugged back, asking the younger girl to stay in the room. "I need to get dressed and eat first." She gestured to her night clothing and her mouth as she spoke.

Celesta shook her head in disagreement.

"Yes," Meena nodded. "Food and clothing." She twisted

her hand away from Celesta's grip and dashed toward the wooden closet that held her dresses.

Celesta waited until Meena glanced back toward her, then made a dramatic show of rolling her eyes and putting her hands on her hips.

Meena laughed. "Fine, fine. I'll hurry as fast as I am able." She pulled out a dress that was simple enough to put on without a maid's help and slipped her feet into it. "Quickly, quickly, quickly," she sang to Celesta as she tightened the front laces, weaving them through the last few holes and tying them closed.

By the time she was finished, Celesta had unrolled the parchment and was studying it closely.

Realizing it was her turn to wait, Meena put her own hands on her hips and tapped her foot until Celesta looked up. "Hurry," Meena waved her hand in small, tight circles.

Celesta rolled her eyes again and dashed toward the door.

Once in the hallway, Meena instinctively turned to her left.

Celesta grabbed her hand, pulling her to the right.

"I need to go break my fast," Meena explained, rubbing her stomach.

Celesta held up the map, gesturing down the other direction of the hall with her head.

Meena tried to stop the smile that came to her lips. Celesta could read the map after all. But Meena wasn't ready to give in quite yet.

Celesta dropped Meena's hand. She opened her eyes even wider as she stared up with a small pout on her lips. She held up her hand, circling her fingertips in the same swift motion Meena had used moments before, urging her to hurry.

"Fine." Meena rolled her eyes. "I can eat later. Let's find

that treasure. You have to lead the way." She pointed to Celesta.

Celesta nodded, opening the map in front of her as she walked slowly down the hall. When they got to the stairs, she continued to hold the map in front of her as though afraid she would lose her way without it.

Rather than tell her to put the map down, Meena gently grasped the girl's elbow to ensure she didn't fall down the stairs.

Celesta paused for a moment at the base of the staircase, comparing the available options to the dotted line on the hand-drawn map.

Meena patiently waited while the girl deciphered its meaning and correctly guided them outside to the back courtyard.

Once there, however, Celesta finally let the map drop to her side.

Meena looked up to see what could have possibly distracted the girl away from her map.

It was not *what*, it turned out—but *who*.

Sol stood in the courtyard, his arms crossed, staring out past the gate toward the forest.

Celesta ran toward him, grasping his elbow as a greeting.

Sol looked down at her, a smile immediately softening his features. Perhaps it was the gentle crinkle of his eyes, or just the full morning light of the courtyard, but Meena thought he looked far less menacing than he had the previous night.

She approached them at a more leisurely pace. Would Sol smile at her if she grabbed his elbow? She pushed the thought out of her mind. She had no reason to go around grabbing people's elbows.

Although Meena was only a few steps away, by the time she joined them, Celesta had already handed the map to Sol and was engaging him in an animated conversation with her hands.

Sol responded in kind, the soft smile still on his face.

Meena could not follow their movements fast enough, but she grasped that they were discussing the map. She saw Celesta put her palm on her chest in the same gesture for a polite request she had made earlier.

Meena stepped into their circle of communication, not wanting to feel left out even if she did not fully speak their language.

"Princess Philomena," Sol flatly welcomed her after a few more interactions with Celesta. He briefly lifted his face, which still held remnants of the smile he had freely given to Celesta.

"Sol," she responded. It felt odd to call him by such a short word when he had said her full name and title. "I see you've been invited to join in our adventure?" Meena asked, guessing at the meaning of their conversation.

Sol raised his eyebrows a small fraction of a space. "I have." He looked down at Celesta again. "Though I am surprised that you could understand as much."

"I was thinking the same of you yesterday. You must have been very close to Aizel and Celesta to be so fluent in their language." Meena felt a twinge of jealousy in her chest. Aizel and Celesta were her friends, too, and she wanted to be close to them.

"It is a language all Majis speak," Sol responded. "We must have a way to communicate when our magic is silenced." A shadow returned to his eyes.

Meena instantly regretted her petty jealousy. "I'm sorry."

The words felt empty, but it was the only thing she could think to say.

Celesta took the map back from Sol, drawing his attention to her as well.

Sol began to shake his head.

Celesta took a step closer and placed her other hand on Sol's arm once again. Her face transformed into the same wide-eyed expression that had gotten Meena out of bed moments before.

Sol slumped his shoulders in defeat. "I guess I'm following this map with you," he said.

Meena smiled at him, glad to see that Celesta had successfully wooed someone else into her early morning adventures.

Celesta happily slipped her empty hand into Sol's. She reached out her other hand toward Meena. It took her a moment to realize she was still holding the map in that hand, and her brow furrowed in disappointment.

"I can hold it," Meena offered, taking the map in one hand and gripping Celesta's with the other. She positioned the map so her fingers held it open and low, in Celesta's view.

The young girl looked at the map, then glanced around the courtyard as though reorienting herself with their mission.

Meena followed the young girl's eye movement, feeling as though she could read exactly what Celesta was thinking. Smiling with an excitement of her own, Meena glanced up at Sol to see if he had noticed the same thing.

Sol's eyes were watching her over Celesta's head.

Meena's smile faltered slightly.

His expression was guarded. His clouded eyes seemed to

be studying her, but he blinked his gaze away as soon as he noticed her looking at him.

Meena shrugged and turned her attention back to Celesta. Sol had chosen to join them on this venture, and she wasn't going to let his complicated eyes stop her from enjoying it.

Celesta slipped her hand from Meena's and pointed to the gate that led to the outer forests behind the castle.

Meena nodded affirmatively.

Celesta put her hand back into Meena's and pulled them toward the gate. Following the well-worn path quickly brought them to the same grassy area where they had flung acorns at Erich and Aizel.

Recognizing the location, Celesta pulled her hands free and ran around looking for any signs of a treasure. She leaned down into the grass, then stood back up with an acorn between her fingers. She turned to Meena, a question in her eyes.

Meena smiled but shook her head slightly. "That's not the treasure." She'd left a clue in the map—which she still held—and she wasn't going to give it away quite so easily.

As if reading her mind, Celesta returned to the center of the glade and took the map from Meena's hand. Sitting on the grass, she studiously bent her head over the parchment.

Meena felt a giggle in her chest. She suppressed it with effort, but couldn't stop the smile that spread across her face. She loved that Celesta was taking this so seriously. For such a young girl, she clearly was not one to give up easily. Glancing up, Meena shared her smile with Sol.

His face was still difficult to read. He was an outsider at the palace, and an outsider to this game she and Celesta had taken to playing together. Meena wanted to draw him in, to see him participate, to see him smile.

The image of herself walking up to him and grabbing his elbow possessively, as a friend might do, came back to her mind. She pushed the ridiculous thought away, but not before her imagination had seen his face smile kindly down at her the way he had done to Celesta. Only when he looked at her, it was different. It wasn't the affectionate smile one would give to a small child. It was a smile filled with . . .

Meena blinked. She needed to act before her imagination made her say something foolish. "Have you ever flicked acorns at someone?" She snapped her mouth closed. She'd been too late to stop the foolishness from coming out.

Sol looked even more confused.

"Generally, when two people are standing next to each other, pursuing the same goal, they discuss things with one another." Meena spoke confidently, hoping her words made enough sense to push the conversation forward instead of discussing acorns.

"Generally?" Sol repeated.

"I don't know how you do things on the Isle—" She paused to correct herself. "In Istroya. But here in Iseldis, we consider it an honor to get to know someone." She wanted to roll her eyes at herself. The words coming out of her mouth sounded so much better in her head.

"In Istroya," Sol responded, "we consider it an honor to receive the trust of a friend, and it is not something taken lightly. With a stranger."

Celesta stood then, saving Meena from attempting a response. Lifting the map so everyone could see it, Celesta pointed to a small arrow.

Meena smiled encouragingly.

Celesta looked around the glade, noticing a trail that led further into the forest. She pointed toward it and looked back at Meena for confirmation.

Meena nodded excitedly. The clues were a perfect mix of difficult and recognizable.

Still clutching the map, Celesta ran to the trail, reaching out to touch the bushy leaves on either side of it.

The morning sun filtered through the canopy of trees overhead, softening the light. Meena breathed in the fresh scents of the forest, happy with her decision not to return to the stale tunnel.

She let Celesta lead the way down the well-worn path. Knowing every footfall herself, Meena delighted in watching Celesta discover it for the first time.

Reaching back to Meena's hand for stability, the younger girl gazed in fascination at the plants around her and the occasional wildlife scampering along the branches. "Is this very different from Istroya?" Meena asked Sol.

"Less sand."

His short answer annoyed Meena, so she decided to focus on the girl in front of her. Celesta responded to everything with such delight, but Meena was sure that she herself was having the most fun. She also couldn't wait to share another secret location with her new friend.

Fortunately, getting to the secret spot was easy and fast as it was all downhill. Climbing back up to the castle would be less fun, but they didn't have to worry about that quite yet. As they were nearing the edge of the forest and the trees began to thin around them, letting the sunlight dance through onto the path below their feet, Meena squeezed Celesta's hand and excitedly pointed ahead.

An ancient tree twisted its way beyond the edge of the

forest. Its trunk was so round that if Meena attempted to stretch her arms around the tree, she would not even be able to reach across a single broad side.

Letting go of Meena's hand, Celesta dashed forward. The old tree had long since died, and much of its inner substance had rotted away, leaving behind a large structure of twisted bark. Celesta, curious and brave, immediately poked her head inside the opening, smiling in wonder as she twisted her neck to gaze up into the empty space. The young girl stepped back, looking toward Meena. She moved her hands, gesturing toward the tree with her brows slightly furrowed.

Meena could see enough of her expression to know what the girl was asking. "My brothers and I discovered this when we were children," Meena naturally explained out loud, though Sol was the only one who could hear her words. Meena pointed to herself, indicating a shorter height with her hand. "We used to hide here and escape to play games away from the castle."

Stepping forward, Meena poked her own head inside the opening of the tree. It was a little bit smaller than she remembered, but still quite large enough to fit both of them comfortably.

Scooting inside, Meena tucked her feet underneath her so Sol could join them as well.

Celesta's mouth had fallen open as she spun around to view the entire space. She was the perfect sized to stand up in the wide hollow of the tree, and Meena remembered having wished she live here as a child.

Celesta turned back to the opening, her hands moving seamlessly as she stared up at Sol.

"Not sure if you can see that," Meena called loudly. "She says to come in."

Sol dropped to his knees in the doorway, blocking most of their light. "It's dark," he said, leaning back to exit the tree before he'd even come inside it.

Celesta grabbed his upper arm, encouraging him into the space.

Sol crawled in, immediately positioning his back against the inner bark of the tree so he could have a clear view of the opening.

Slouching forward, Meena indicated some long cracks on the opposite wall of bark. Celesta followed her movements, pressing her face up against the cracks. Like slotted windows in a battle tower, the cracks offered a perfect and protected view of the road leading up the hill to the palace.

Celesta pulled back, looking up at Meena with her mouth in a rounded shape of excitement and fascination.

Meena's chest once again filled with happiness. It was so much fun to share her favorite things with someone who appreciated them. Following Celesta's lead, she pressed her face against one of the cracks. It was the perfect place to spy, as the shadows and folds of the old tree completely hid the fact that someone was peering through cracks in the bark. They used to come here and pretend they were guarding the kingdom from a Majis invasion.

Meena exhaled. Her lungs remained compressed and empty.

She had forgotten about that particular childhood game. She and her brothers had always known the evil Majis would return in their lifetime to wreak vengeance on the five kingdoms. Even as children, she had taken great pride in preparing herself to defend Iseldis. Ian often bragged that he would never let the cruel, powerful magic-wielders oppress the ordinary quotidian people.

Meena shook her head.

None of it was true. Rather, some of it was true, but it was all inside out from what she had always believed.

Her world was crumbling around her, and she didn't know when she would stop tumbling. Still struggling to breathe, Meena felt a light sweat break out on her face and arms despite the chill that shivered down her spine.

She could not free fall forever while the crumbling world sucked people she loved into its cracks.

Gareth would surely retaliate soon, and he would target Iseldis—the kingdom that knew he'd tried to murder its princes and that harbored his fugitives. He would strike soon.

Her father needed to get Sol to Falqri. Immediately. She would talk to him. Not that she could make a difference. Her father knew the urgency of this matter more than she did. But she had to talk to someone about it.

Meena finally inhaled, breathing deeply into her lungs. She would do what little she could. At the moment, she could keep Celesta entertained and happy despite the heavy air that lingered throughout the castle.

Forcing a smile, she turned back to her young friend.

Celesta pushed her fingers through one of the cracks in the bark, trying to find out how far her hand could fit through.

Picking up a stick, Meena started absently scraping away at the soft dirt at her feet.

Sol instantly noticed her actions.

Meena felt her mouth twist into the awkward smile she couldn't hold back whenever she had a secret.

Sol reached forward, scraping at the dirt with his hand.

"She has no idea," Meena whispered.

"She will," Sol mouthed back.

After a few more moments, Celesta turned back to face them.

Meena watched the surprise, comprehension, and excitement that ran through the girl's eyes as she looked from the ground to the map lying just outside the tree, then back to each of their faces.

"Do you want to find a treasure?" Meena almost squealed in excitement.

Celesta took the stick from Meena's hand and furiously dug into the dirt.

Meena smiled over her bent head. Celesta effortlessly joined in every game Meena came up with. They didn't need words to enjoy spending time together, and she loved it.

"You are enjoying this more than she is," Sol whispered.

Meena laughed. It was just like one of her brothers jesting at her expense. Lifting her arm in the tight space, she gave Sol a gentle punch in the shoulder.

She pulled her hand away quickly, however, her fingers tingling uncomfortably. They didn't hurt since she'd hardly touched him. But she had made physical contact with him. Her stomach felt light and airy, her cheeks suddenly a little warm in the stuffy space.

Sol's head snapped toward her. His forehead was wrinkled in confusion, but his mouth had the slightest quirk of a smile.

Meena rubbed the back of her hand against the small of her back. The tingling sensation didn't go away despite the slightly rough texture of her linen dress. She heard herself laughing still, but it sounded hollow and loud, and she couldn't remember what she was laughing at.

She looked away quickly.

Sol was just a boy. A boy like any of her brothers.

"Very good digging," she said to Celesta.

The girl was still intent on her task and hadn't seen the interactions taking place behind her back.

Meena kept talking to cover her embarrassment. "I'm sure you'll find something soon." Her eyes remained glued on Celesta, keeping Sol out of sight.

It was just . . . he wasn't a boy. He was a man. And he most certainly was not one of her brothers. In her most secret dreams, Meena imagined wedding an adventurer who would take her across the five kingdoms. As a child, she'd believed that her life as an adult would be more exciting than the games they played. The older she grew, the more she realized those games were childish fantasies. Fantasies that weren't true.

For a single moment, she imagined joining Sol on his mission to Falqri. She would wear a dark cloak to cover her silk dresses from view, and she would help him uncover the clues that would lead straight into the heart of Gareth's strongest fortress.

Meena didn't know how long her mind had wandered, but she was saved from further embarrassment by the sound of the stick scraping across a hard surface.

Moments later, a very excited Celesta held a dust-covered wooden chest in her hands.

From the corner of her eye, Meena could see that Sol was still watching her, his face as expressionless as always. This old tree had been large enough for several children to play inside, but it was far too small for two adults. "Let's head back to the castle and we can open the treasure there," Meena said.

Sol lifted his eyebrows, then looked pointedly at the girl between them.

Meena followed his eyeline down to Celesta.

She was sitting on the floor, the wooden box already open in her hand as she reached for the treasures inside.

"Or we could wait a moment," Meena whispered, her heart melting.

As usual, Sol did not respond verbally.

Celesta lifted the first item from the box. It was a carved wooden donkey. Meena had freshly cleaned the softly sanded surfaces of its short, round body. The toy had been hers for as long as she could remember. While she felt a small twinge of regret at giving the beloved plaything away, the look of joy on Celesta's face was completely worth it. Besides, Celesta was family now. Meena had outgrown the toy and was giving it to her younger sister.

As Celesta reached into the box for the next item, Meena looked up again at Sol. Rather than watch the excitement of the treasure, his eyes were scanning the opening of the tree and the long cracks near his head.

Meena wanted to tell him that they were safe for the moment—they were deep in the very heart of Iseldis. But it seemed that Sol was a person who was always on guard.

Sol frowned.

Meena instantly felt more alert, and her eyes darted to the opening of the tree.

Then she heard it too. A sound from the road.

Just as she had when she was a child, Meena turned and squinted against a crack in the bark. Her throat swelled closed as a group of travelers rounded the bend. She squeezed her eyes tightly shut, hoping that she was dreaming. Opening her eyes, she looked again.

If she was dreaming, then this was a nightmare straight out of her childhood.

Row upon row of soldiers on horseback galloped up the road toward the castle. They were riding in a tight formation and moving quickly. Even the horses' hooves moved in an intimidating repetition, as though their movements were one. In the front, a single rider rode ahead of the others. Since Meena's eyes had been attuned to the murky darkness, she was nearly blinded by the pristine white of his jacket and helmet as they flashed under the bright afternoon sun.

She couldn't look away.

The captain rode under the banner of Chendas. These soldiers were from King Gareth. And from the look of it, they were not coming in peace.

Meena gripped the bark in front of her as her head swam and her stomach turned.

Noticing that something had changed, Celesta tapped her shoulder.

Meena threw a smile on her face as she quickly turned around, hoping that Sol would not frighten the girl. Celesta had spent weeks as a prisoner in Gareth's castle. Meena couldn't let the soldiers find the escaped girl. And she couldn't let the happy, adventurous girl in front of her set eyes on the soldiers that had once held her captive. Celesta would instantly recognize the Chendas uniform and colors. She had to make sure that the girl did not look back out of the crack again.

"We should head back to the castle now," she said, her eyes wide and smile big. She pointed to the treasures on the ground and then back up the hill toward the palace.

Sol had stopped moving, his posture tense, ready to

spring into action. His eyes still scanned the area, then came back to Meena.

And she had to get back to the castle as soon as possible to warn her father.

But surely someone had seen the actual army riding through their kingdom and reported it to the king?

"No one else knows that Chendas is our enemy yet," Meena spoke through the same smile on her face.

"Get her back to the palace," Sol said, his lips twisting up into the most awkward smile Meena had ever seen. At least he understood she was trying to protect Celesta. Although, with a smile like that, the younger girl would instantly know something was wrong.

Fortunately, she was happily putting the toys back into her treasure box.

"The path back is hidden from sight," Meena whispered in response to Sol. "Come with us. It will be safer for everyone."

Sol nodded. He tilted his head toward the door. "Go first. I'll guard the rear."

Celesta looked up at them with concern on her face. She'd noticed something was wrong.

Meena threw her arm around Celesta's shoulder. Placing her hand above her eyes, she pretended to squint into the distance—back toward the castle, not the road—as though she were about to lead them on another adventure. Making her painful smile even bigger, she gave a confident nod.

Celesta nodded back, pointing to the castle and pretending to scan the trees around them.

The hoofbeats of the horses thundered past on the road below them. Meena couldn't tell if the pulse in her body was her own frantic heartbeat or the reverberation of the hoofbeats below. She hoped it was the former so that Celesta would not notice what was happening.

Raising her finger to her lips, Meena mimicked a tiptoe as she slowly crawled toward the door of the tree cave.

Celesta's eyebrows rose high, and she nodded in agreement, mimicking Meena's actions.

Without a brief glance over her shoulder to Sol, Meena took Celesta's hand in her own and set a pace as quickly as she dared while still pretending to play.

The steely determination on Sol's face remained fixed in her memory. Knowing he was behind her gave her strength.

Nonetheless, she was breathless before they even began ascending the hill back up to the palace. She waved it away, pretending to be tired.

Celesta merely took the opportunity to pretend to be the stronger of the two, and she set out ahead, forging her way fearlessly up the path.

For one brief moment, Meena exhaled, allowing the panic she felt inside to show on her face. Fortunately, the steep angle of the hill below them and the surrounding trees hid the running trio from the passing soldiers below.

CHAPTER 10

"Come in, quickly." The guard at the back gate waved them into the palace courtyard. Sol immediately turned to help him close the heavy gate and bar it safely.

Two other guards raced across the courtyard, heading toward the back stables. The air was thick, fraught with tension.

The princess was breathing heavily, but she had a smile on her face and a protective arm around Celesta's shoulders.

Gesturing with her free hand, Celesta asked what was happening.

Sol lifted his hands to respond. He had to leave the castle unnoticed. His mind was too busy building a strategy to tell the girl anything but the truth.

"Nothing to worry about," Meena's voice cut into his thoughts. She was clearly speaking to Celesta, but looking at Sol.

Thankful for her quick thinking, Sol repeated her words with his hands.

"The king called a surprise meeting with his advisors," Meena continued. "So everyone is rushing to make it happen."

Celesta nodded. Sol didn't think she looked convinced, but at least she'd accepted their explanation.

"Can you hide her somewhere safely?" Sol asked. "I need to find Aizel and make sure she stays out of sight." He didn't want to reveal that he planned on leaving the castle as soon as possible.

"Of course." Meena nodded, gently guiding Celesta toward the palace stairs.

Sol took a step toward the castle ruins. The best way to leave would be by the tunnel.

"They are meeting in the grand hall," the gate guard said.

Sol stopped. The grand hall would definitely be in the palace behind him, not the ruins ahead.

"Not the council room?" Meena's voice sounded behind him. She sounded confused.

Sol turned back to face them.

"The contingent from Chendas is so large—" the gate guard explained.

Sol saw Celesta staring at the guard's lips as he spoke. She understood too much.

Meena must have noticed as well. She quickly cut off the guard's words with an enormously fake smile and a quick shake of her head. "I need to make sure my friend is safe and calm," Meena said through clenched teeth as she gestured toward Celesta. "Then I'll join the others."

The guard nodded, forcing a shaky smile to his lips as he understood what she meant. "I don't believe my king wanted you present for the meeting."

Sol saw the flash of anger that sparked through Meena's eyes. "Go," Sol said quickly. Celesta's safety came first.

Meena exhaled with a huff but turned her charge back toward the stairs and disappeared into the palace.

Sol nodded to the gate guard, then hurried after them. It would be foolish to leave without knowing what was happening.

His instincts led him quickly to the great hall. It was a simple matter of following the layout of the palace halls and paying attention to the direction the guards moved in—and where the servants moved away from.

In the rapid pace of his thoughts, he realized that he'd just let the Iseldan princess take charge of one of the most important people in his life. To his own surprise, he truly believed Celesta would be safe with the woman he'd recently considered an empty-headed enemy.

He didn't have time to ponder this feeling, though, as he approached his destination.

The meeting appeared to have started. The door to the great hall was closed, with two soldiers standing guard at either side. One of them, however, gripped the door handle tightly, holding it closed while he argued with Aizel.

"Let me in," she commanded.

Sol could sense the fury in her voice despite its quiet tone. He hurried toward them, anxious to know what was happening and to keep his friend safe.

"I'm sorry, my lady," the guard responded. "Prince Erich will have my head if I let you into this room."

"And I will have your head regardless." Aizel drew herself up, inhaling menacingly.

The guard paled. His eyes watched her hands, which she had raised in front of her.

He seemed to be afraid she would attack him with magic.

Surely Aizel knew better than to attempt harmony magic while in such a state?

Sol rushed forward. "Erich's in the meeting?" he asked.

Aizel spun around, her green eyes snapping fire. "I will not let them take him again." She blinked. Sol saw the terror in her eyes masked by her fury.

"And I will not let them take you again," Sol said. "Erich is a prince in this kingdom. He is surrounded by supporters."

The cowering guard nodded emphatically, appearing quite grateful for Sol's interception.

But Aizel spun back toward the door. "Then let me in. I am part of this family now, and you cannot deny my order."

Sol reached forward to firmly squeeze Aizel's shoulder. He wanted to reassure her, but he was also unsure whether she was about to physically throw herself at the guard.

"They will kill you on sight. You are the threat to them, not Erich." Looking over her shoulder to the guard, Sol asked, "Is there a place we can watch the proceedings without being seen?"

CHAPTER 11

$\mathcal{A}$s Meena entered the palace, Celesta squeezed her hand, refusing to budge. The girl might have been young, but she was far too good at reading people and lips to allow herself to be coddled.

Meena turned and crouched until her face was level with Celesta's furrowed brow. "Everything is going to be well." She squeezed her friend's small hand reassuringly. Though she did not know if her words were true, she knew she would do everything in her power to make them true.

The silence in the castle was deafening. Heavy footfalls and closing doors sounded all around her, but the joyful chatter of servants and nobles was suspiciously absent.

Celesta huddled close to Meena as they wound upstairs and through the halls of the family wing. Meena hated when her family coddled her—she was the youngest and the only girl—and she felt bad that she had not explained the situation to Celesta. The poor girl was probably imagining a situation far worse than the truth. Meena pinched her lips closed in helplessness. This time, the real situation was probably the worst possible thing that could happen.

Instead of going to the bedrooms, Meena brought Celesta straight to the family salon. It was the safest place in the castle. Not only was it high in the center keep, but it was the place she always went to seek comfort. Queen Cara spent many hours here, working over correspondence and managing the kingdom and household from the worn wooden desk against the wall. At the moment, her mother's desk was empty. The queen would be in the great hall, supporting her kingdom, not hiding away.

At the sound of their entrance, a matronly woman entered the salon from the other side of the room. Her fore-head was creased with worry as she bustled toward them across the room.

"Mistress Marie," Meena said, keeping her tone forcibly light. "Could you see to it that Celesta gets a nice, warm tea?"

The fear drained from Marie's face as she smiled warmly at the young girl. "Of course, my lady." She stepped forward and held out an inviting hand. "It would be my pleasure. And I might be able to squeeze in a treat from cook too."

Celesta reached out with her free hand, placing it in Mistress Marie's. Her other hand remained tightly in Meena's. She bit her lip, looking back at Meena with concern, unwilling to be relinquished without knowing what was going on.

Meena squeezed back. "I don't know what's happening," she said truthfully, emphasizing her words with a shake of her head and a shrug of her shoulders. "But I will find out, and I will bring Aizel back to you."

Celesta nodded in understanding and released Meena's hand. Meena gently touched the young girl's wild curls and smiled softly, this time for real. "I'll make sure everything will be well."

Marie pursed her lips. "And what can I get for you, my princess?" Her question was innocent, but her voice held a note of displeasure.

Meena shook her head. "Nothing. Just keep her safe and distracted."

Marie had worked at the palace since before Meena was born. She narrowed her eyes at the princess. "You mean 'we.' We will keep her safe and distracted."

Meena shook her head, backing toward the door.

Marie raised her chin and her voice. "I've been told to keep you safely here."

"Not if you never saw me." Meena threw the words over her shoulder as she dashed out of the room. The large hall was on the opposite side of the palace, and Meena did not care that her shoes slapped against the stone floor as she ran. Her heart was racing, pounding in her throat. Without Celesta at her side, she did not have to hide the terror that seemed to be squeezing her from the inside out. She didn't care that she shouldn't be flying so fast inside. If she went any slower, she would explode. Besides, it was an unusual event, and she didn't have to worry about silly rules. But she relished the opportunity to break this one. It was one thing she could control, and it helped to ease her mind.

~

~

~

Sol glanced around the small room adjacent to the great hall. Just like the tree he'd been in quite recently, it was a place where one could easily hide and view an area without being seen. Specially designed holes on the back of a wooden carving allowed the room's occupants a clear view of everything that went on in the hall below.

"You are so gracious to welcome us, King Frederich." The councilor's loud voice carried directly into the small room occupied by Sol and Aizel.

Standing in the center of the great hall, the councilor stood facing a raised dais, upon which sat the king, his wife, and their four sons.

A single empty chair at the end of the line indicated where the princess would have been seated.

"Had I had more notice of your coming, Councilor Younn," the king replied, "I would have been better equipped to prepare a welcome for you and your large company."

Sol heard both politeness and a barbed threat in the king's words.

A line of Chendas soldiers paraded quietly into the room from a large open door at the end of the hall. As though practiced in advance, the soldiers lined themselves around the four walls of the massive room.

King Frederich only had four guards stationed around the dais. The formation of the Chendas soldiers blocked all exits from the room, cutting the king off from his own men.

Sol squeezed his hands into fists.

"I am pleased to see that all of your children look well," the councilor said. His eyes seemed to scan the row of chairs. Sol was some distance away, but it seemed the man stared particularly long at Erich.

"Your concern is appreciated, but I doubt it is the reason for your visit," Frederich replied.

"My dear Frederich," Councilor Younn said, dropping the honorific title. "My King Gareth was comforted to hear news of Aden's miraculous cure. Is that not reason enough to send a delegation?" Even as he spoke, soldiers continued to march into the room behind him, building up their human wall another layer deep until two rows of soldiers lined the room.

"Gareth's comfort comforts me," King Frederich responded. Sol admired the imperious tone of the man's voice, even when he was clearly outnumbered in his own home. "However, it seems Gareth recently attempted to harm one of my own children. I was hoping you would have more clarity on that matter."

"My king sends his deepest apologies for any misunderstanding that has happened between your great houses." The councilor bowed low, swinging his arm as though in a performance.

"Misunderstanding?" Frederich emphasized the single word.

The councilor lifted his head, moving back into a standing position. But before he could respond, the side door of the great hall slammed open.

"Princess, you cannot—" a guard's voice was cut short as it entered the great hall.

From his limited view, Sol could only see an unruly commotion in the line of Chendas soldiers who stood in front of the door as Meena pressed her way through them. She smiled brightly as she walked across the hall and ascended the dais to join her family.

～

MEENA GAVE her father a respectful nod before she sat on the large chair beside Erich. She hoped her dramatic entrance had not flustered him, but the regal stability on his face never wavered as he made eye contact with her. She would have entered more quietly if the guards at the door hadn't tried so hard to keep her out.

"I apologize for my late entrance, Father." Meena spoke loud enough for most of the room to hear. "I was . . . seeing to someone."

"The councilor was apologizing for Gareth's misunderstanding."

Meena turned to face Councilor Younn. His average height and build were overpowered by the thick quilted doublet he wore, which seemed to add an entire hand's width to his girth.

"As I was saying . . ." The councilor bent forward, though Meena had no idea how it was possible through the thick layers of fabric surrounding his middle. "My king sends his deepest apologies for any misunderstanding that has happened between your great houses."

As the councilor apologized with flowery words, Meena risked a glance to Erich at her side. He lounged comfortably in his seat, resting his head on his hands and looking almost bored.

Meena wanted to pinch him. These men had attempted to literally chop off his head barely a sennight prior.

Erich seemed completely unperturbed, but Meena could see that his half-closed eyes were watching Younn intently.

She was relieved to see they had been sensible enough to keep Aizel out of sight.

"He has been under great pressure preparing the kingdoms for the return of the Majis," the councilor continued his carefully rehearsed lines. "It was a lapsed moment of judgment. He sends these gifts to you as a sign of his goodwill."

Four soldiers stepped forward, placing elaborate silver platters on a small table below the dais.

"He sends us sweetmeats as an apology for his lapsed judgment?" King Frederich's controlled rage was beginning to surface.

Meena tapped her fingers against the wooden armrest of her chair, playing out a melody only she could hear. Chendas soldiers continued to pour through the main door, lining themselves up three deep around the room.

Standing from his chair, Erich sauntered to the edge of the dais and lifted the lid from one of the platters.

"Erich." Ian's voice held a note of reproach from the seat next to their father.

Younn watched Erich's movement through heavily lidded eyes.

"These look delicious," Erich said, reaching down to grab one.

Two of the soldiers standing next to the councilor took a half step forward.

Meena's frantic fingers tapped faster. "Bring me one," she called to Erich, her voice light. Keeping the forced smile on her face, she bit her tongue so she wouldn't say anything further. It was little wonder the king of Chendas had wanted to murder her brother. She rather felt like doing so herself.

Erich took a bite of the sweetmeat and stood back up. He

groaned as he chewed it. "The best I've ever had. Send my dear friend Gareth my thanks."

The two Chendas soldiers relaxed back into place beside the councilor as Erich returned to his seat.

Her brother was a nincompoop. No one else would have the spite to dangle his existence in front of the enemy who wanted him dead.

Sitting beside her, Erich handed Meena a pretty little morsel of dried fruits dusted in sugar.

She smiled her thanks as she accepted it, shooting a glare at Erich that he appeared not to notice.

"As a sign of his goodwill," Younn repeated, then stopped.

Meena barely caught the sly wink Erich sent her way. He'd successfully distracted the councilor from King Frederich's growing anger.

"As another token of his goodwill," the councilor corrected himself, "my king has offered Iseldis his close and personal attention. As we speak, squadrons of his own soldiers are making their way to the coast, ready and prepared to defend you should the need arise."

Meena absently raised the sweetmeat to her lips, taking her cue from Erich to remain as unconcerned as possible to continue toying with Younn.

"And if I do not wish for Gareth's aid in the defense of my kingdom?" King Frederich asked. His words were crisp but controlled.

The councilor dipped his head in acknowledgment. "My king would take personal offense at your refusal of his offer of reconciliation."

Meena choked on the bite in her mouth. She coughed loudly into her hand, attempting to clear her airway. The councilor was threatening to make them prisoners in their own kingdom, but her mind could not even fathom the thought as she coughed.

Erich jumped from his seat and started to pound her back.

Meena sputtered loudly as the morsel dislodged and continued peacefully down her throat. She heaved in great gulps of air, pushing Erich's fist away.

"Princess?" the councilor asked, concern lacing his loud voice.

"I am well." Meena held up a hand to stop his questions, keeping her face turned down. She wasn't ready to look at the room yet. She'd just made an absolute fool of herself in front of countless strangers. "I was enjoying it so much I ate it too quickly."

"Would you like another?" Younn asked.

"No!" Meena put a hand on her chest, forcing a cough to undermine the strength of her rebuke. "Please, carry on."

King Frederich sent a shrewd look to Meena.

She smiled weakly. He probably thought she'd faked the choking, but she couldn't explain to him here and now that it had been real. Although, she couldn't deny the excellent timing of drawing everyone's attention her way while her father processed the threat.

"What other signs of goodwill does Gareth wish to bestow?" Frederich asked.

"Getting greedy now, Your Majesty?" The councilor's smile made even Meena angry. "I jest, I jest." He held up a placating hand. "My king has three other offerings. The soldiers you see here have been gifted to you for defense of the castle, as well as my humble self." He bowed. Again. "I will aid you with my knowledge to the best of my ability."

Meena struggled to breathe, although she couldn't tell if it was from the fear that gripped her heart or the scratching feeling in her throat. It would be difficult to get Sol out of the castle with their new guests.

"What an honor," King Frederich replied through clenched teeth. His hands gripped the arms of his chair, his white knuckles contrasting with the growing red that covered his face.

"Finally," the councilor continued, "King Gareth will personally oversee all incoming and outbound ships of trade, so that you can focus solely on the needs of your people during this difficult season."

If Gareth controlled the outbound ships, Sol would never make it to Falqri. And they would have no hope of destroying the store of magic.

King Frederich stood slowly. From his place on the dais, he was the tallest man in the room. Even the councilor had to lean his head back to see up at him. "I will not be made a prisoner in my own castle." He spoke slowly, a burning rage fueling every word.

Meena had never heard him so angry before. Ever.

"Father—" Aden started to speak, but the king cut him off.

"You can tell your king that his aid is not wanted here."

Meena noticed the front line of soldiers on the back wall around the dais step forward in formation, placing hands on their sword hilts. Behind them, every other soldier in the second row lifted a crossbow. The soldiers who had moved were strategically placed behind the dais, and it appeared her father either hadn't noticed them or chose not to.

The four guards stationed around the dais had definitely noticed. They grasped their own sword handles, ready to defend.

"Father." Meena jumped up, ignoring the part of her mind that told her to keep her mouth closed. The only thing she could do was stall for time before her father declared war on Chendas and sacrificed his life in the process.

"Philomena." He never used her full name.

"Father." She did not falter as she walked toward him across the line of her seated brothers. "I think you should try the sweetmeats before you completely reject King Gareth's kind apology."

Meena recognized the shock on her father's face—it mirrored the shock she felt in her own mind. She silently begged him to join her on this surprise adventure. If she had enough time, she could think of something.

"They really are exquisite." Her mouth continued to blabber about the ridiculous candies as her mind furiously looked for a way to get Sol out of the country as soon as possible without suspicion. Preferably in a way that did not involve the death of anyone in her family. "Like something from a feast, or a wedding even."

Smiling at Younn, she swooped down to pick up another sweet from the tray.

"Imagine these at a wedding. Our cook could never hope to compete with something this elegant."

She heard the restless sound of the soldiers shuffling their feet. She was running out of time.

"Philomena, you should not have come here," King Frederich stepped forward, reaching out toward her. "She is beside herself. Erich, take her to her room."

"Wait." Meena held up her hand, forcing her body to calm itself so she would be taken seriously. "Do you think King Gareth would be kind enough to send us more of these sweetmeats in time for my wedding next week? Surely as a token of his continued goodwill, the king would personally see to our wedding trip down south."

The room fell completely silent.

Meena's mouth went dry. She was speaking her thoughts faster than she could think them, and she wanted to burst into laughter at the controlled shock on her parent's faces. She couldn't believe she'd shared her silliest dream out loud. Of course she had imagined having an exciting romance with the heroic stranger who wanted to save their kingdoms, but now she had proposed it in front of a room full of threatening soldiers and her entire family.

King Frederich dropped to his chair as though his legs could no longer support him. His expression remained as passive as ever, of course, but Meena could see a thousand thoughts running through his eyes. Every muscle on his face appeared to be straining in an effort to not raise an eyebrow at her.

"The princess is getting married?" The councilor also leaned forward, his smile still disgustingly wide. "This is the first we have heard of it."

Meena felt her face flush under her father's intense stare, but she played it off as embarrassment in front of the councilor. "Well, that's because it only just happened last night." She smiled and fluttered her eyelashes. Her thumb started tapping out a furious beat against her thigh, and she clutched her hands together to stop the frantic motion. But the nervous energy merely transferred to her foot, which began drawing circles on the stone floor at her feet.

"And who is the honorable choice of King Frederich's only daughter?" the councilor asked.

At that, King Frederich's eyebrows really did go up. "Pray, enlighten the room, Meena, and share your good news."

130

Meena opened her mouth. Now that she needed it most, her ever-present voice seemed to have betrayed her. She swallowed, glancing quickly around the room with her eyes only. Her head was still bowed toward the ground as she couldn't trust her expression.

Every eye in the room was trained on her. Even the grim soldiers in their lines looked very invested in the conversation. A small smile flitted at her lips as she realized how ridiculous the situation was. Fortunately, happiness was the best emotion to show for an announcement of marriage, so she embraced the smile as she lifted her head. "Yesterday evening . . ." Her voice was strong and clear. "With my father's permission, of course . . ." She nodded toward her father, blinking at the right moment so she wouldn't have to make eye contact with him. "Lord Sol-ah-no and I pledged ourselves to be wed." She stumbled over Sol's name, realizing too late that she shouldn't share his identity. Hopefully no one would notice the slip.

She shot her father a quick glance, though, hoping he had picked up on it.

"Lord Solano?" Younn looked confused.

"From Allys," Meena glibly supplied, as though everyone should know Lord Solano.

"Solano Gilart," Erich added. "Son of Lord Gilart. Cousin to the king of Allys."

"Indeed." The councilor recovered himself quickly. "Lord Gilart has so many sons, one forgets . . . often stumbles over their names."

"An understandable mistake." King Frederich nodded graciously at Younn.

Meena exhaled a small sigh of relief. Her father had turned to their guest and was backing up her claim.

The tension in the room had shifted as the soldiers against the wall relaxed back into their original formation.

"And how does this joyous union increase the goodwill between Chendas and Iseldis?" the councilor asked.

"I don't know." Meena shrugged flippantly. "But Solano and I were planning to take an immediate wedding trip to Falqri. It's rather selfish, really, but I was hoping King Gareth would allow for us to leave from the Iseldis port if he is controlling the outbound ships." Meena kept talking. "I know Falqri is a favorite destination of His Majesty. I've never visited there myself, and I've always wanted to see why the king loves it so much!" Meena clapped her hands together. She was pushing the topic of Falqri too aggressively.

"His Majesty will be most pleased," the councilor responded. "Especially if you would deign to visit him in Chendas with your new husband."

The weight of what she was proposing settled on Meena's chest. She was buying time for her family and kingdom, but she was also placing herself at the whims of a man who had tried to kill multiple members of her family. Iseldis would be too burdened to come to her aid should she need help.

King Frederich's fingers curled around the armrest of his chair. "The White Palace is a considerable distance from the fort and would be very much out of their way."

Meena smiled weakly, forcing herself to breathe. This was a simple negotiation. It was not as though her life and kingdom were riding on it. Except they were. Her mouth moved to swallow, but the lump in her throat refused to move. Her fingers returned to their habitual tapping as she tried to recall feeling amused at the situation. She could not panic now.

Meena imagined herself sneaking into the White Palace

of Chendas, dressed in darkly colored breeches and a hat that covered her hair. She would slip into the king's office and slyly take a magic-filled item from his secret desk drawer that she would discover by a stroke of luck. Then she would make her escape, leaving through the servants' hallways so as not to be discovered by the guards. Fortunately, she had not seen any guards in the palace at all, which made her secret mission that much easier.

The sound of clanking armor and shifting feet brought her back to the present moment. The councilor cleared his throat, and the row of soldiers behind him simultaneously shifted in place as though reminding them of their presence.

"I'm sure the happy couple will be safer coming to Chendas after their wedding trip regardless. I will let His Majesty know to expect them by the first day of harvestreign?"

"Yes," Meena said before her father could ruin their plan —which was currently working fairly well. Her voice was loud but still carried a small squeak she hoped no one noticed. She could find a way back to Iseldis after they had accomplished their mission in Falqri. The important thing at the moment was getting Sol into the enemy's fortress.

"We would invite you to join us for dinner, Councilor," King Frederich said. "But I'm sure you have traveled far and fast today and would be more comfortable seeing to your men than entertaining an old monarch like myself."

"You are too kind, Your Majesty." The councilor bowed, dipping nothing more than his head at his shoulders. His eyes lingered on each member of the royal family, sending a ghosted smile to Meena last. "May your marriage be long and prosperous, Princess Philomena."

She dipped her own head imperceptibly in thanks.

Younn left the room, and his soldiers filed out after him.

Meena waited until every soldier had left the room before she turned to face her family.

"An intriguing plan, little sister." Erich was the first to speak. He quirked an eyebrow at her. "But who's going to tell Sol?"

CHAPTER 12

Sol could feel his own heart pumping so aggressively in his chest he wondered if it was trying to escape his body. "No," he growled. "No."

"I think it's a resourceful solution," Aizel said. "Unusual, yes, but crazy enough it just might work."

"No." Sol could force no other word through his paralyzed lips.

The soldiers in the room below followed the councilor out the main door, slowly emptying the great hall.

"She is the best option you have. Will you not even consider her?" Aizel pressed.

"No." He couldn't tear his eyes away from the princess standing on the dais below, her back to her family. Sol couldn't see her face.

"You're beginning to sound like a whining child," Aizel said.

Sol did not deign to offer her a reply. He needed a moment to think before opening his mouth again.

"I can understand why you are shocked, but Sol . . ." Aizel moved closer to him. "You have to do this. For Istroya. For our families."

Sol shook his head. "It would never work."

"It's the only option." Aizel's voice was desperate. "Robin said you can't get to the fort by land, and now even the sea is closed to you."

"Then I'll walk down the shoreline."

"That would take weeks. There're cliffs."

"I'll climb them."

"She literally offered you a direct route to the fort, and access inside it. Your life is not the only one at stake!"

Sol felt a fire in his head. "Everything I've done has been a sacrifice for my family, my people. You cannot accuse me of avoiding hardship. She's a Quotidian princess. At best she'll be an additional responsibility, at worst a distraction."

Aizel sighed. "Her family is in danger, too. She's opened a door for you. Don't slam it closed without consideration."

Aizel brushed past him and left the dark side room.

Sol clenched his fists, angry at his body for betraying him. When he'd first heard the princess's plan, his heart had soared. Perhaps it was hope, perhaps it was anticipation, perhaps it was longing. The feeling, however, was definitely a weakness.

"I guess I should go find him," Meena's voice came from the great hall. "At least before half the castle congratulates him on a wedding he knows nothing about."

Sol backed away from the hidden window, shrinking into the darkness behind him.

He could not talk to her until he'd hidden away the foreign feelings in his mind and body.

His knees bumped into the chair behind him. She didn't

know he was here, and she would be unlikely to search for him in this particular room.

He sat down. The cool stone wall of the castle was directly behind him, and he leaned his head back against it.

He would find a way. He had never backed down from a challenge, and he would push against the obstacles in his path until he'd overcome them or been destroyed by them. He didn't have any other option. His life had no other purpose.

His peaceful solitude was interrupted a few moments later when the door quietly opened.

Sol sat up instantly.

A beam of light illuminated the very person he was trying to avoid.

"Sol!" Meena said loudly. Clearly she was just as surprised. She glanced toward the window to the great hall, then back at him. "What are you doing here?" she hissed.

Sol didn't respond. The use of this particular room seemed obvious.

She approached the window, peering out into the hall below. "How long have you been here?"

"Long enough."

She winced.

A quiet voice from the hall below filtered up to them. "You don't intend to let her follow through with this, right?"

Sol stood and approached the window to see who was speaking. It appeared to be the crown prince.

He looked down at the princess standing quite close to him. She didn't look like a princess. Not that he'd ever met a princess before. Her hair was long, dark, and straight. He didn't remember the color of her eyes, and he couldn't see them from the angle she was facing. He did remember the way her eyes crinkled in laughter over Celesta's head, though.

She seemed like a normal woman. Just one who was loud enough to talk over an entire room full of hostile soldiers.

"Why are you here?" Sol asked.

"Shhhh." She kept her eyes on her family below.

"You do realize she just stalled a continental war." That was Aden. He and Erich were the only family members who remained seated.

"We can't let her sail to Falqri with some Majis we've only just met." Onric paced across the dais.

"I dislike your flippant use of the word Majis. It sounds as though you are insulting my wife." Erich had his leg over one arm of his wide chair.

"I don't think we can stop her," Queen Cara declared. "She stepped in at a critical moment, placing herself in danger, and came up with a solution to buy us time. Really, she did better than any of us."

Sol looked back at the princess. He had not expected her mother to be the first to support her.

Meena had a small smile on her face.

Sol thought she deserved it. Her action had been brave and resourceful.

"This is not the proper place for this discussion." King Frederich stepped from the dais.

The rest of the family followed him, their voices masked by the sound of their footsteps.

"You came here to listen to what your family said of you?" Sol asked.

Meena shrugged, turning to him. "So you heard everything?"

Sol nodded.

"What do you think?" she asked. She bit her lower lip as she looked up at him.

Sol felt his throat tighten. He knew from experience that if he opened his mouth, "no" was the only word he'd be capable of saying. And looking into the anxious eyes of the woman in front of him, he could not bring himself to immediately deny her request.

"I know this is sudden," she said, filling the silence. She began to inhale through her nose and kept doing so until her entire body stretched taller. "And . . . I know it is uncomfortable and awkward." She spoke more quickly as she went on. "It's not an actual proposal. Well—I mean, I am proposing that we wed, but it would only be a counterfeit marriage. We would have a big wedding so everyone—especially the councilor—believes it, and we would pretend to be madly in love." She looked at her hands.

Sol's frown deepened. His racing heart had calmed of its own accord, and he wanted to believe it was because he'd willed it. Surely he was not so weak that her words were having any sort of effect on him.

The princess inhaled again, turning her face away from him. "It would be in name only, of course. For the sake of your people and mine."

Sol crossed his arms, instinctively leaning away, spacing his feet just a small bit further apart so his center of balance was lower. Not that he expected her to physically attack him—he just felt more in control when he was prepared for whatever might come at him. He had to refuse this. He didn't want to refuse it. He didn't want to agree to it.

She was too beautiful to be marred by his callousness.

He pressed his foot against the floor below, trying to find

an outlet for his pent-up energy. Her beauty had nothing to do with it.

She was spoiled.

Naive.

Immature.

Loud.

"This is absolutely not something you have to do," the princess continued. "It was just the only way I could think to get you inside the fortress to complete your mission as soon as possible. I did tell the councilor that we would be spending our wedding trip at the fort. That made him believe that Iseldis still trusts—or more like fears—Chendas, but it also gives you a chance to gain full access to the fort. If you were my husband, no one would know it wasn't real, and you could be shown anything you asked to see. But you already knew that because you heard it the first time I said it. I'm talking too much."

He noticed her hands were moving rapidly, or at least her fingers were. Each thumb was rapidly touching the finger-tips of its respective hand in quick succession, bouncing back and forth in each direction. The knowledge that she was nervous loosened the tension in his chest.

Brown. Her eyes were a soft, dark brown. He could see them now in the dim light of the window to the great hall.

He would not give in to this weakness. He knew better than to follow something as fleeting as a feeling. He clenched his jaw, squeezing his teeth together in anger at his body for giving in to such weakness.

"I'm sorry." She broke the moment of silence, dropping her eyes to the ground. "It was a foolish suggestion. We'll tell the Council the wedding has been called off and find another way to get you into the fort."

She leaned away as she walked around him toward the door.

Sol turned after her. If he let her leave, he would never find the courage to ask her to reconsider.

"It is not a foolish suggestion," he finally blurted out.

The door was halfway open. She stopped.

"It is a resourceful solution. A genius idea. Better than anyone's." Sol tried to remember what others had said about Meena's plan. "It is our best option."

She closed the door and turned around. He could not see her face in the darkness.

"Is that a yes, then?" she whispered.

"Yes," Sol replied.

The tension in his body dissolved into lightness.

CHAPTER 13

$\mathcal{M}$eena stood below the dais in the great hall. She wore the deep purple dress that had been made for Ian's dance during the last silverreign. There had not been time to create a new dress for the occasion. Not that it bothered Meena. The last few days had been more than full, planning a wedding in public and a dangerous mission behind closed doors.

The hall around her was full of nobles, relatives, and friends from the palace and city. King Frederich had shared the full extent of their political situation with their most trusted inner circle, but for the most part, the hundreds of witnesses had no idea the wedding was anything other than a love match.

From the upper balcony, a group of musicians played joyful tunes. The happy sounds flooded the room, lifting the spirits of nearly everyone present.

The usual palace guard stood in their strategically appointed positions. Each one, however, was flanked by a "visiting" soldier from Chendas. The councilor himself stood on the dais next to the royal family.

Lord Gilart and two of his sons had traveled multiple nights from Allys to stand on the dais as well. As close friends of the Sirilian family, they had been informed of the situation and gladly welcomed Sol into the family whenever the councilor was present. Even Aizel and Celesta, masked under layers of millinery and face powder, stood with the Gilart family as Sol's sisters.

Meena was not sure if the Gilart family knew or believed in the full extent of the chaos- and harmony-magic users, but they were happy to participate in a plan that undermined King Gareth.

In all, the moment was exactly as Meena had imagined her wedding to be. Though in her dreams, the face of the man standing before her was always hazy. Now, it was very clear. Too clear.

Meena stared at Sol's face as though she were a woman in love. It was not difficult. She could see every small detail of his appearance and disposition, and she liked what she saw. His freshly shaven skin made him look younger, though it revealed the firmly pursed expression of his lips. This was a boy who had been forced too soon to play the part of a man. Meena wanted to place her hand on his cheek, to ease away the constant rigidity in his face and posture.

She could feel his intense gaze watching her from under hooded lids, but she flicked her eyes away, afraid he would read her thoughts if she met them.

As the music ended with a triumphant flourish, Queen Cara stepped forward to stand in front of the couple.

Meena drew her eyes back to Sol's face. Suddenly, her

hands felt cold and sweaty at the same time. She wiped them on her dress, hoping no one would notice the motion.

Sol looked solemn. More than solemn—stern. Meena felt a strange flutter in her chest as she swallowed, smiling sweetly up at him to ensure at least one of them was performing this correctly.

Scanning around the side of his face, she took in his curling brown hair. He kept it shorter than most of the men she knew, less than a hand's length long. A stray strand fell across his forehead, and her chest relaxed. The unruly curl softened him, proving that he was indeed human.

Finally, when she had taken in his whole face, she brought her eyes to meet his. Her heart thumped in her chest, seemingly loud enough to be heard in her own ears. Hopefully, he could not hear it.

His intense eyes were a rocky green. Not the bright gem-like color of Aizel and Celesta's eyes, but a mossy green, streaked with gray.

He stared back at her, hardly blinking. His gaze was direct, but guarded. He seemed to be as intensely focused on her as she was on him.

For just a moment, Meena imagined if this truly was the wedding she had always wanted. The only thing out of place was the small wrinkle between Sol's eyebrows. Perhaps, for a moment, she could pretend it was a wrinkle of excitement and responsibility. That the man she was marrying truly wanted to marry her. That he was looking at her with eyes of love and honesty.

Meena started, coming back to the moment. Sol was not the husband she'd always dreamed of. He was a stranger.

Even if this wedding was a farce, it was likely the only wedding she'd ever have. She was a princess, and the attendants believed it was real. And with the precarious future of her kingdom, it felt selfish to imagine a real wedding in the future. If she ever had the chance to marry for real, to someone who truly loved her, it would be in a small and private place, surrounded by beautiful trees and a blue sky and with no deception to mar its loveliness.

Sol still had the small wrinkle between his eyebrows. Meena wanted to reach up and gently massage it with her finger. They were in this together. She scrunched her nose at him, reminding him to relax.

His eyes lost the guarded look for a moment as he reacted to her expression, but he did not relax enough to smile.

"You may join hands," Queen Cara whispered.

Sol lifted his hand, holding it palm up.

Meena swallowed back the overwhelming feelings of disappointment that threatened to spill out. Lifting her hand, she placed it in his.

A spark of energy ran down her arm at the contact. His hand was warm, wrapping around hers in a gentle grip. Meena squeezed back firmly.

She would not let her hand lie limply in his as if she'd had no part in this arrangement.

She had proposed this marriage, for the good of everyone they loved even if not for herself and him.

And though her head knew it was not a real marriage, her heart couldn't help but wish that it was.

Queen Cara lifted her own hands, placing a long yellow strip of silk around the couple's joined hands, looping it around them multiple times.

Sol lowered his eyes to watch the movements.

Meena did the same. But as her mother continued to wrap the full length of silk into a beautiful weave around their hands and wrists, Meena found her eyes glancing back up at Sol.

She was struck once again by how young his face was. If she were going to marry someone, it would be someone like him. Someone who was close to her in age. Someone who took themselves seriously and cared deeply enough about those he loved to spend his life working for their good.

When she had tied the yellow ribbon closed, Queen Cara placed her hands around theirs. She paused for a moment, as was customary, silently offering her support and well wishes for the new couple.

"May this union, beginning in companionship, grow into joy," she whispered. Her words were vague, but they also sounded like something a mother would say if her daughter truly was getting married.

With a small smile, she leaned forward and placed a soft kiss on Meena's cheek.

Meena swallowed loudly. The moment was as beautiful as she'd imagined it would be, except for the hollow bloom in her stomach.

Queen Cara lifted her eyes to Sol's for a moment, and Meena felt her mother squeeze their hands as she nodded to him.

Sol nodded in return as Meena felt his grasp on her hand tighten.

When her mother stepped back, Meena's father took her place. He surrounded their bound hands with his own. His eyes, crinkled softly in affection, met Meena's.

"May this union be for the good of our peoples," he whispered.

Blinking, he turned his gaze to Sol.

Sol inclined his head slightly in response to the intensity of the king's gaze.

The king placed one hand on Sol's shoulder. Leaning toward Meena, he used his other hand to softly pull her into a hug.

Meena leaned into him, twisting the upper half of her body as her hand was still bound to Sol's. She saw her father gently shake Sol's shoulder as he pulled her close.

Meena swallowed as her father stepped away. He was trusting them to accomplish this. He was trusting in her and in a complete stranger.

She brought her eyes back to Sol.

This time, his eyes met hers, clear and confident. His hand still gripped hers tightly inside the cocoon of ribbon.

They were in this together.

Meena smiled as an elder monk stepped forward. He carried a scroll, which he opened when he stood in front of the couple.

"Do you know the words of the betrothing?" he whispered to Sol.

Sol shook his head.

"I will lead, then," the monk responded. He whispered the first words from the scroll, then paused for Sol to repeat them.

"I choose to bind myself to you," Sol repeated slowly. His voice was low but carried strongly. "Under the eyes of the people gathered here today, I pledge my life, happiness, health, and belongings to thee. May these witnesses see that I keep my promise to thee for all time."

Meena could feel his muscles tense through their joined hands as he spoke the last words. A promise he did not intend to keep.

Meena's own hand began to feel uncomfortably wet and hot. She hoped Sol hadn't noticed.

"And you?" the monk whispered.

"I know the words," Meena replied. She'd memorized them in her ninth silverreign. Her tongue suddenly felt dry, and time seemed to stop as she tried to pry it from the roof of her mouth. "I choose to bind myself to you." Her voice was loud, but it squeaked a little. She inhaled, but her lungs still felt desperate for air. She couldn't say the words out loud and not mean them. She paused. *For the purpose of our joint mission.* Adding the words in her head gave her strength. "Under the eyes of the people gathered here today, I pledge my life, happiness, health, and belongings to thee." *During this time, as we work to accomplish the same goal.* "May these witnesses see that I keep my promise to thee for all time." *My promise being to protect them as is my royal duty.*

As soon as the words had been said, Meena felt her body relax. They'd done it.

Meena let the next several minutes wash over her in a haze. She and Sol stood in front of the dais, their hands still bound, as their guests approached and continued to offer them well wishes. Meena did her best to smile even when the older married couples leaned in to offer advice about a happy union. It all sounded the same to Meena, and she couldn't tell if everyone was repeating the same few platitudes or if she was just too tired to listen properly.

≈

≈

SOL WATCHED as an endless wave of guests lined up to greet them—or greet Meena, rather, since no one there actually knew him. He watched the princess laugh anew each time an older man patted her on the cheek, told her to stay young forever, and called him a lucky man. She thanked each older lady who told her the secret to lasting happiness was to laugh together often.

Lords and ladies, advisors and relatives each came forward to touch the yellow binding around their hands and whisper some quick message that got lost in the noise of the crowd.

Sol tried to remember to smile if anyone directed these well wishes at him, but after the first few, every face seemed to look the same.

Every face except for that of the raven-haired beauty standing at his side. She was too bright and happy. Untouched. He was afraid to squeeze her hand for fear she might break.

He didn't want to watch her crumble at the first sign of hardship. She'd never known a single difficulty. And here he was, about to take her into the hands of a heartless enemy, away from the protective father and brothers who had squeezed his shoulder, slapped his back, and given him imperious looks.

His head started to throb. His plan had been so simple and straightforward. Now it was more complicated than he'd ever imagined. And why had Meena not looked at him a single time since she'd spoken the words that bound them together?

Finally, the musicians started to play again as trays of mouthwatering food were brought into the room and spread out on the tables. It still took an agonizingly long moment for the final members of the crowd to congratulate them before the lure of food and drink called them away.

Sol felt his shoulders sink, not in relaxation but exhaustion. His arm was stiff from holding his hand up, and his hand was numb from not moving.

Finally, she looked up at him.

Sol turned to face her. He desperately wanted to tear his hand out of the silken prison and hide from the watching eyes of everyone in the room.

"I've seen some couples keep the binding on for the entire wedding feast," Meena said, as though she had read his mind. "But I'd rather enjoy the food before our travel tonight, if you don't mind."

Sol fumbled for the end of the yellow ribbon, pulling it loose as fast as his free hand could move. "Food is a smart decision."

"You don't need to look like you are trying to escape from my side," Meena whispered, lifting her hand to help untie the ridiculously long length of silk.

"Right." Sol slowed his frantic movements, glancing at her face.

She was focused on the ribbon, and he could not read her expression.

*a*s the third round of wine was poured, Meena felt Sol's gaze on her.

She nodded back at him imperceptibly. It was time to leave.

Onric approached them from around the table, Ashlin at his side. He leaned down between them, a wide smile on his face. "Once again, I'm stuck here at the palace while one of my younger siblings leaves on a dangerous trip."

"Defending the palace is actually your one responsibility," Meena responded with a small smile of her own. "Besides, something tells me you are jesting, and you don't truly want to leave the city this time." She looked up at Ashlin.

"Take care, little sister." Onric dropped his jesting voice as he put his arm around her, though he kept the smile on his face. "Best of luck." He turned to Sol. "Keep us informed. And keep her safe."

Sol nodded in response.

When Ashlin reached out, Meena jumped from her chair and threw her arms around her friend.

"You can do this," Ashlin whispered in her ear.

"Of course I can," Meena responded, her throat tightening. "All I have to do is be a princess, something I'm particularly good at."

Onric joined in the hug, squeezing Meena between himself and Ashlin.

Erich approached next.

Sol stood awkwardly, not joining in the group hug.

Erich placed a hand on his shoulder. "If she talks too much, just pretend to be asleep. It's always worked for me."

"I heard that," Meena yelled, poking her head out of the hug she was still tightly entangled in. She caught a look at Sol's face, hoping he wasn't taking her brother seriously.

But Sol nodded to Erich—with no hint of humor—as though he thought Erich was actually giving him advice.

"He's jesting!" Meena said, twisting her head as Erich threw himself into the family hug. "I don't talk that much," she continued, but she was not sure her voice carried beyond the bodies now surrounding her.

Another small person wiggled into the center of the hug, and Meena embraced Celesta, half hugging the little girl and half protecting her from the aggressive nature of the rest of the hugging.

Before her vision was cut off by someone's arm, Meena saw Ian approach her new husband and speak to him. Together, they looked properly solemn. They would keep each other great company.

But she would be the one keeping company with her solemn partner.

Which reminded her it was time to leave. They wanted to start their journey before night fell.

Wiggling her way out of the crowded hug, Meena moved to Sol's side. She slipped her hand inside his arm and smiled up at him, like a new wife would do to her husband. She could feel him stiffen momentarily at her touch, but he quickly brought a smile to his face. He wasn't a very good actor, but she hoped he would get better at faking smiles that didn't look so forced in the future.

"Shall we set out on our wedding journey?" Meena asked, smirking sweetly. It was too tempting to jest with his seriousness.

He nodded—seriously, of course—and patted her hand. "It is time."

Meena ignored the fluttering in her stomach. She wasn't actually setting out on her wedding journey. She was setting out on a real mission with a real cypher. One of these two things was far more exciting and far more preferable than the other.

Turning toward the front door of the hall, Meena gently led Sol through the crowd. The people around them separated, cheering and clapping as the married couple made their way to the door.

Meena smiled at the many faces she knew, nodding and waving at the cheerful send-off.

Sol's arm under her hand was hard as a rock. His pace was swift, and Meena could feel the discomfort rolling off him.

Taking her other hand, Meena placed it on his arm as comfortingly as she could. "Slow down. You are doing well," she said as loudly as she dared, covering her words with another blushing smile up at her new husband.

Sol leaned his head down toward her. "So many eyes," he whispered in her ear.

Meena smiled without faking it. The heat of his breath on her ear seemed to warm her entire body. She leaned into him as they walked the rest of the hall, grateful to be experiencing this together.

The crowd spilled over into the front courtyard, and Meena continued to smile and wave as she and Sol slowly made their way to the waiting royal carriage.

The noise of the crowd lessened considerably as soon as she stepped inside it. Sol had used his hand to help her up the step. She gripped it tightly, not letting go as he followed her inside.

Someone shut the door behind them, and Meena sat down thankfully on the back bench, leaving enough room for Sol to sit next to her if he chose to.

Sol's eyes quickly scanned the carriage, but he sat down next to her.

Meena relaxed into her position, pleased that he had chosen to remain united even though they were hidden from view.

The crowd let out a joyful cheer as the carriage rumbled forward.

"That ought to have fooled the councilor," she said, turning to Sol.

He exhaled, still stiff.

Realizing her hand was still clinging to his, Meena relaxed her hold.

He immediately slid his hand out of her grip and placed it on his knee.

Meena turned her face away, feeling her cheeks heat in embarrassment. Not that she was ashamed. It was just, perhaps he'd sat next to her because it was his only choice with the way she'd been holding his hand. "The hardest part is over now," she said lightly, masking her feelings.

"Hardly," Sol responded.

"I was jesting," Meena said, exhaling as her shoulders fell. "At least the next part of the mission won't have quite so many eyes." Her words were a touch bitter.

"I should hope not," Sol responded.

Meena felt his gaze turn to her, and she glanced back toward him.

"That was truly terrifying," he said.

Meena smiled a small smile. "You do know there will be a grand reception to celebrate our union when we arrive at the Falqri Fortress?"

"If you grip my arm there as tightly as you did just now, I think I can remain standing," he responded.

The interior of the carriage was darker than the evening light outside, but Meena thought she detected a hint of a smile on Sol's face. A real one.

"Are you jesting?" she whispered.

"I'm not sure," Sol responded. "But I do know I can handle the rest of this mission as long as you are there to lead us through the receptions and dinners and dancing."

Meena nodded, turning her head away from him. "That is one thing I can absolutely take care of." She leaned her head against the wall of the carriage, feeling less unsettled than before.

She might not be defending the castle or leading the elite guard like Ian and Onric and Erich, but she could do something. And maybe she could even do it better than they would have.

She closed her eyes. The journey would take several

hours into the night. Her last conscious thought was a sweet reminder that Sol had attempted to make a jest.

CHAPTER 15

*W*hen the carriage finally pulled to a halt, Sol opened his eyes. He had not fully slept on the ride, but he felt moderately rested.

The princess was still fast asleep, her head buried in her arms, leaning against the wall to her side. She did not stir as the carriage jolted in place and someone opened the door from the outside.

"We've arrived at the monastery, Your Highness," the servant said. His voice was tired, and his face remained clouded in the darkness outside.

"Thank you," Sol responded, feeling awkward. No one had addressed him with a title before, and he realized he would have to get used to it. The feeling it elicited was closer to anger than pride.

The servant stepped away, leaving the door open.

Meena was still asleep.

With a growing panic, Sol realized he would have to be the one to wake her. He could not fully see her in the darkness, but he looked her over for a moment while deciding the best way to go about this.

"Princess?" he whispered.

She didn't stir. Not that he was surprised, since the louder noises of the servant and horses had not disturbed her.

Reaching for her shoulder, he gently placed his hand on it. "Princess," he whispered a little more sharply.

Still nothing.

Twisting his wrist, he gave her shoulder a single shake.

She exhaled, making the smallest noise in the back of her throat.

Sol immediately removed his hand.

As she inhaled deeply, she lifted her head and slowly stretched her body awake. "Have we arrived?" she asked.

"Yes," Sol answered. He backed himself out of the carriage, waving the hand that had touched her through the cold night air. His skin tingled from the warm contact of her shoulder.

She followed after him.

He held out his hand to help her find the step, but she must not have seen it. She held the sides of the door frame and sleepily jumped to the ground, bypassing the carriage step completely.

Sol walked by her side, subtly letting her take the lead. He'd never stayed at an inn before, though he was told this was more of a monastery turned army camp. "I used to love this place," she whispered.

"Used to?" Sol asked, leaning over her to keep his whisper quiet.

A servant walked past them, carrying a small chest of

Meena's belongings. "I'll explain later," she whispered back up at him.

She kept her hands tucked into her own arms, likely for warmth, instead of holding on to Sol as she had at the palace. He found himself instinctively walking closer to her, half a step behind to keep her safely within view. It was definitely not because he wanted to be near her.

"Welcome, Your Royal Highnesses." A large, imposing man bowed graciously as they entered the main door of the monastery.

"General Gautho," Meena responded. She sounded awake and alert, as though she had not just traveled in an uncomfortable wheeled cart for hours. "You did not have to greet us personally. It is quite late."

"I would not have missed the occasion to wish you well," Gautho responded. "Nor have I had the pleasure of meeting Lord Solano—eh, Prince Sirilian now, of course."

Sol willed himself to remain confident and unmoving under the cheerful man's shrewd gaze. He nodded his head, unsure how to respond to the man's statement.

"I have trained with many of the young nobles from Allys. I find it surprising that I never worked with you," the general continued.

Sol pressed his tongue against the roof of his mouth. "My brothers showed more skill in combat, I'm afraid." He tried to smile, to play off the words as light. He was afraid the man would see through his defensiveness. They had only just begun their subterfuge, and their first opponent was already doubting him.

"He's being modest, General," Meena said, playfully swatting Sol's arm.

Gautho's gaze softened into a smile as he turned to

Meena. "And yet he has won the hand of a princess." His eyes turned back to Sol, glinting through his smile. "Frederich's only daughter. There must have been some other skill which won her affection? I would love to hear more."

Meena tucked her hand into Sol's arm then and leaned her head against his shoulder. "Shall I not choose whomever I wish? Some other time, General. Our ship sails on the early tide, and today has been long. I am exhausted. I must beg you to show me our room."

"Of course, Princess. The invitation still stands, Prince Sol, if you would like to share a drink and relax your muscles from traveling."

Sol smiled down at Meena. He had no desire to be alone with this Quotidian soldier. If they had been at the fort, he would have gladly accepted, hoping to glean information through their conversation. For now, however, he placed his hand on Meena's back. "I would prefer to retire with my wife." He felt Meena's spine stiffen, but she twisted her neck and looked up at him with an adoring smile. If he hadn't known she was acting, he would have completely been tricked by her performance. For a moment, he hoped the rest of the mission would offer many more opportunities for adoring smiles.

Once they were in a small room on the upper level of the monastery turned fort, Sol closed the door behind them. He looked over it as Meena brought a lit candle to the bedside table. Sol was disappointed to see there was no locking mechanism on the door. He strode to the window. He could see the stars blearily through the glass, but the window itself did not open.

"Admiring the stars?" Meena asked, approaching his side.

Sol looked down, offended that she would think him

capable of doing something so frivolous. "This window does not open. Which means we are safe from intruders, but also that we are limited to a single escape route."

The princess glanced around the room. "The door?"

He nodded.

"When I was a child, we used to visit the monks here," Meena said. The candle behind them lit her hair, but not her face. "The good men patiently let us race through the halls and courtyards. I imagine I could still get from the back gate to the front courtyard by several different routes." She stopped abruptly.

He said nothing, looking down at her face in the shadows, unsure what she was trying to tell him.

"I'm sorry. You're probably not at all interested in the layout of the monastery, I was just rambling on about why I used to love this place."

"I am, in fact, very interested in how this room is connected to the back door, and where the back door is located," Sol responded. "Used to?" he asked again.

"I haven't tried racing through the halls since the soldiers took over. I'm not sure they would be as patient about it."

Sol nodded. "You're likely correct. And I'd rather not find out."

"The back door is easy to access from here. It is down the hall in the other direction and across the gardens."

Sol felt his shoulders relax. It was time for sleep. Stepping to the bed, he pulled back one of the blankets.

Meena had not moved from the window, her arms crossed in front of her.

"Can I take this one?" he asked, moving toward the door, blanket in hand.

"Take? Yes. Why?" she asked.

He spread the blanket on the floor in front of the door, assuming his actions would be explanation enough.

"Sol, I don't think anyone is going to attack us this night," she said, moving closer to the bed.

"We are always susceptible to attack," Sol replied, removing his leather shoes.

"They know who I am. They think you are my husband. I mean, you are my husband. For all they know, that is." She closed her mouth.

"I am not willing to take that risk," Sol said, spreading himself on the blanket fully clothed.

"You don't have to sleep on the floor," Meena tried again.

Sol felt the awkwardness of their situation. He had no intention of becoming close to the princess when they were alone, in any form. "I've slept in worse places." He crossed his arms over his chest and closed his eyes, hoping to deter further conversation.

"Would you at least like a pillow?" she asked.

He opened an eye.

She was holding out a feather-stuffed sack.

He shook his head. "I've never used one. It would probably hurt my neck." He closed his eyes, but not before he'd caught the look of confusion on her face.

She remained unmoving for several seconds. Then, finally, he heard her light footfall.

He kept his eyes firmly closed as she moved around the room. He heard the mattress crunch as she sank into it. And he could see through his eyelids when the room darkened as she blew out the candle beside the bed.

Leaning his head toward the door, he opened his eyes in the darkness. He listened to her breathing until it settled into a slow rhythm. Not only did she sleep deeply, she fell asleep quickly.

Sol exhaled, wishing he could afford such a luxury. Reaching out, he touched the door, ensuring it was latched closed.

With his hand against the wood, he finally closed his eyes and allowed himself to relax. It was several minutes before his mind stopped racing through the various situations he should remain prepared for throughout the night.

Finally, he drifted into a light sleep.

CHAPTER 16

$\mathcal{M}$eena woke early when a hand shook her shoulder. She groaned into her pillow, keeping her eyes closed until she realized Sol—her new husband—was gently asking her to wake up. She rolled over, instantly wide awake.

She clutched the blankets to her shoulders, despite the fact that she was still wearing a full chemise and underdress. Sol wasn't her real husband, after all, even if they did have to share a room for the next several days.

She needn't have bothered. His back was already turned. He was fully clothed and appeared to have been awake for some time. His blanket was folded on the floor. His tousled curls, however, stuck out at all angles.

Slipping out of bed, she slid her travel dress over her head and fastened it in the front. In the interest of speed and secrecy and safety, she had declined bringing a lady's maid. The councilor had insisted they would provide someone to assist her in Falqri. Meena was fairly certain he had meant "watch" rather than "assist."

Turning to Sol, Meena gestured for him to come closer with her hand. "Lean your head forward," she said.

"Why?" He turned to face her at her words but moved his head back, the exact opposite of what she had asked.

Meena snorted. "Because your hair looks slept in."

"It was slept in," he retorted.

"Just let me fix it." Meena reached up to the top of his head, though she had to stretch her arm up to do so.

He sighed audibly and slunk his shoulders forward.

Gently running her fingers through the short lengths, Meena separated some of the thick, wide curls. It only took a few shakes of her hand to encourage them to stand on their own and fill in the flat spot he'd created from sleeping. "Much better," she said. The casual touch had calmed her, even as it brought a happy twinge to her stomach.

Sol lifted his hand and ruffled his fingers close to his scalp as she had done. "I'll remember that tomorrow morning," he mumbled, turning away from her.

Meena felt the happy twinge in her stomach pop in disappointment. She'd liked the familiarity of touching his hair. It would be better if he took care of it himself. She squeezed her fingers into a tight ball against her palm. He needed to get a little more comfortable with her or this would be a very difficult trip.

Through the rest of the short morning, Meena chatted easily with General Gautho, who had also risen early to see them off. When he asked pointed questions about how she and Sol had met, she deflected by describing the wedding in great detail.

The sun had barely risen over the sea when the captain of

the ship came up to the monastery. He informed them the ship was ready and the tides favorable.

Meena bid Gautho a cheery farewell to compensate for Sol's monosyllabic goodbye.

The ship, a merchant's vessel, was a short distance from the shore. Meena assumed it was a trading ship from Falqri as the captain spoke with a noticeable staccato rhythm. The ship had a wide, rounded hull designed for transporting goods rather than speeding through the water. It was a fairly large vessel, requiring two masts.

Meena bunched her skirts in hand and hopped from the sand into the grounded rowboat that waited to take them out to the larger ship.

Sol leaned down, putting his shoulder against the small craft to push it off the sand.

"Your Highness, please." A sailor rushed forward, leaning down to take over the task. "We may not have the sleek caravel you are used to, but you are our guests."

Sol ignored the man's plea and helped him slide the rowboat until it floated on the light waves. He splashed through the shallow water and leapt over the side of the boat to sit opposite Meena.

He grabbed the oars and swung them into place. "Thank you for your aid," he said to the sailor. "I will see my wife safely aboard."

"Is it that hard being a prince?" Meena asked as soon as they were out of earshot.

"I'm not enjoying it," Sol replied heavily, pressing against the oars.

"You just need to be in control." Meena knew she was somewhat correct, but she hoped he knew she was jesting.

"Is that such a bad thing?" He looked up at her, letting the craft carry its own momentum forward for a moment.

"You did well," Meena replied. "I was afraid you would offend that sailor by ignoring him, but your excuse was well thought out."

"My excuse to take care of you?"

"Taking care of me is always a good course of action. It never has to be an excuse." Meena spoke the light words before her mind realized that Sol would take her too seriously.

Sol remained silent for the rest of the short trip.

Once on board, they were welcomed stiffly and given a brief tour of the upper deck.

The captain climbed aboard a short while later, directing the sailors on where to stow Sol and Meena's personal chests.

He turned to a door on the upper deck, opened it and stood aside. "The Sapphire isn't used to transporting royalty, but she's a good ship. You'll have my cabin, of course. It's small, but I hope you will be comfortable here."

Meena stepped past his open arm into the small space.

Small was too generous a description. The closet she stood in consisted of a thin bed—barely wide enough for a single person—and enough room to stand right next to it.

As soon as Sol entered the room beside her, neither of them could move.

"It is quite cozy," the captain said behind them. "But it is the best space on board. Cozy is perfect for two young people in love."

"I'll sleep with the crew below decks," Sol whispered in her ear.

Meena hoped the captain couldn't hear the quiet words. She grabbed Sol's arm, squeezing it with a small shake of her head. "Thank you, Captain," she said. "We do not want to take your space. Surely there is room for us elsewhere on board?"

"Just the main galley below, where everyone else sleeps. And, well . . ." He paused for a moment, scratching the back of his neck. "I don't suppose the crew would mind too much, but I think Your Highnesses might have a different perspective."

Meena swallowed. Suddenly, the small room felt like a palace. "Thank you for your generosity, Captain."

"I'll let you get settled in." The captain left, closing the door behind them.

"This will not work," Sol whispered. The back of his arm rubbed against her shoulder.

Meena felt her face grow warm, but she didn't want to move her arm as that would only bring attention to their closeness. "This has to work," she said. "They would be suspicious if we separated. We'll make it work somehow." She spun around in place, trying to find an extra finger's width of space in the tiny room. The movement also gave her a chance to resettle her arm into a place where it was not pressed up against his. "We can take turns sleeping at night," she said. "It will be like standing guard."

"I hadn't thought of that as a solution," Sol replied. He sounded as though he would consider the idea despite not being excited about it.

"It will be a test." Meena kept talking. The tingling in her shoulder was distracting, and she didn't want to scratch it in front of him. "If we can handle this together, surely we can get through anything."

"Let us go see the rest of the ship." Sol unlatched the door behind them and slipped out.

Meena followed, oddly disappointed about leaving the small space with him. The sooner she could accept he would never relax around her, the easier her life would be.

CHAPTER 17

Sol spread himself out on the floor of the tiny cabin. He had to bend at the knee so his head and feet would fit between the two close walls. It wasn't completely uncomfortable. The constant rocking of the boat kept him rolled against the wall, which meant no one could open the door without waking him. Perhaps he would be able to sleep deeply because of that.

"Goodnight, Sol," Meena whispered from the bed just above him.

"Goodnight," Sol whispered back. He could not remember the last time someone had offered him a nightly greeting.

He woke with a start sometime later when a hand touched his shoulder. He sat up instantly. "What's wrong?"

He could feel the princess kneeling by his side, her knees pressed against his hip.

"It's halfway through the night." She yawned. "At least I think it is."

Sol tried to make out her face in the darkness. Her voice was calm and sleepy. Perhaps she was talking in a dream. He'd heard of it happening, though he'd never witnessed it.

"Go back to bed, Princess," he whispered.

"It's your turn to take the bed," she replied. "I'll take the floor."

"You were serious about that?" Sol asked. "It sounded like one of your jests."

"I can't let you sleep on the floor every night." She sounded offended.

Sol wasn't sure what to respond to that. He'd intended to sleep on the floor every night. He'd never even considered asking someone else—especially a woman and princess—to take the more uncomfortable option.

"We are in this together," she said after a short pause. "I expect you'll need sleep even more than I, by the time this is over. Take the bed."

"That's really not necessary," Sol protested.

Meena dropped to her elbows and rolled on her side, curling up on the floor. "I'm too tired to move again." She yawned. "Goodnight."

Sol realized his only options were to take the bed or sleep next to her on the floor. While he was tempted to do the latter, he knew he'd never get any sleep, so he pushed himself up and rolled onto the thin pallet.

When Sol woke the following morning, the tiny cabin was empty. Slipping out the door, he stretched his folded limbs to their full height. A cursory glance at the deck around him provided no sight of the princess. A sparkle of laughter rang out above the low groans of the wooden ship, and Sol followed the sound below deck.

Meena was sitting at a small table with three sailors and

the captain, laughing over a bowl of thick stew. "That's truly how you became a sailor? It didn't scare you away from the sea for life?"

"I had no other choice, my lady," the captain responded. His back was to the ladder, and he did not see Sol's approach. "There were too many mouths to feed at home—I couldn't go back." He leaned over the table. "Between you and me, I still think she's out there, swimming the waves in wait for me."

Meena laughed again, snorting over her bowl of food.

Noting Sol's presence, the three other sailors stood from the table, heads nodded in respect.

"Your Highness!" The captain who'd been recounting his tale turned his head and jumped from his seat. "Sit. I'll get you something to break your fast." He grabbed his own empty bowl and left Sol at the table with Meena.

"You don't all have to leave," Meena called after them.

"We've bothered you long enough," the captain replied. "The captain'll have our hides if we don't get back up to deck."

"Aren't you the captain?" Meena asked, laughing.

"Precisely," he said.

One of the sailors set a bowl of stew and roll of bread in front of Sol. Then the crew swung up the ladder, leaving Sol and Meena alone.

"They seem quite eager to leave us alone," Sol said, glancing at the empty ladder.

"They seem quite eager to leave *one* of us alone," Meena said.

Sol caught the smile on her face as she said it. "Are they afraid of me?" he asked.

"You are a prince now," Meena whispered. "And you scowl."

Sol felt himself scowling harder at her words, but he couldn't stop it. "What does my face have to do with it?"

"Your face is quite perfect as it is," Meena said. "Behind it, there's a brave man who can both infiltrate a castle by himself and spend his morning hunting for treasure." She reached out and touched a finger to the spot between his eyes. She rubbed it gently. "You can scowl all you wish."

Sol instinctively leaned away from her touch. Her words made him uncomfortable. He'd spent his life avoiding notice, but she'd taken that away from him.

His face felt cold the moment he broke contact with her finger.

She pulled her hand back quickly, turning her focus to the half-eaten bowl in front of her.

He rubbed his face, picking up the roll of bread with his other hand. He didn't dislike her touch, and he hadn't meant to offend her by rejecting it. Maybe next time he would try not to lean away.

"Did you sleep well?" Her voice was high, confident but not personal.

Sol nodded, his mouth full of food.

"I can't quite get used to the constant pitching of the boat." She grabbed the edge of the table as the bow of the ship dipped slightly faster than usual. "Does it bother you? I can't decide if it's terrifying or exciting."

Sol shrugged. He hadn't really thought about it.

"You were a diver like Aizel," she continued, seemingly undeterred by his lack of conversation. "You are probably much more comfortable with the sea, then."

Sol nodded. The waves were much calmer in the deeper

water and, for the most part, the ship rocked gently over them. Sol swallowed the food in his mouth. "I am very comfortable below the water," he said. "I know nothing of wind and sail. The rocking is new for me."

When Meena didn't respond immediately, Sol glanced up at her. She was grinning at him.

"What?" Sol asked, feeling suddenly very exposed.

"Nothing." She scraped the side of her almost-empty bowl. "I just like talking."

"I noticed." Sol felt a small smile tug at his lips.

"I mean, I'm sorry. I do talk a lot." She pushed her bowl to the center of the table, her expression falling.

Sol felt his own smile disappear with hers.

"We should be making plans while we have the time to do so," she said.

Sol shook his head. "We can't discuss it here," he whispered, glancing around the room to make sure no one had entered unnoticed. "Your talking is good. It makes us look real."

Her face brightened.

CHAPTER 18

"*D*on't wake me up tonight," Sol whispered to Meena as he latched the door closed behind him.

"Who is going to be doing most of the work once we reach Falqri?" Meena asked.

"What do you mean?" Sol responded.

"Who is going to be skipping sleep, sneaking around the city at night and constantly watching our backs to keep us safe?" Meena knew Sol could not see the hands she had on her hips, but she hoped the hissing in her whisper properly conveyed how seriously she wanted to be taken.

"I assume you are speaking of me?" he responded.

Meena kept her mouth closed, for once choosing to let her facial expression convey what she wanted to say.

Then she remembered Sol couldn't see her face.

"Obviously." The snide comment had less of an impact after the awkward pause, though. "Sol, you are the central piece of this mission. Please sleep on the bed. All night. And then neither of us will lose sleep."

"I don't think I'm going to sleep much either way."

"Because you will be constantly alert against an attack?" Meena said. "I see the way you look at every space we enter, how you are always aware of who else is in the room. Let me guard the door tonight. We won't have much time for sleeping in Falqri."

"You are a rather heavy sleeper," Sol said slowly. "Thank you for offering the bed, but I don't think even a storm could wake you."

"I'm already lying down." Meena dropped quickly to the ground in front of the door as she spoke. "Did you know I can sleep anywhere?"

"I've noticed." Sol must have sat back on the thin pallet as Meena heard it creak.

She smiled. Winning felt good. "Do you think all married couples argue about their sleeping arrangements?"

"I'm sleeping," Sol replied.

"It probably helps prove we have a real marriage if any of the sailors can hear us through the walls," Meena said.

"If they were listening, you just gave it away."

"Right. Sorry."

"Goodnight, Meena," Sol whispered.

Meena could feel the end of the conversation in his voice. She settled comfortably against the hard floor. "Goodnight, Sol."

Meena fell asleep quickly. Spending the day wandering the ship's deck in the warmth of the sun had been both exhilarating and exhausting. She'd enjoyed watching the green forests and rolling hills of the Iseldis coastline as they sailed south toward their destination. But her eyes were begging for a rest.

She slept soundly until she found herself in the middle of

a dream about the ship sinking. In the dream, she stood on the deck, watching someone climb the roped rigging as a storm raged around them. Lightning struck. The ship pitched. And the person in the rigging lost their grip and fell toward her through the air.

Meena woke up screaming. The body had hit her. Something was on top of her.

Sol leapt off her. "Meena, it's me. I fell off the bed—did I hurt you?"

Meena stopped screaming, drawing in huge gulps of air as she sat up. Her body was overheated with sweat. "I don't feel any pain."

A thunderous clap sounded above them. The ship rolled again, tossing Sol against her. This time, he was prepared. He caught himself with his hands on the wall before his body slammed into hers.

"We're in the middle of a storm."

"So it wasn't a dream," Meena murmured. She looked up at the low roof of the small cabin, expecting to see rain leaking through it or lightning burning it off. But all she could see was darkness, and the outline of Sol's head close to hers.

"I'm going to see if I can help," Sol said, standing despite the ship's motion. He reached down to help her to her feet.

She leaned against him as she frantically reached for the wall to stabilize herself.

Rain pelted their faces as Sol opened the door.

"Stay here," he yelled over the noise as he slipped outside.

Meena stepped out after him, holding both sides of the door frame to keep herself standing. Rolling around in the tiny cabin by herself did not sound appealing.

The ship pitched again, and Meena found herself tipping

forward. Her arms strained against the door frame as she attempted to keep herself from falling face forward. Water sloshed over the rail in front of her as the ship righted itself and then pitched in the other direction.

Meena swung back inside the room and fumbled for the door.

On second thought, rolling around inside the tiny cabin sounded far preferable to rolling over the side of the ship into the raging sea.

Jumping onto the bed, she curled herself in the blanket, wound her arm through a tall post attached to the wall, and huddled into a ball. The makeshift handle and walled corner of the tiny room kept her fairly stable against the constant motion of the ship.

This was decidedly less pleasant than watching the sunny coast of Iseldis drift by.

She closed her eyes. It didn't make much of a difference since the cabin was dark, anyway.

Her stomach churned as the ship rose and fell, then landed back in the water with a breath-defying jolt.

It felt like an eternity before the door swung open, letting in rain and seawater along with a very wet Sol.

"It's bad," he said, forcing the door shut behind him.

"I can feel that," Meena responded, her arm already bruising from how hard she was clutching the perpendicular post of wood. "How bad? Sinking bad?"

"The storm was unexpected," Sol replied. "We've been traveling close to the shore for speediest passage. That was a mistake. We are now too close."

"So yes, sinking bad." Meena's stomach churned again.

"More like crashing into rocks bad."

"You really didn't soften the blow," Meena muttered.

"I didn't hear that," Sol yelled, still bracing himself against the wall.

"Nothing!" she responded. It felt good to yell. Her stomach stopped rolling when she yelled. "So we just wait it out?"

"That's one option," Sol replied.

"Can't we use the sails or something to go in the other direction?" She knew it was probably a foolish suggestion. She knew nothing about ships or sails or navigation in stormy weather, but talking was better than silence. Or listening to thunder and waves.

"I don't know about sailing, but the wind is pushing us into the shore, so I don't think that would work."

"What other option is there?" Meena's throat felt hoarse. Her stomach started to churn again, despite the yelling.

"There is one last resort I'd rather avoid," Sol responded.

"You can get us out of this with your magic?" Meena didn't dare yell the secret out loud, so Sol didn't hear her question.

The ship shuddered, stilling in the waves but shaking in place. A deep, low groan from below sounded over the noises of the storm.

Meena screamed.

Sol pushed himself off the wall and sat on the bed next to her, throwing one arm around her shoulders and grasping the handle above her.

"It's time for that last resort," Meena yelled. "We just hit something." She said the words out loud, hoping Sol would refute them and calm her fear.

He said nothing, but Meena could feel his arm and chest relax around her.

She shivered.

He tensed as the ship rocked again, but still said nothing.

She could feel reverberation from his chest as though he were speaking, but she heard nothing.

"Please try the last resort," she repeated in a louder voice.

"I am!" he responded. "It's a little difficult right now. Think of something calming!"

Meena closed her eyes. The handle she clung to was firm, but her body rolled against it at the whims of the ship. Water from Sol's clothing had seeped through her dress, but she could also feel the warmth of his arm around her shoulders.

As the next wave hit, his arm flexed around her, helping her remain stable against the motion.

She inhaled. Calming thoughts. His arm was calming. This was not the adventure she'd asked for, but it was exciting. They were in this together, and she was looking forward to spending the next several days with Sol, even if they were difficult.

His chest vibrated again, and it sounded as though he was humming, or even singing a song.

Meena breathed deeply, hoping his magic would work.

A slight wind rustled over her ear, and she shivered. Not even the air was stable.

The wind picked up, wrapping around her head and bouncing off the wall next to her. She buried her face in her elbow, protecting her eyes from the blowing gale, all calm feelings gone.

Surely the roof had been torn off the cabin and the storm was raining down upon them. It was the only explanation she could think of for the intensity of the wind that still circled her.

"The door!" Sol yelled, pushing away from her.

She clung to the wooden handle, accepting her fate as it

came to her. There was no point in leaving the cabin now. The ship was done for.

She heard the door slam open, slapping the cabin wall.

The wind whipped around her head once more and then disappeared.

Meena kept her face covered, waiting for the inevitable water to reach her toes.

The door slammed shut again, and the ship rolled. Meena waited for it to bounce back. Sol had left her.

She inhaled a shaky breath.

A very wet arm wrapped around her shoulder again, and she started in surprise. "Sol!"

"The storm won't die immediately, but that should keep us from the rocks below," he yelled in her ear.

"What did you do?"

"I asked the wind for help."

CHAPTER 19

$\mathcal{S}$ol dozed fitfully throughout the night. He didn't want to admit the princess had been right about his needing sleep. He'd slept so soundly the storm hadn't woken him until he'd been thrown off the pallet onto the sleeping girl below.

Hopefully he hadn't hurt her, but everyone was bound to be a bit bruised and battered today.

He left Meena sleeping—still curled in the corner of the bed—and went to see how the rest of the ship fared.

The calm water looked like glass, as though it had not been an angry tempest the night before. Walking around the deck, he could find no sight of the shoreline. The wind had taken them back out to safety.

"It's a good thing we reinforced the hull," a sailor said from further down the deck. "That scrape could have done us in."

Sol stepped toward the talking crew members. He avoided a pool of water and stooped to pick up a tangled length of rope. His fingers pulled at the knot as he continued his way across the deck.

"You survived the night, Your Highness?" the captain called out to him.

Sol nodded stiffly. Being called by his newly acquired title was disconcerting.

"Are we far off course?" he asked, looking over the torn sail the two men were mending.

"No," the captain replied. "Nothing a little tacking can't fix."

Sol knew tacking referred to moving a ship into the wind, but he had never understood how the actual maneuvering worked. The sailors seemed to enjoy talking with Meena; perhaps they would not mind explaining it to him. He loosened another knot in the tangled rope, keeping his hands busy while he thought of the words to ask his question.

"Your Highness." The other sailor stepped forward, taking the rope from Sol. "You needn't concern yourself with cleaning the ship. The captain'd have our hide for letting royalty take over our responsibilities." He winked at the captain.

"I don't think the fresh bread survived the storm, but there's still plenty of stew and porridge to keep you sated. Head below and find some food, Your Highness."

Sol did not pride himself on conversing easily with people, but he did know when he was not wanted. With a nod to the sailors, he made his way below decks.

The other two members of the crew nodded politely when he entered. Just like the previous morning, they hurried up the ladder as soon as possible.

Sol ate quickly. Usually, he preferred to be alone, but something about the confined spaces of the ship weighed in on him. He finished eating and went back up to the captain's cabin.

Knocking gently, he waited for Meena's invitation before he opened the door.

Her cheerful face greeted him with a welcoming smile.

Sol closed the door behind him. His shoulders relaxed, though he had not noticed they were tense.

Meena sat on the edge of the bed, plaiting her hair into a braid. "Good morning," she said cheerfully.

"Good morning," Sol responded, leaning his lower half against the bed while leaving as much space as possible between them. "Did you sleep well?" His mouth quirked into a smile as he realized his question was a silly one.

"The most relaxing night of my life, I think," Meena responded with a smile. "Although I cannot figure out why every part of my body aches." She stretched her arms over her head and winced. "I think my arm and shoulder are one giant bruise thanks to this slat of wood, but I must admit, I'm very glad it was there to cling to. Though it does seem like an odd addition to the room." She looked around the room, the rest of which was quite simple in its construction.

"I think that's its very purpose," Sol said.

"Oh!" Meena touched the handle with what looked like a new appreciation. "That makes so much more sense. I suppose if one sails often, they would know to expect stormy seas."

Sol nodded, enjoying her cheerful temperament. He did not take correction well from others, yet here she was, amiably learning something new from him after nearly dying at sea the night prior.

"Were you being humble yesterday?" she asked. "You said

you don't know much about sailing, but you seem to be quite knowledgeable on the topic."

Sol shook his head. "Truly, I know nothing about sailing. I wish I actually did. But because I knew how to swim, learning the ropes on a ship was never a necessity for me."

Meena wrapped the braid around her head, tying it in place with a large kerchief. "Do you never learn things that are not a necessity?"

Sol frowned. He'd never thought of it that way. "When your constant survival is threatened, you don't get much of a chance to learn things for the enjoyment of them."

Meena frowned back at him. "I'm sorry. If I knew anything about sailing, I'd tell you all I know."

Sol couldn't stop the smile that came to his face. Her words sounded flowery and empty, but he believed she would do exactly as she'd said. The tiny cabin felt larger than the main room below deck, and he was glad he'd come back here.

"Was learning to wield magic a necessity?" she asked.

"Yes and no," Sol responded. "We were only useful to the Quotidian if our magic could expedite the speed of necessary work."

"Why don't the Quotidian use their own chaos magic to get work done?" Meena asked.

Sol noted that it was an astute question. "Chaos magic must be powered by chaos, and most are not keen on inflicting pain upon themselves for the purpose of using their magic sustainably over the course of a day or longer." Sol clenched his jaw. "They do relish using it in shorter bursts, though—when it is convenient to draw the chaos from someone else's pain."

"Do you remember learning magic?" she asked. He was

thankful to move the conversation into a lighter area, whether she realized they were doing so or not.

"I don't recall learning it," Sol responded. "It is something that always was. It was in the tales my grandmother whispered as she rocked me to sleep. It was in the rules my parents enforced to keep us away from the notice of the taskers."

"When you put it like that, it sounds so beautiful. Other than the taskers part, of course. Just that it always was. I always . . . I never . . ." She stopped talking.

Sol waited for her to finish her thought.

"I always thought it was something to be scared of. A power that would destroy Iseldis and my family and even me. I just—I never thought it could be something different. I'm sorry."

Sol nodded. She was right. She had been wrong, even if she had not been the one to twist the truth herself. "I don't remember the first time I used the harmony within me to wield the magic, but I do remember when I discovered how it worked, I used it discreetly to do things I didn't want to do, like clean the water pail or shake out the blankets."

Meena smiled at his memory. "What fun things do you do with it now?" she asked.

Sol exhaled. It seemed it would be impossible to keep this particular conversation from becoming sad. "As soon as the taskers know you've learned to channel it, they collar you with a chaos-powered gem so you cannot use your voice and therefore cannot access your magic."

"Oh." Meena looked down at her hands. "Aizel told me about that."

Sol held his breath. He hadn't meant to share that much, and he did not want to carry the weight of her sympathy or guilt or whatever other emotions were warring across her face.

"I'm sorry," she said. Looking up, she added, "Not that I have any understanding of what that was like, but you did not deserve to grow up under such a cruel set of rules."

Sol released his breath. He was neither offended by her words nor hurt further by them. "No one does," he responded.

Her eyes opened a little wider. "Which is exactly why we are here." She tilted her chin down in determination.

Sol nodded in response. He had put all his energy into getting to the fortress, and now he was mere days away from arriving. He still needed to refine the final pieces of his plan.

First, he needed to get a layout of the fort, which hopefully would be easier to access than the palace in Chendas. The magic receptacle was probably in some sort of underground dungeon area with limited access. Only a select few of the soldiers would be aware of its existence, and even fewer would know of its purpose. But it would be heavily guarded.

"What is our plan for destroying the stored chaos magic in Falqri?" Meena asked, interrupting his thoughts. "We have not discussed it in detail yet, and we only have a few days left to know what we are doing. Shouldn't we talk about it now while we are on the ship?"

Sol let her talk, barely paying attention. "I can't make a plan until I see the fort. And it would be best not to discuss it. We never know who is listening."

The princess glanced around the tiny room. "Alright," she whispered. "But how will I know what to do?"

"What do you mean?" Sol asked.

"If we don't discuss the plan, I won't know what my part is."

"You've already done your part," Sol explained, confused at her questioning.

"We haven't even arrived yet, though. What did you expect me to do once we got to Falqri?"

Sol did not have an immediate answer to that question. "I wasn't expecting you to do anything."

"Do you plan to do this entire thing by yourself?" Meena asked. "Do you know anyone in Falqri? Surely you'll need help."

"Yes," Sol responded to her first question. "And no. This plan will most likely fail. I don't think you realize what that means."

"What plan?" Meena asked, her voice rising a bit. "Of course it will fail if you don't accept help."

"Failure means death, Princess," Sol said bluntly.

"I know," she responded, standing from her seat on the bed and stepping away from him to lean back against the wall.

This created a little more distance between them, but now Sol could clearly see the expression on her face. It was not necessarily a view he appreciated.

"I don't want you to die," she continued. "I don't want my family to be destroyed by this chaos magic. I saw my brother get cursed by a Majis—" She stopped speaking with a groan, covering her face with her hands. "See, I still can't even say it right. A Quotidian mage. I feel as though I've been swimming in a beautiful sea, but I never put my head under the water to notice the murky sea floor below is rotting away. Now I've seen it and I can't unsee it."

"I'm not sure what you mean," Sol said as she took her hands from her face.

"Never mind. It's just a feeling I don't yet understand."

Sol stayed silent.

"Let me help you," she said. "I don't know if I have any skills to offer, but at the very least I can put all my fancy dresses to use and distract the other nobles so you can do some cyphering."

"That actually would be helpful," Sol replied. He'd expected her to interact with the other members of her class —a task he had no comfort in doing—but he had not considered working together on it strategically. The less she knew about this mission—the less anyone knew about this mission —the better.

"Should we assign a sort of language to use?" Meena asked. "A way to secretly signal to each other whether a conversation is merely social or part of the mission?"

Sol shook his head. "I don't think that will be necessary."

"But what if I'm talking to someone and you need me to keep asking the questions?"

"The less we communicate about this, the better," Sol replied. Working together was too risky. He would do this alone.

"I'll follow your lead, then." The princess relaxed her stance. "I am here to aid you—not get in your way."

"Thank you." Sol exhaled. "Are you hungry?" he asked, quickly changing the topic of conversation.

"Starving," Meena replied, moving to the door.

"The fresh bread got soaked last night, but the stew is hot," Sol said as he stood from the bed.

"Sol." Meena stopped in the doorway, blocking his passage. "We are on this ship for four more days." Her face lit up. "Why don't you ask the sailors? We are literally stuck here with nothing necessary to do."

"Ask the sailors?" His mind was still on their conversation, and he had no idea what she was referring to.

"About sailing!" she explained. "They know everything there is to know about it, or at least more than either of us."

Sol hesitated. The sailors had not been overly friendly with him, and he didn't blame them. He was playing the part of royalty. He had a title he despised. He would despise himself too if he were in their position.

"They seem friendly enough," Meena persisted despite his reticence.

"With you, perhaps," Sol responded. The princess had a title too, yet somehow the sailors overlooked that and enjoyed her company.

She looked over her shoulder at him, brown eyes open wide and lips curved in a welcoming and happy smile.

Of course the sailors enjoyed her company. No one could be intimidated by her energetic personality. Sol wanted to be angry at the ease with which she carried through life. Perhaps that was what she meant when she said it felt as though her whole life had been spent above the water on a beautiful sea. He was jealous of her, yes. But he could not be angry at her. In the short time he had known her, she had constantly focused on making Celesta happy, protecting her family and kingdom, and now aiding him. It was little wonder the sailors loved her. "They have been less friendly toward me," he tried to explain when he realized she was still waiting for him to speak.

She turned back around and led him through the door onto the deck of the ship.

Sol followed her, still deep in thought. His spatial awareness remained sharp, fortunately, or he would have walked right into her back when she stopped abruptly a few steps later.

"It's so beautiful," she said, her voice barely more than a breath. Her hands were clasped at her chest as she stared out at the calm, glassy sea. Tilting her head back, she closed her eyes. "The sun. The water. The stillness."

Sol looked from her to the ominously peaceful water. If he hadn't witnessed its recent storm, he would have called it beautiful as well.

"I was so scared last night." She turned to him. "Thank you for asking the wind—"

Realizing what she was about to say, Sol leaned forward, covering her mouth with his own in a kiss.

Her whole body stiffened with shock. She grabbed his upper arms but did not pull her face away.

"I am so sorry," Sol whispered after ending the awkward but not unpleasant kiss. His hands instinctively held her waist since there was nowhere else for them to go.

Meena still clutched his arms, her eyes wide with shock. "Please don't apologize," she whispered. "I . . . What . . . Ohhhhhh. I almost said it, didn't I?"

Sol nodded. He could hardly hear her whisper despite the quiet stillness around them. "Perhaps we should have a secret language after all."

"If that is one of the secret symbols, I'm not complaining." She still had not taken her hands from his arms.

He stepped back, forcing their contact to end. "I am so sorry, Princess."

She ducked her head, awkwardly slipping her arms around her own waist. "I can't believe I almost said that out loud. It was so foolish of me."

Before Sol could respond, a loud whistle sounded from further down the deck. "It would seem the real storm hasn't stopped yet," a sailor yelled.

Sol wished he could dive into the sea and disappear for a moment. He was glad he'd stopped Meena from finishing her sentence about the magic he'd used, but he hoped the sailors were still far enough away they hadn't heard any of that conversation.

"Good morning, Tillon!" Meena called, her voice loud and cheerful. A little too cheerful. She quickly made her way across the deck of the ship to join the sailors.

Sol followed her.

"I see your monstrous mer-friend visited us last night to wreak havoc on the ship," Meena called as she walked.

The captain sputtered in laughter. "Good morning, my lady. Glad to see you are none the worse for wear. Perhaps my nightmares came true after all."

"What happened to the sail?" Meena asked, pointing to the work in their hands.

"The wind and the waves seemed to be at odds with each other last night, in a way I've never seen before. Perhaps it was the mer-monster's doing." He paused dramatically. "Anyway, we tried to use the sails to make use of the favorable wind, but you can see the result." He gestured to the torn sail.

"I'm glad we survived, even if the sail failed us." Meena said.

"The winds were strong, but they still pulled us through." Tillon pointed to the full sail on the other mast. "Bertha there stayed put."

Sol looked over to the sail, noting the angle of it against the current breeze. He was glad his wind had gotten them out of the storm, but he was still confused as to how the ship had worked against the waves even with the wind on their side.

"Bertha?" Meena burst into laughter. "You named the sail? And you chose to name it Bertha?"

"Can you think of a better one?" Tillon asked, bristling.

Meena shook her head. "Who's this then?" She gestured toward the down sail.

"This here is Maximilien, but don't you dare laugh at him now—he gets offended easy, see."

Meena shook her head, covering a snort with her hand. She looked over at Sol and raised her eyebrows.

Sol scrunched his brows back at her in return, uncertain what she was looking for.

"Tillon." Meena turned back to the sailor. "What kind of cloth are sails made from to withstand such a powerful force as wind?" She reached down and touched the sail.

"This one here is canvas," he responded.

"And Bertha?" Meena pointed to the other sail.

"Canvas as well."

"Are they made with anything other than canvas?" Meena asked.

Tillon looked confused. "No. All sails are made of canvas. It's the only fabric strong enough for it. They say leather would be better, but it would be too heavy and too expensive. So it wouldn't be better." Tillon paused. "Why do you ask, my lady? Are you interested in sailcraft?"

"Yes!" Meena replied. "Well, not particularly. I just like learning new things." She sent a pointed look back to Sol.

He raised his eyebrows in return, finally understanding. Looking back at the sailor, Sol cleared his throat. "Tillon," he said, "you seem to know much about sailing. Could you explain how tacking works?"

"Tacking?" Tillon replied. "It's the first thing a sailing lad learns, and it's easy as climbing the rigging."

As Tillon launched into an explanation of the maneuver, Meena subtly glided away, climbing down the ladder toward the kitchen.

Sol smiled at her back and sat down on the nearly dry deck. He picked up the piece of tangled rope he'd had earlier and settled in to listen to all he could hear.

CHAPTER 20

Meena pretended to watch the distant landscape draw nearer on the final day of their journey. In reality, her eyes barely registered the bright blue sky above or the hazy outline of the far-off shore.

Her hand slowly ran up and down the ship's railing, her fingernail gently prying at a loose sliver of wood.

Sol had been acting particularly awkward since they'd kissed three days prior. He'd been skirting around her without touching her—a surprising feat in the small space they shared—and he continued to address her in a formal manner.

He had been spending most of his time with the sailors, asking them questions and helping them around the ship.

Meena, on the other hand, had done little since then but think about kissing Sol again. Their relationship was merely a strategic partnership, but apparently that hadn't stopped her heart from dreaming about more. Especially during those rare moments when Sol seemed carefree enough to smile.

She, too, had done her share of shadowing Tillon and his crew, participating in whatever tasks they would permit. Despite the looming danger, these last few days had felt as though they were outside of time. She loved strolling the small deck, jesting with the sailors, and having no responsibilities.

And she loved the rare moments when Sol seemed to set aside his constant vigilance and enjoy the same thing.

But it wasn't just his smile that made her heart pound more quickly. There was something incredibly attractive about the way he approached every action with a thorough intensity. His eyes never appeared dull or vacant. Where he looked, he looked with purpose.

Meena wished he would look at her more often. She wanted to be seen by him.

She yanked on the splinter, breaking it away from the wooden rail.

Clearly, she had developed feelings for him. And it was even more clear that he did not return those feelings. Otherwise, he would not be so ashamed of having kissed her.

Holding the long splinter between her two hands, she snapped it in half. It broke easily with little resistance.

"Tighter, Solano—tighter!" Tillon's voice sounded down the deck behind her.

Meena turned, leaning her side against the rail so she could more comfortably observe the latest lesson.

Sol grasped a rope that was looped through an iron stay and attached to the top of a sail. He pitched his weight against that of the unfurling sail, struggling against the rope.

"Aye, that's it. We'll make a sailor of you yet, lad!" Tillon encouraged.

Sol's face glistened with perspiration as the other end of the rope slowly lifted the hefty sail up the mast.

"Now!" Tillon called.

Sol wrapped the rope around the iron stay, deftly overlapping it in a sailor's knot that would hold through any storm. At least, Meena assumed it would hold.

She threw up her arms and cheered as the intensity on his face melted into a smile of success.

He glanced up at her, seeming surprised that she was watching.

She smiled in response, still clapping.

As a child, she'd had the opportunity to learn whatever interested her. Happy as she was to see Sol enjoying himself, a small part of her heart ached for the serious little boy who had been too busy trying to survive that he'd never had time to do anything unnecessary.

She longed to give that to him. To give him the time and space to explore something because it interested him or fascinated him. Even though she missed his company and attention, she was happy to stand back and watch him become a sailor for the brief time they had aboard.

It was not his fault that she had fallen in love with him.

Feeling her cheeks turn warm, Meena quickly twisted her body around, slamming her stomach into the railing so that her back faced Sol.

She did love him.

She'd only been married to this stranger for a handful of days, and her entire body wanted to be near him. Her heart wanted what was best for him. Her mind wanted to know everything about him, on this day and every day in the future while he grew and changed.

A shadow blocked the bright sun from her eyes, and she turned to see Sol standing next to her at the railing.

Her skin tingled at the sudden lack of sunlight falling on it. Pretending that it was too bright to look up into his face, she started scratching on the railing in front of her with a piece of the broken splinter.

It was the first time he had sought out her company since the kiss. But, in typical Sol fashion, he merely stood next to her and said nothing.

Meena tossed the piece of splinter over the rail and into the water below. She still had the other half to spin between her nervous fingers.

Hopefully he could not understand what she'd been thinking when she'd realized she loved him.

Or at that moment, right then.

She was thinking about being in love with him, and he was even closer. If he could read her mind, it would be in close proximity. Perhaps there was something about magic users where they could read thoughts with their magic.

Meena's heart raced as she shook her head in an effort to free herself from her spiraling thoughts.

Everyone had the potential to wield magic. She was being fearful and ridiculous.

He still hadn't explained why he had approached her, and Meena was done with her thoughts.

"Falqri truly is beautiful," she said, focusing her eyes on the red coastline, which was slowly coming closer. "I was here as a child, but all I remember is being overheated and constantly asking for something to drink or a fruit to eat. There was this delicious yellow one—I forgot what it was called, but it was sweet and tangy at the same time, and I couldn't get enough of it."

"Foreboding," Sol said.

"The fruit?" Meena asked, confused. "It was delicious. I'm sure you'll love it."

"The landscape," Sol responded. He pointed to the looming cliffs ahead. "It looks foreboding."

Meena stared out at the soft rounded sandstone that lined the shore as far as she could see in either direction. She tried to imagine seeing the layers of yellow, cream, and red through Sol's eyes. The height of the cliff itself *could* be described as ominous, but Meena also thought it was more than that. "Majestic," she said, speaking the next word that came to her mind.

"Uninviting."

"Strong," Meena said. "The sharp edges and rounded corners have withstood the test of time. Powerful."

"Blood red," Sol responded instantly. "Tired. Worn down."

"Now you are just being wrongheaded because you enjoy it." Meena looked up at the man standing next to her. This she felt comfortable with. Perhaps she was the one being wrongheaded.

Sol returned her gaze. He was not smiling, but the lines in his face were relaxed. "I wasn't being wrongheaded—I was being honest."

"As was I." Meena tilted her chin up ever so slightly.

The corner of Sol's mouth tilted up. "Whose words are true if the words contradict each other?"

"We were not contradicting each other," Meena said quickly. "We were . . . discussing things from different points of view. But I still stand by what I said. You were being contrary for the sake of quarreling."

"Which you shouldn't mind because you enjoy quarreling," Sol said, his eyes still on her.

Meena punched his arm softly with her fist. "You are purposely making me angry." She drew her hand back instantly. Her knuckles tingled. She rubbed them with her other hand to wipe away the overpowering sensation.

Sol, too, lifted his hand, rubbing the place on his arm where she'd touched him.

Meena quickly looked away. "The cliffs are not blood red," she said quickly, bringing the conversation to safer waters. "They are rust red. They look like pieces of iron someone has left out in the rain."

"Is that not ominous, still?" Sol asked. "I don't find anything comforting about rusted iron."

"It's less ominous than blood."

"One is direct, the other insidious, like the purposeful tarnishing of something that was good. Breaking it down over time, ruining what it once was."

Meena looked back at Sol. He was no longer poking fun at her. His tone was too serious. "I don't fully follow, but I would like to understand what you mean."

"I was speaking of the cliffs." Sol grabbed the railing with both his hands, leaning out over it slightly and away from her.

He was hiding something from her.

Meena leaned forward, desperate to be included and instinctively trying to see his eyes, which were turned away from her. "You can tell me."

"There is nothing to tell."

Her heart once again broke for the young boy whose world had been constructed of cruel realities. "If you do not wish to tell me, I will not force your voice." She reached a hand toward his arm, stopping before she made physical contact again. "But I am here, and I can listen. Want to listen. Will listen." She dropped her hand, pulling it away from him.

"Princess." Sol turned from the rail, dipping his head in a gesture of respect as he quickly walked away.

Meena had the distinct feeling he had not done so out of deference, but merely to hide his face from her.

She exhaled, dropping her elbows on the railing to hold her weight. She felt like a child, like Sol was protecting her from some horrible truth just as she had tried to do for Celesta. "I am not so unscathed by the world that you must hide things from me." She spoke over her shoulder to the empty air behind his back, but her words were quiet and the waves were loud.

She did not repeat them.

He did not turn around.

Meena returned her gaze to the shore, watching its rapid approach by herself.

The ship dropped anchor a short length from sand, and she and Sol were given the first rowboat ashore.

Sol occupied himself with helping the sailors load their chests on the small rowboat, which hung over the side of the ship.

Grasping the rail for stability, Meena jumped, swinging her legs up and over the rail until her feet landed on top of it. Her skirts bundled up underneath her, but she carefully rotated her body until she was sitting on the rail, her feet hanging over the edge of the ship to get into the sailboat below.

"Allow me to help, Princess," Tillon said, appearing at her side.

"Thank you, friend." Meena accepted his hand as she slid off the railing, landing unstably in the rowboat.

She held tightly to Tillon's hand for a few extra seconds as she caught her balance in the swinging boat. "Thank you," she repeated, looking up at the sailor on the other ship. "It was a breathtaking voyage."

"Breathtaking is one way to put it," he responded with his ever-quick smile.

"I hope we will travel with you again for our return trip?" Meena asked. "Only next time without the storm, please?"

He laughed at that. "I'll do my best, Princess. Enjoy your stay in Falqri."

Sol climbed over the railing a few moments later and sat in the center of the boat to help row.

Staring at his back, Meena waved goodbye to the other sailors still on deck as they made their way to the shore.

Minutes later, the rowboat bumped against sand, as close to the dry ground as it could get. Meena swung herself over the edge of it on her own before Sol could offer her his hand.

Dropping her feet into the ankle deep water, she bundled her skirts as best she could and waded the final few steps to shore.

Sol naturally helped the sailors lift their trunks from the bottom of the rowboat.

The Falqri Fortress loomed overhead. It was constructed of the same red sandstone that spread along the cliffs all the way down the coast, as far as the eye could see.

Standing directly below it, Meena tilted her head far back and took in the low profile of the wide building. It appeared to be built into the cliff rather than above it. A thin path swung back and forth up the cliff face, connecting the shore to the city above.

Sol wordlessly dropped a chest by her side in the sand and returned to the boat for another.

Meena could see nothing of the city itself, as the fort and cliff hid it from view. But she could see various people making their way up and down the long road, leading carts and hauling loads of goods from the beach around her.

Sol returned to her side a moment later, dropping another chest. A sailor behind him deposited their third and final piece of luggage.

"If royalty doesn't work out for you, you could make your fortune at sea." The sailor dipped his head as he splashed back into the water.

"Thank you, Esven," Sol said with a sincere smile. "Safe seas to you."

The sailor winked at Meena. "Though it seems you've already found yourself quite the fortune."

She rolled her eyes as she waved back at him.

Sol did not acknowledge the man's brash comment. He turned to stand next to Meena, his expression serious. She could see his eyes quickly taking stock of the area around them, just as she had done.

"Who is meeting us?" he asked.

"I have no idea," she responded. "The councilor said we would be met at the shore and taken to our lodging. He insisted on arranging everything as a *marriage gift*." Meena spoke the last two words with contempt.

Sol's eyes still scanned the light crowd of moving people in front of them, but he picked up on her meaning instantly. "He must keep us constantly under his thumb."

"It will likely be some gruesome Falqri captain who doubles as both innkeeper and prisonkeeper." Meena let her imagination play on Sol's observation. Their keeper would likely search all their chests for hidden weapons and put them up in a dark room half dug out of the ground, as she'd heard was the Falqri way to avoid the sun's heat indoors. "We are little more than hostages of Chendas."

"It would be more accurate to say your family is being held hostage," Sol said.

Meena tensed. He was right. Iseldis was under King Gareth's thumb, and by traveling alone to the strongest hold in the five kingdoms, Meena and Sol were placing themselves in a precarious position.

"We must give him no reason to think we are suspicious on any account," Sol continued. "Be the princess you are and we should not raise any concern." Sol turned back toward the sea, distracted by the sound of another incoming rowboat.

Meena let him speak, knowing she would have no trouble playing her part. It was him they were both concerned about, and he knew it. But she enjoyed hearing him talk in multiple sentences at once and didn't interrupt to correct him.

She did, however, notice two people walking toward them.

"Like this?" she asked, slipping her hand under Sol's arm and smiling up at him, drawing his attention back to her. They had to re-establish some sort of relationship before they were on display once again. If Sol was not comfortable with her because of the kiss, she had to sell their ruse. Perhaps if she led the way, he would continue to relax enough to smile more often.

"Exactly like that," Sol responded, his arm stiff. "Though it's only necessary after our keeper arrives."

"Keepers, I think," Meena responded. "And they've

arrived." She gestured lightly toward the man and woman quickly approaching them.

"So they have, Meena mine." Sol spoke quietly, his mouth somehow smiling and tense at once.

"Meena mine?" Their keepers were only a few steps away, but Meena couldn't help but tease Sol for the silly name he'd called her. He was going to have to try much harder to convince anyone they were in love.

He didn't respond, but she could feel his arm tense as he prepared to meet the newcomers.

"Prince and Princess Sirilian?" the man asked pleasantly.

Sol didn't answer immediately, so Meena held out her free hand. "You must be our keeper?" Meena asked.

"Your keeper?" the woman replied, confused.

"Innkeeper." Meena quickly fixed her slip of tongue.

"Your Highness." The man bowed over her hand. "Falqri would never offer a *princess* such as yourself a mere inn. You and His Highness will be guests in our home. Which, I can assure you, is far finer than an inn."

The man's smile was disarmingly charming. Wearing the white and purple of Chendas, he appeared to be only a few seasons older than she and Sol. His eyes twinkled with mischief, reminding her with a pang of Erich. She missed Erich. And because of it, she liked this man. Instantly. Which she knew was ridiculous because he was her actual enemy. But apparently, her feelings and her mind had stopped consulting with one another.

Squeezing Sol's arm for stability, she looked between the man and woman in front of them. "And you are?"

"Jules." The man bowed again, sweeping the hat off his head in an elaborate flourish that reminded Meena once again of Erich. "And this is the most perfect woman in all the kingdoms—except for yourself, of course—who was gracious enough to bind herself to me, my darling Ezra."

The woman's severe expression relaxed into a small smile. She was tall and full-bodied. Her stiff dress and cloak, along with her tightly braided crown of hair, gave her an intimidating air. If Jules was charming, this woman was frightening. Her smile softened her demeanor by the smallest degree. "You are one of the most prominent captains in the king's army. The binding was not a difficult choice to make."

"I always hoped our union might be one of true love." Jules pretended to wipe away a tear. "But at least you love me for my many accomplishments—and that is love, is it not?"

Meena smiled, enjoying his dramatics. If he could jest so easily around his wife, she could not truly be that intimidating.

Sol placed his hand over Meena's, pressing it against his arm. "Thank you for keeping us." His hand was damp and warm.

Meena squeezed Sol's arm with her hand, both in an attempt to reassure him and encourage him to remove his sweaty grip. It had taken him long enough to find his voice.

"Here we are, keeping you on the shore," Jules said, playing off Sol's words. "Surely you are tired and hungry. Come. We've hired a cart for the chests, and another for our rears." Jules winked at his wife.

Ezra rolled her eyes. "It was a good jest the first time you used it, Jules."

"It's the first time they've heard it, so it's amusing for them." Jules spoke to his wife as though Sol and Meena were not standing right in front of them.

Meena laughed appreciatively, looking at Sol to share in the mirth.

His face was stony. She couldn't see the expression in his eyes as they were shadowed under the tilt of his brow.

Jules, however, grinned at her. His own eyes sparkled at her appreciation of his jest.

"I am both exhausted and starving," Meena said, her voice cheerful and loud to compensate for Sol's reserved presence. "Please lead us to the cart for our rears."

Sol's arm flexed under her hand.

Meena slipped her hand free under the pretense of lifting her skirt across the sand. Her mouth quirked into a smile she couldn't hide. If she'd embarrassed Sol with her mention of 'rears', she was not sorry for it. In fact, she rather enjoyed it and hoped she would have the opportunity to embarrass him again.

Jules held his wife's hand, swinging it widely back and forth as they worked their way across the sand. Meena noticed with jealousy that Ezra did not bother to lift her skirt, nor was she tripping on it. Upon closer inspection, Meena saw that the hem of the other woman's skirt was higher than her own. She hoped it was a Falqri fashion she could adopt while living in the sandy environment.

Sol followed a step behind Meena, and she threw him a quick smile. She reminded herself he was both displaced from his familiar surroundings and social standing. She resolved not to get angry with him for tripping over his tongue in social settings. That was the one thing she could help with on this mission, and she intended to do it well.

"How long have you been here at the fort?" Meena asked Jules, keen on keeping the conversation flowing.

"Not long at all," Jules replied. "We were in the capital at Chendas until very recently."

Meena felt the world shift around her. Her legs stumbled as they adjusted to walking across solid ground.

Sol grabbed her upper arm, steadying her before she fell. She threw another smile over her shoulder to thank him. He dropped his hand as soon as she moved forward again.

If Jules had been in Chendas recently, he could have been present when Erich was nearly executed. He could have participated in that awful event.

Meena clutched her skirts. "How recently?" she asked, keeping her voice light despite the crack that accompanied it.

"We arrived in Falqri at the end of silverreign," Ezra responded.

Meena exhaled. Her brother had not been in Chendas until greenreign. Jules had not participated in Erich's imprisonment.

He still could have been there when Aizel or Celesta had been captured.

Meena's chest tightened. For all his charm, she had to remember that Jules was a minion of Gareth. As delightful or charming as he and Ezra might seem, they were still the enemy.

She hoped they did not know about the chaos magic and Gareth's cruelty toward the Majis. Jules and Ezra seemed like genuine and kind people, but she steeled her heart against them.

Though Jules kept up a constant chatter as their cart slowly rambled up the cliffside road, Meena had difficulty hearing the words he said.

Sol remained stony and silent at her side.

214

Ezra occasionally spoke a word or two, but only when her husband called on her to affirm his facts and stories.

The fort loomed overhead as they criss-crossed their way up the cliffside road. The uneven sandstone gradually transformed into a carved brick wall. Long, thin slits made up the windows of the lower levels of the fort while short, pointed triangles lined the upper wall.

"Was the fort built *into* the cliff or *out of* the cliff?" Meena wondered, not realizing she'd asked the question out loud until Ezra answered her.

"Both, I presume," he said. "Anywhere you see individual bricks, such as the towers or battlements, were added to what the cliff already provided."

"I've never seen triangular battlements before," Meena said. "Are those a Falqri tradition?" Meena nudged Sol, who sat at her side.

When he looked down at her, she blinked twice, slowly. It was the communication they had agreed upon for warning the other when they were discussing parts of the plan.

Sol's gray eyes appeared a shade darker as he furrowed his brow.

"I have not been in Falqri long enough to know," Ezra responded.

The wagon bounced as they rounded a corner. Meena grabbed at the wooden bench she was sitting on. The uncomfortable feeling she had been trying to forget snaked its way back into her stomach. Ezra was from Chendas, not Falqri.

"The triangle shape seems as though it would be a poorer choice for defense," Sol said slowly. He bit his lower lip and twisted his neck back to stare at the fort as the wagon finished turning around the tight corner. "A rectangular shape would provide more coverage."

"You seem very interested in the fort's defenses," Jules said. "Are you looking for its weaknesses?" He glanced over his shoulder at Sol. "Are you planning to attack it?" His mouth was smiling in jest, but his eyes appeared uncomfortably sharp.

"No," Sol sputtered as he looked to Meena. He blinked, furiously.

They had not agreed upon a meaning for that many successive blinks, but Meena knew he was asking for her help.

"You are really in command of this entire fortress?" Meena directed her question at Jules. It was not difficult to fill her voice with awe and respect.

She saw Jules's chest puff out as he inhaled. "A tremendous responsibility." His words were modest, but Meena could hear the pride in them.

"Interesting." Sol gave Meena a sidelong glance. "Interesting that a soldier from Chendas should oversee the largest port city in Falqri."

Jules glanced over his shoulder again. Meena could see one of his eyebrows suspiciously raised.

She nudged Sol with her elbow. That was too pointed of a question to ask.

"Not surprising at all," Jules responded more slowly than usual. "Falqri is known for its great warriors, and Chendas for its great strategy. It only makes sense that we would combine our strengths."

Sol scooted a touch further away from Meena. It seemed he did not like her warning jabs in his side.

"The soldiers here must really respect you, then." Meena

directed her words to Jules but sent a glare toward Sol. She blinked once. Once meant they were simply making conversation.

"They do," Ezra responded for her husband, slipping her arm into his and nudging his shoulder with devotion and pride.

Staring at the gentle contact between Jules and Ezra, Meena suddenly felt very cold. She could feel the ocean breeze blowing freely in the space between her and Sol. She let the conversation dwindle.

As they finally entered the city gates, two guards stopped them on the way in. "Oh, it's you, Captain," one said, standing up stiffly and nodding in a salute. "Sorry to stop you."

"Thank you, Rivard," Jules replied kindly. "You are supposed to stop everyone who comes through these gates —even me."

The cart rode through, and Meena let her attention turn to the small city that comprised the fort.

The structures, composed of clay and sandstone, ranged in color from creamy whites to rusty reds. Most of the buildings were indeed built low to the ground, with sand piling around their outer walls. Other than that, it felt very much like the Iseldan capital she'd grown up in. Tight rows of small houses gave way to open marketplaces. Surrounding it all, the thick wall of the fort protected everything and everyone inside the city.

The lighter and warmer colors were different from what she was used to, especially the pale, soft hues of the Falqri clothing. Everyone in Iseldis seemed to favor deep, dark tones. It appeared as though everything here, from the buildings to the clothing to the people, had been shaped by the constant heat of the sun.

They were only a few turns past the operating section of the fort when the cart stopped in front of a sprawling sandstone manse. It was set against the wall of the fort, overlooking the city inside it. The sprawling courtyard in front of the house was covered in sand and beautifully arranged stones. Small bulbous plants in a pale green color brought a charming sense of life to the dry environment. Short, stocky trees with long, thin, willowing leaves lined a path to the main entrance.

"Beautiful, isn't it?" Jules asked.

Meena turned to him. "I've lived my entire life in a castle, and I've never seen a more welcoming home. Is this your family's estate?"

"No. Not sure who had it last, but they were thrown out. King Gareth certainly knows how to take care of his own," Jules replied.

Meena kept the smile on her face even as the joy in her stomach turned to horror. Her own father provided housing for all the commanders in his army, but she didn't know if he'd ever thrown someone out of their home to accommodate the soldiers. She'd never even considered it as an option before.

It seemed as though every moment of joy she found here was unraveled by another reminder that she knew so little about so many important things. Exhausted, she accepted Sol's hand as he helped her down from the cart.

He seemed completely unperturbed at the admission of having removed people from their homes, which meant he'd either known of the practice or was not surprised by it because such horrors were common to him.

Meena squeezed his hand, refusing to let go of it as she stepped onto the ground. She was glad to know now, but she didn't like to think of how many other uncomfortable truths she'd been protected from. She only knew she would find them, one by one, uprooting everything she had previously known.

CHAPTER 21

*S*ol followed Jules, Ezra, and Meena into the extravagant home they would be staying in.

The climate of Falqri reminded him of Istroya, and he felt at home in the dry heat amongst the round, stubby plants.

He did not feel at home in the opulent sandstone manse. It reminded him of the houses inhabited by the taskers on Istroya.

Interestingly, he did not remember feeling so disgusted by the palace of Iseldis. Perhaps he had been too focused to notice his surroundings, or perhaps the large castle felt less opulent because it was less a home and more a small city. He did remember feeling overwhelmed by the sheer number of people who lived and worked in the palace. It had a function that served many people.

This particular large home was eerily empty. Sol felt that its only purpose was to impress.

He pushed aside the tired frustration he was feeling and brought his mind back to his present mission. All he wanted was a room to himself, a long nap, and the freedom of darkness so he could explore the city on his own.

He followed Jules through the halls of the home, keeping note of every turn they took and how far they were from the main entrance. Occasionally, he saw windows in the outer walls that would be surprisingly easy to escape through. The house itself had been built several hand-lengths deep, so the ground outside was nearly as tall as the base of the window.

"Would you care to join us for a game of quugot?" Jules asked, stopping at the open door to an inner courtyard.

Sol began to shake his head.

"Surely they are tired from their travels, dear," Ezra said, reading his mind. "You must let them go rest. We can play all the quugot your heart desires during the rest of their stay."

Jules turned back to them with a rogue smile. "Of course, of course. They surely want to go to their rooms."

Sol smiled his thanks, relieved. He was exhausted.

But Meena caught his attention, blinking twice.

She wanted to find out more information, even though she, too, was likely exhausted.

Impressed at her dedication and not wanting to be outdone by her, Sol gave her a slight nod.

She smiled warmly at him before turning back to their hosts. "We would love to join you for a game of quugot. You will have to teach me the rules, as I've never played it."

Sol nodded his agreement, thankful Meena had spoken for them. He raised his eyebrows at her, hoping to communicate that she had done well.

Meena blinked back at him in response.

"Magnificent!" Jules threw his arms out wide. "Ezra and I make a formidable team, but we will take it easy on you just this once."

Meena slipped her hand into Sol's arm as they followed their hosts through the beautiful house. "That sounds intimidating, but I never back down from a challenge," Meena said. "Is it a fun game?"

"It's deceptively simple," Jules responded. "But don't let that fool you. It's very fun."

Sol did not care about the game, but he did care about gaining information. If they asked the right questions, they could confirm that an important shipment had recently arrived from Chendas. He could also learn about the rotation of the soldiers and where he was most likely to find the magic receptacle.

If he had calculated correctly, the chaos mages should not currently have any Majis prisoners. Insofar as they had been able to track on Istroya, the mages only took two at a time to steal magic from. They chose those with a good propensity for magic or those who would not be missed for the labor. Sol had a powerful affiliation with magic, and he guessed from Neven's age that the man had been chosen for the latter reason.

It had been over fifteen years since the taskers had chosen his father. If they had come for another pair of chosen, it meant the previous pair were dead.

Sol forgot about his exhaustion, reinvigorated as he was by the justice he sought.

"It's a simple game, really," Jules explained as they stopped in the inner courtyard. He handed a pouch to Sol. "You merely toss this pouch into that casing." He pointed to a small ring of stones a good distance away.

Sol accepted the pouch, quickly noting the way it was tied closed with multiple loops and knots. The weight of it settled between his fingers, shifting in a pleasant way. "Sand?" he asked.

"Yes," Jules responded. "Gives it a good weight to work with. Try it."

Sol looked at the circle he was supposed to hit. Swinging back his arm, he felt the weight of the pouch and gave it a solid push through the air.

The sand-filled bag arched through the air and landed with a satisfying thud on the ring of stones.

Meena clapped at his side. "Let me try it," she said, holding out her hand to Jules.

Jules gave Meena another pouch. "That was a good shot, Your Highness," he said to Sol. "It would only give your team a single point. If you land it in the center of the circle, you get three points. First team to twenty points wins."

Meena threw the pouch into the air. It landed with a much softer thump in the sandy spot at the center of the circle of stones.

"Ha!" she yelled. "I like this game."

Jules laughed out loud at her obvious pleasure. "The two of you start over there, so we stand on opposite sides."

Meena leapt forward, pulling Sol along with her. "We have to win," she whispered, cozying up to his shoulder.

"Isn't it just a game?" Sol responded, glancing back at their competition. "I thought we were here to . . ." He waited for her to look up at him before he blinked twice.

Jules and Ezra were laughing about something together and did not seem to notice the quiet conversation happening across the sandy courtyard. Sol took note of their infatuation with each other. It could be a useful tool for distracting them in the future.

"We can't just lose," Meena hissed. "We need them to respect us."

Sol looked back over his shoulder. Jules was kissing Ezra's fingertips, as though they were the only two people in the world. Earning their respect was not his highest priority.

"I don't think that's necessary," Sol replied, picking up the sand pouches from the ground at their feet. "We don't need their respect, just their information." He said the last part so quietly he could not even hear himself.

"It's a good thing I'm a fair shot, then," Meena muttered to herself. "I'll have to win this on my own."

Sol raised his eyebrows. "I never said I intended to miss."

"Good." Meena put a dazzling smile on her face, but it wasn't for him. They had reached the mark, and she spun back toward their hosts, her skirt energetically wrapping around his legs as well as her own.

Jules and Ezra earned five points on their first round. Meena growled in despair each time their opponents landed a shot.

"Are shipments from the other kingdoms difficult to receive in such a remote outpost?" Sol asked, trying to sound casual.

"He thinks this is remote," Jules said to Ezra. "We should take him further south. The prince has likely never seen an actual village before."

Sol rolled his eyes. He was no prince. And he was from a small island. It was his turn, so he lined up to take his shot.

"We got this, Sol," Meena whispered very intensely at his side.

He let the sandbag fly through the air.

"Have you received any shipments from Chendas, recently?" Meena called across the playing space. "I've been waiting for months to see the latest dresses." She trailed off in a whoop of joy as Sol landed a three-point shot.

"A caravan from Chendas arrived three weeks ago," Jules replied. "The new silks are stunning. Wouldn't you agree, my dear?"

Ezra smiled at her husband, stepping forward to take her shot. "Anything you purchase for me is stunning."

Sol stored that information in his head. He did not doubt Robin's information, but it was nice to know that the caravan had arrived from Chendas within the likely timeframe.

"Well asked," he whispered as Meena prepared for her next throw.

Her shot landed to the side of the target.

"You distracted me," she hissed as she stepped back. "But thank you."

Sol stepped to the mark for his turn.

"Please get three points," Meena said loudly.

Jules laughed, but his laugh turned into applause when Sol landed a three-point shot.

"Yes!" Meena shouted with glee. "Are we free to explore the city tomorrow?" she asked, weaving her excitement into the question.

"Your word is our command," Jules responded, missing his next shot.

"Except for three evenings from now," Ezra said. "The fort always celebrates the Goldenreign Feast, and we would be honored for you to attend."

"It would be our honor to attend," Meena graciously responded.

Sol also took that piece of information into his plan. A night of celebration and a disturbance in the routine would be the perfect time to empty the magic receptacle—if he could locate it by then, of course.

Sol inhaled. His mind relaxed, turning over the new information as his body enjoyed the movement of the game.

Meena shouted in glee every time either of them scored a point, and Sol found himself enjoying the sound of her excitement.

"We only need one more perfect throw," she said encouragingly as he took his place again. "You can do this."

Sol paused, looking to his side at the vibrant woman cheering him on. Whether they won or lost, tonight was a victory. They had made it this far, and he would do everything in his power to bring down the reign of the chaos magic users. "Let's win," he said to Meena.

"Yes!" she yelled. "That's the spirit!"

Jules laughed at her exuberance, and even Ezra cracked a small smile.

Sol refocused on his immediate goal, taking careful aim and tossing the sand pouch confidently into the air.

He remained hunched in position, waiting to see where his shot would land.

It was a perfect three-pointer.

Sol stood, throwing his fists up in front of him. Victory felt wonderful.

"That's twenty-one!" Meena called out. "We win! I knew you were the best partner!"

Sol thought his chest might explode with the feeling of joy that coursed through him.

Meena slipped her hand in his arm and tugged him toward their opponents. "I hope you were not going easy on us, because we are the best team to ever play quugot!"

"I will demand a rematch," Jules said. "But we did not go easy on you." He slipped his arm around Ezra's waist. "We could never be so devious."

Sol had a feeling he was merely placating Meena, but he couldn't blame the man. Watching Meena's happiness made him happier than he'd ever felt on his own. "Thank you for the game, and for having us in your home," Sol said. "I think it is time we find our rooms for the night."

"Of course," Jules responded. With his arm still around his wife, he led them back down the hall.

"The servants should have had time to unload the chests into your room," Ezra explained.

She only indicated a single room, which made Sol slightly nervous. Rich married people did not share the same room. Why else would they have such large houses?

Jules and Ezra stopped at an open door in a quiet section of the house.

With a quick glance, Sol confirmed that it was a single room. With a single bed.

"Ah, to be young and in love," Jules said to his wife. "I wish we were newly wed again." Tilting his head, he kissed his tall wife.

Meena squeezed Sol's arm, and he felt his face growing hot. Not in embarrassment, of course—but the kiss reminded him of the moment he'd shared with Meena. The moment he had enjoyed far more than he was willing to admit. The moment that had distracted him from his purpose for too many days already.

"How long have you been married?" Meena asked innocently.

"Three months," Jules responded. "It feels like yesterday and a lifetime ago."

Sol snorted.

Meena pinched his arm again, and he quickly turned it into a cough.

"Thank you again for having us in your home," Meena said, covering up his awkwardness. "I hope to win many more games of quugot against you." Her sweet voice held a confident challenge.

Sol tugged at the collar of his shirt. She was a distraction. He had worshipped his father, then lost him. He would never make that mistake again.

Even if he miraculously succeeded in his mission—and remained alive—there was far too much left to do to spend any time wooing a princess. Even if that princess could get him to enjoy something as simple as a tossing game.

"I'll send you my maid, Princess," Ezra said.

"Tomorrow, my love, tomorrow." Jules winked at Meena. "She has no need of Laila tonight."

"Goodnight," Sol said firmly. He needed to end this conversation. And he needed to get a certain princess out of his head so he could make plans for the next day.

"You like them," he whispered when they were finally alone in their room, dropping her hand from his arm. He didn't dare speak too loudly.

Meena paused for an awkward moment. "I was playacting," she whispered. The look she gave him was filled with confusion. "Ensuring they like us."

"Your laugh was too real for that to be playacting," Sol responded. He knew his words were petty, but he had to put distance between them.

The princess jumped back as though she had been slapped. "And you know me well enough to know my laugh?" she said, clearly hurt. "I suppose you were playacting out there as well? Meena mine?" She spat his words from the beach back at him.

He brushed past her, walking the perimeter of the room.

This was good. This was back to a relationship he could control.

The relief and joy he'd experienced from winning the game were gone. His muscles were back to their usual tense state.

He stopped, checking the window and curtains to ensure they were locked and closed. That the room was safe. "Actually, I was hoping they would be a bit more like the keeper you described on the shore earlier. A big, nosy man keeping his watchful eye on us at all times. Then we would not have to worry so much about faking this relationship behind closed doors."

Meena gasped at the harshness of his words.

He went to the door to ensure it was also locked.

She turned her back to him and sat on the corner of the bed, reaching down to remove her shoes.

Sol waited for her equally harsh response, but she said nothing. After several moments, he felt a small pit form in his stomach. She'd never been voluntarily quiet for this long before. Somehow, he knew she would not speak to him again for the remainder of the night.

That would be good. Preferable even. But his stomach still felt twisted and empty.

He kept his back to her while she readied herself for bed. A wadded-up blanket landed at his feet, and a pillow followed soon after.

He spread the blanket next to the door, waiting until she blew out the candle before he allowed himself to finally lie down and relax.

As he laid his head down on the pillow, it felt as though it fell straight through the floor. His body was firm on the ground, but his mind kept falling in a loop.

He closed his eyes, but the sensation grew worse. It reminded him of being back on the ship, gently rising and falling with each wave. That was likely the cause of it, just readjusting to sleeping on solid ground again.

He did not recall experiencing this after having sailed from Istroya, but he had felt many more unpleasant things on that trip. Perhaps they'd overpowered the odd sensation in his mind.

He wondered if Meena was experiencing the same thing. He hoped it was not upsetting her.

He could check in with her and ask. When he tried to open his mouth, his tongue seemed to swell, stuck in place. She was likely already asleep and didn't want to be disturbed.

CHAPTER 22

Sol was not in their room when Meena awoke the
next morning. She struggled into one of her
fancier gowns, unsure what the activities of the day would
entail. As she fumbled with the laces behind her back, the
door creaked open with a light knock.

"My lady sent me to see if you needed anything?" a bright
voice said.

With her hands awkwardly pulled over her shoulders,
Meena shuffled around to face the door.

The lady's maid appeared to be a handful of years older
than Meena. Her dress was well made and looked new. "Let
me help you with that," she said immediately.

"Thank you," Meena replied. "I seem to have tied myself
into knots."

"Of course you have," the maid took the laces from
Meena's hands and deftly worked them where they were
supposed to be.

"What's your name?" Meena asked after a moment of silence.

"Laila, my lady," the maid responded. She offered nothing more.

"You arrived at the perfect moment," Meena said, smiling politely, though the woman behind her back could not see it.

Laila said nothing, but she grunted as she tied the laces closed. "Would you like me to help with your hair?"

"Please," Meena responded. She moved forward to sit at a small table against the wall.

Laila followed behind her and immediately started undoing the thick braid in Meena's hair.

Meena relaxed into the maid's touch. She'd been solely responsible for her hair maintenance since she'd left Iseldis, and it was luxurious to leave the laborious task to someone else.

Having removed the braid, Laila carefully used her fingers to separate out any large knots in Meena's hair. Though the occasional tug pulled on Meena's scalp, the maid performed her task gently and thoroughly.

"Did you come from Chendas with the captain and his wife, or are you from Falqri?" Meena asked, trying to think of something they could talk about. While she was used to having help getting dressed and ready, she was not used to doing so in silence.

"I've never set foot outside of Falqri," Laila responded. Her words were crisp and quick. She kept her eyes firmly on her hands as she worked.

Meena bit her lower lip. This table had a small mirror, just like the one at home. It was tilted back so Meena could see her own face and that of Laila's behind her. She was used to using the mirror to chat and connect with whomever was doing her hair. She preferred to dress herself when she did not have to wear something elaborate, but occasionally she would ask for help from one of the palace maids. Or occasionally her mother stepped in so they could have some time together in the morning, just the two of them.

Meena didn't need to talk—and she wasn't going to force someone else to speak with her—but it felt so uncomfortable to have a complete stranger working on her hair and touching her head.

Laila had switched to a wooden comb and was slowly running it down the length of Meena's waist-long hair. The gentle pressure of the comb felt relaxing on her scalp.

A knock sounded on the door, and this time the newcomer waited until Meena answered before entering the room.

"Come in!" Meena looked up, watching in the mirror as Sol entered. "Good morning!" She'd forgotten why they'd been upset at each other the night before. She was so relieved to see a familiar face that she welcomed him enthusiastically.

Sol stepped across the room, covering the small space quickly with long strides. He stopped at Meena's side, standing close enough to touch her shoulder.

Meena looked up at him, moving her head slowly so as not to disturb Laila.

"I would love to discuss the day with you, Meena mine," Sol said. He smiled widely and blinked twice.

Meena turned to look over her shoulder at the maid behind her. "I can take it from here, Laila. Thank you for your help this morning." She smiled warmly, eager to make the other woman like her.

Laila dipped into a curtsy without making eye contact. "Yes, my lady," she said. She turned toward the door, then stopped awkwardly for a moment, the hair comb still in her hand.

Sol, who was now standing directly in front of Meena—and very closely to her—held out his hand.

Laila gave the comb and quickly dropped into another curtsy before leaving the room.

As soon as the door closed, Sol turned back to Meena. "Our hosts are planning to take us on a tour of the city today." He did not sound excited at the prospect.

Tired of twisting her neck, Meena settled back into the chair, using the mirror on the desk to make eye contact with Sol. "And?" she asked, unsure what he was upset by.

"I cannot waste valuable time exploring the local merchants. I need to observe the fort and see if I can learn information from the local soldiers." Sol tapped the comb against his hand, positioning himself behind her so he could clearly see her face in the mirror as well.

"You need me to distract Jules and Ezra today so you can be free to explore on your own?" Meena clarified.

"Precisely." Sol exhaled. He lifted the comb and ran it through her hair.

Shocked at the ease of his action, Meena froze. "I can do that," she said. Her fingertips tingled. She thought it was probably due to the excitement of having a responsibility that would help in their mission.

Her scalp tingled as well, but that was just because the comb was gently pulling on her hair.

Sol repositioned the comb, running it through the exact same strands he had just done. His face was deep in concentration.

Meena smiled as she watched him through the mirror. Sometimes she had no idea what he was thinking behind his mask of silence, but in that moment she was confident she knew exactly what he was thinking. He was strategizing his plan for gathering information today. And he clearly had no idea he was also brushing her hair.

His eyes were active, but not in a defensive and guarded way. Rather, they were focused and alert, intent upon his own thoughts. He looked younger, his face relaxed to fit his actual age instead of carrying the weight of the world.

Meena closed her eyes, blinking rapidly for a moment. She was not ready to drop her gaze from his face. She inhaled, wishing for a moment that this was her real life instead of her fake one.

Sol looked up suddenly, catching her eye in the mirror. His eyes instantly tightened, and the line of his mouth went rigid. He pulled the comb from her hair and nodded briefly at her as he set it on the table.

"Thank you," she whispered, sad that the moment had ended. Though, in the life of her dreams, it would have been better if he'd chosen to participate consciously rather than by accident.

"Are you ready?" he asked.

She nodded, standing from the chair. "Let's get started. Best of luck in your search today."

Sol led the way to the bedroom door, and Meena quickly braided her hair over her shoulder as she followed him out.

"Good morning, royal guests!" Jules's voice echoed down the hall as though he had been waiting for them to leave their room.

Meena gasped in surprise, not expecting such a jubilant welcome so quickly. She felt slightly better to see Sol looking startled as well.

"Good morning, good captain!" Meena called, recovering quickly and stepping forward to meet their host.

Jules and Ezra swept down the hallway toward them.

Meena's jaw dropped when she saw the elaborate clothing they were both wearing.

"What is the occasion?" she asked. "You both look so lovely." She fingered her simple braid self-consciously. At least she had worn one of her better dresses.

Jules bowed graciously as he came to a stop in front of them. The decorative chain of his captain's uniform clanked delicately as he straightened. "Does one need an occasion to impress the loveliest princess in all the lands?"

Meena smiled at his charm, feeling both flattered and patronized.

"I hope you slept well?" Ezra dipped into a subtle curtsy, her stiffly tailored gown accentuating both her height and the long, imposing line of her nose.

Suddenly, Meena realized that Laila must take after her mistress. Rather than feel intimidated, Meena had the desire to break through the cold woman's icy exterior. "It was amazing to sleep on a real bed again after so many days at sea," she answered. "Though I must say, the world still feels like it is rolling under my feet."

"You've become a true sailor, then, Princess," Jules said. "That feeling will eventually go away." He winked. "At least it should."

Meena laughed properly, feeling more like herself.

"Are you ready to see the finest sights in all of Falqri?" Jules asked.

"Yes!" Meena replied. "At least I am. I believe my husband has some plans of his own today."

"Oh?" Jules asked, looking expectantly at Sol.

Sol nodded. "I am very interested in the architecture of the fortress," he said. "I was planning to get a closer study of it."

Jules stepped forward, offering Meena his arm as he stood between her and Sol. "I can show you the fort any other day—that is hardly pressing. Besides, how could you refuse to spend the day away from your beautiful wife?"

Meena, her hand gently holding Jules's arm, shook her head. "If anything, we need a little space from each other. We did just spend five days with each other on a tiny ship."

Jules looked at her in horror. "The two of you newly married and already tired of each other?" He looked to Ezra. "Can you imagine?"

Ezra shook her head. "That must be terribly sad."

Meena thought she looked more judgmental than sad.

"No." Jules put his other arm around Sol's shoulders. "Today, we celebrate. I insist." He stepped forward, literally pulling Meena with one arm and Sol with the other.

Meena grimaced at Sol behind Jules's back, shrugging apologetically.

Sol did not seem to notice her silent communication. His lips were set in stone, and his eyes brewed ominously.

MEENA WAS EXHAUSTED when they returned home that evening. "I didn't know walking could make me so tired," she hissed as soon as they were alone in their room for the night.

"Although I suppose it was more than the walking. We did a large amount of talking, eating, looking, admiring, and laughing. Also, the sun was very hot today, and I feel like that makes me tired more quickly."

Sol nodded. He remained by the door, silently testing the latch to ensure it was closed.

"My feet are in pain," she continued. Without making it as far as the bed or a chair, she sank to the floor, immediately releasing her feet from the leather coverings. She stretched her toes. "That feels so much better."

Sol still stood awkwardly by the door.

"Do your feet hurt?" she asked.

"Yes," he responded. But he made no move to enter the room or remove his shoes, as though he should not be there.

Noticing his discomfort, Meena stood, bouncing on her feet to alleviate the pain. "Sol, come in. We've spent enough nights in the same room. Be at ease." She reached out, wishing she could grab his arm and pull him into the room.

"I am not uncomfortable," he responded. "I'm thinking."

"Sol," Meena spoke again. "I'm sorry I couldn't think of something fast enough to cover for you this morning."

That seemed to catch his attention, and he looked at her. "He was very forceful about us both coming with them, wasn't he?"

Meena nodded, not needing to ask who Sol was referring to. "He couldn't know, right? Why we are here?" She barely whispered the last words.

"We will have to be extremely careful to give him no cause for suspicion," Sol said. His eyes had wandered again, and a familiar wrinkle appeared between them as he tensed his forehead.

"Can you not be here, right now?" Meena asked, wishing

she could take away some of the stress he carried. She instinctively stepped closer to him, wanting to reach out to him. To hug him. To be present with him.

Sol looked around the room, confused. "I am here," he protested, pointing to the ground at his feet.

"You are here," Meena said, her voice light with jest. She poked his shoulder, feeling that it was the safest way to reach him physically. "But your mind is certainly somewhere else." She tapped the side of his head.

"We did waste an entire day. Doing nothing," Sol responded. His face still looked grumpy, but he did not lean away from her touch.

"It was not nothing. We learned the major layout of the city and observed the shape of the fortress walls, and I saw the way you looked at the soldiers and noticed the rotation of the guards and the control of passage through the main gate."

Sol sighed. "It's so little."

"I'm sorry I failed you this morning," Meena repeated.

"You did not fail me," Sol said, lifting his eyes back to her. "This is my burden to carry."

"But who is going to carry the weight of you?"

"No one," Sol replied. "I have no weight to carry, no ties binding me down."

"I am here," Meena spoke quietly. She had already offered her help, multiple times. She couldn't force her way into a place he wanted to hide from her.

∾

∾

MEENA'S EYES stared up at him in the dim candlelight. They were open and earnest and bright.

Sol swallowed. He wanted to lose himself in those beautiful brown eyes. She kept offering to help him, but the longing in her eyes seemed to offer something more.

Sol blinked, tearing his eyes away from hers. She was a Quotidian princess. He needed to run before he fell under her spell.

She had asked him a question.

"I don't know what you mean," he replied, retreating into himself.

"Is it always a burden to lay down ties?" she asked. She leaned ever so slightly away from him, as though she could sense his reticence.

Sol turned away. He couldn't make her sad. He hardly knew her, yet his heart broke at the sight of her disappointment.

He did not want to examine the question she was asking.

He desperately wanted a moment to set aside his burden, to forget the injustice of the world and just enjoy being with a person who made him laugh. Her. Enjoy being with her.

She was a distraction.

"I don't have a choice," he finally said, his voice intentionally rough. "I cannot set aside the pain of my people while they still live in it." Sol closed his eyes, hoping she would end the discussion and let him be.

Thankfully, she was silent.

"I am going back out." He walked into the room, throwing open the window on the far wall. The cool breeze of the evening air calmed his heated skin.

"Tonight?" she asked. "Again?" She followed him across the room.

He looked out into the darkness below. They were on an upper floor of the building, but the stone buttresses outside would be easy to navigate. "I cannot sleep until I have made progress."

"Shall I come with you?" She ran back into the room, stooping down to pick up her shoes.

"No," Sol responded. His chest loosened. Perhaps it was the selfless offer to go out once again on her aching feet, or perhaps it was the knowledge he would soon be alone and free to move about as he pleased in the darkness. "One of us needs to be well rested for tomorrow."

The princess walked back to the window, stifling a yawn with the same hand that held her shoes. "I'll leave the candle burning so you can see which room to come back to."

Sol swung both legs over the window frame and started to lower his body down the other side. "Don't bother," he whispered. "It might alert someone it shouldn't. I'll find my way back to you."

His body instantly felt overheated again. He slipped further, searching for safe footing in the darkness before he let go of the window frame.

He needed to memorize this route so he could navigate it easily with the princess by his side in the event they needed to rapidly escape.

The princess. Meena.

He wanted to feel guilt for walking away from her conversation, but she didn't understand. She couldn't understand. He wanted to talk her to, but he could not burden her with his worries. She had never experienced what it was like to live on Istroya. To lose someone she loved. To feel the betrayal of attachment.

Yes, they had proven to be helpful to each other thus far. And his mind was already including her in his constantly prepared escape routes. She was someone he would take care of. She was like his family now. But that did not mean he could love her.

He felt a solid stone ledge beneath his feet.

Just before he dropped his hands from the ledge, he thought he heard her whisper.

"You don't have to carry it alone."

It was likely just his imagination.

CHAPTER 23

"You must have your union dedicated by a Sophist," Jules insisted. He and Ezra had once again pounced on them the moment they showed their faces the following morning.

"Union?" Meena asked.

"Sophist?" Sol said at the same time.

"A wise woman. Her name also happens to be Sophie," Ezra explained.

"Why don't they just call her Sophie the Wise?" Meena asked.

"Oh, you've heard of her, then?" Jules jumped in.

"No, it's just that her name seems complicated—"

"Her name isn't important," Jules spoke over her.

Meena glanced up at Sol, raising her eyebrows. They had not yet seen their host lose his temper.

Sol shrugged, but a small smile played on his lips.

Meena relaxed, turning her attention back to Jules, who

was still speaking. Even if she and Sol were at odds, they could still laugh over the same things.

"Every union in Falqri is dedicated by her. It's a must-have experience." Jules smiled benevolently.

Meena had little desire to spend the morning focusing on her supposedly real marriage, but Jules's benevolent smile made it clear he would not be refused. "Did you have your marriage dedicated by this Sophist?"

"Of course." Jules took Ezra's hand, gazing at her fondly. "And see how it worked for us. Two people have never been so happy."

Meena bit her upper lip for a moment. The adoration on Jules's face made her chest inflate with jealousy. "And remind me, how long have you been married again?" she asked, her voice a little sharp. She knew the answer but wanted them to say it out loud.

"Three perfect months." Jules's eyes were still on his wife.

Ezra rolled her eyes, but she didn't pull her hand from his.

Neither seemed to notice the irony Meena had pointed out. Their devotion clearly stemmed from their newfound infatuation with each other. She glanced at Sol again.

"Three months is a significant length of time." Sol's face was serious, but his loud whisper was clearly meant to be heard by everyone within earshot.

"To Sophie's it is." Jules turned back to them.

"Perhaps I could come with you to see this wise woman, but I believe Sol-ano has some business to attend to."

Jules burst out laughing.

"You can't dedicate a marriage when only one member of the party is present," Ezra explained as Jules wiped tears from his eyes.

"Can you imagine what Sophie would say?" Jules asked Ezra, still chuckling. "That union surely wouldn't last—and I mean you no offense, but I think the two of you could use all the help you can get."

Meena straightened her back as she opened her mouth in shock. "What do you mean by that?"

Jules lifted his hands. "I mean you no disrespect, Princess. I was merely observing that you and Prince Sirilian are quite new at all this, and a special blessing could secure your future happiness together."

Meena bristled. "I think our future happiness would be more assured if Prince Sirilian could attend to the business he needs to see to."

"Business?" Ezra questioned.

"Just some letters and such to see to," Meena said vaguely. "He has only just become a prince and is still getting used to his responsibilities."

"Responsibility doesn't start until you are home from your wedding trip," Jules countered. "You cannot risk the future of your marriage for a seemingly urgent task. Come."

Meena refused to budge. The Goldenreign Feast was just over a day away, and Sol still hadn't even discovered the location of their target, much less developed a plan for getting through the soldiers defending it.

"Unfortunately," Sol finally said, supporting her support of him. "My brilliant wife is right. King Frederich and Prince Onric specifically asked me to return with a detailed report on how you have managed to create such a well-prepared defense system."

"What with the upcoming Return of the Majis and all," Meena added. "Defense is our highest priority in Iseldis."

Jules's smile seemed to falter at the mention of the fort.

"If that is all you are after, I can have any of my men write that up for you in an afternoon." He stepped between them, tucking Meena's hand under his arm. Placing his other arm around Sol's back, Jules forced them to step forward. "To Sophie's!"

Meena leaned her head back, sharing another quick glance with Sol.

Jules was definitely trying to keep their time occupied.

∿

∿

∿

THE WISE WOMAN'S home was made up of the same cream-colored sandstone as most of the buildings in the city.

It was also built partially below the ground, requiring them to descend a handful of steps before pushing open the worn wooden door.

Meena entered the cool room with some excitement, squinting at the loss of light. It was not completely dark, but it took a moment for her eyes to adjust after the bright morning sun. In other circumstances, she would have thoroughly enjoyed the experience of having her union dedicated by a wise old woman. She decided to enjoy this unique experience as it was.

Sophie was surprisingly tall, but her shoulders were stooped and her movements slow. A loose gauzy fabric covered her hair. She greeted Jules with familiarity.

"Didn't I just see the two of you?" she asked, looking between Jules and Ezra. "Are you having problems already?

Your marriage is still very young. You have to give it time to grow along with you."

Meena instantly liked the woman for pointing out that three months of marriage was not very long.

"Oh, no, Sophie," Jules protested. "We are not here for us." He stepped aside and gestured toward Meena and Sol.

Sophie eyed them with a neutral gaze.

"This is Princess Philomena of Iseldis and her new husband, Prince Solano," Jules introduced them.

"I had heard of your union," Sophie said. "Though I did not expect the honor of seeing you so shortly afterward myself." She smiled.

Jules beamed, seemingly pleased with himself for arranging such a fortuitous meeting.

When he said nothing further, Meena broke the awkwardness. "It would be an honor for us if you would be so kind as to dedicate our union."

"Of course," Sophie replied. "Give me a moment." She disappeared behind a curtained doorway.

Meena took in the room around her. The harsh sandstone was softened by draping fabrics and bright plants. Cushioned chairs lined the walls of the room, but no one was currently making use of them.

"Do we need to do anything?" Sol whispered to Jules.

"No," Ezra responded. "She'll be back in a moment."

"She takes care of everything," Jules said reassuringly.

Sol did not look reassured, but Meena was thoroughly intrigued.

A few moments later, Sophie returned holding a thin bouquet of dried herbs. She held them in her hands, crushing the leaves lightly between her fingers as she approached Sol and Meena in the center of the room.

Meena caught the scent of the herbs and breathed in. It reminded her of the forests back home, but there was a touch of the desert in the smell as well.

"Face each other," Sophie instructed, gently gesturing with her hands to direct them.

Feeling embarrassed, humored, and relaxed, Meena turned to face Sol.

The woman said nothing, and it seemed as though she wanted something more from them.

Meena took a step so that she and Sol were closer together.

Sophie nodded. "Now, if you would hold each other's hands."

Meena looked up at Sol. His stony expression was easy to read. He was not enjoying this. She held out her hands, keenly aware of Jules and Ezra's presence.

Sol lifted his hands, placing them stiffly under Meena's.

The woman said nothing for several long breaths.

Meena could feel both her face and her palms warming. Sol's hands remained completely motionless under her own.

"Captain and Lady Levek, I believe this moment may be more meaningful to our friends if you were not present."

Meena almost snickered. She definitely liked this woman.

"Of course," Jules said, bowing his shoulders and head. "Whatever you wish—we would be happy to comply." With an arm extended to his wife, Jules led her across the room. "Let's go next door to visit your favorite seamstress, shall we? Perhaps find you something new?"

"I don't have a favorite seamstress," Ezra replied.

Meena's body relaxed as they left the room.

Sophie waited a few more moments before speaking. "Having bound yourselves to one another, do you wish to recommit the vows you made?" she asked. The words were formal and sincere.

Meena swallowed. It had been hard enough to bind herself to Sol the first time, knowing it was all a ruse. Somehow, the idea of lying in the presence of this sweet woman felt even worse.

Meena's forehead tensed.

Sol squeezed her hands.

She looked up at his face, expecting to see him scrunch his eyes and blink twice. The sooner they got this over with, the sooner they could continue their mission.

Instead, Sol shook his head at her.

Relieved, Meena nodded in understanding. "We are not prepared to recommit our vows." She watched Sol's face as she spoke, ensuring that they were thinking the same thing.

His hands relaxed under hers.

Meena turned to face the older woman.

Sophie slipped the covering from her head, shaking out her long, white hair. "That's what I thought." She waved at their joined hands.

Meena slipped her hands out of Sol's, wiping them on her skirt. "What do you mean?" she asked.

"I could feel your discomfort the second you walked through my door. I just needed to ensure it was a discomfort with each other and not with me."

Meena looked back to Sol. If they had been so obviously uncomfortable with each other that a complete stranger could comment on it only moments after meeting them . . .

"Your secret is safe with me." Sophie winked.

"What secret?" Meena asked, alarmed. The room was growing oppressively hot as the late morning turned into noon.

"There is harmony in both of your hearts," she answered cryptically, "even if there is not yet harmony between you."

"What do you mean?" Meena looked from Sophie to Sol.

Even the unflappable Sol looked concerned.

"If ever I can help you, please feel free to ask." She dipped her head. "Now . . ." She turned away, slipping behind a different colorful wall hanging. Meena had assumed it was decorative, but apparently it also covered a door.

"Should we go?" Meena whispered.

Sol shook his head, watching the door where Sophie had disappeared.

She returned a few moments later, carrying a folded parchment. "I believe this is from a friend." She handed the paper to Sol.

He took it and slid it under the top layer of his doublet. "Thank you for your service," he said.

"Go to your friends and assure them that your union has been dedicated."

Sol turned toward the door, moving quickly. His hand covered his chest where the letter lay.

Meena did not blame him. She was eager to know what information had been sent to them. But she spared a moment to smile her thanks to Sophie before she hurried after Sol. It was good to know they had at least one ally in Falqri.

As soon as they stepped back out onto the street, Jules appeared in front of them, smiling expectantly. "Are you dedicated?" he asked. They must not have gone to the seamstress after all, though Meena did notice a sewing shop across the street.

"She said to tell you we were," Meena replied, using the

woman's exact words, still uncomfortable with the thought of lying.

Jules wrinkled his nose, sniffing and smiling at the same time. "I knew you would love it." He pulled Ezra into a close side hug. "How special that we got to be here to witness it. If you don't mind my asking, what did she dedicate you to?"

Meena looked up at Sol. She had no idea what a union was supposed to be dedicated to, so she could not make up an answer. This custom was not common in Iseldis.

Sol shrugged. "I don't recall." He looked at Meena as though she were the reason he had not been paying attention to the woman's blessing.

Even though she knew it was fake, she couldn't control the flush that spread across her cheeks under his adoring gaze. She smiled shyly back at him, playing her part.

"You must know!" Jules insisted. "Let's go back and ask her."

"That's not necessary," Sol said.

"Come." Jules walked between them and jumped down the stairs.

Meena followed, Sol and Ezra close behind.

"Wise One." Jules bowed as he entered the room without knocking. "These two lovebirds have already forgotten what you dedicated their future to?"

Sophie raised her eyebrows, deepening the creases that crossed her forehead. "To the future, of course."

"I'm sorry?" Jules asked, confused.

"I dedicated their future to the future. That their harmony may ever increase."

Jules nodded. "That is beautiful. Thank you for your time." He bowed again and turned to leave the room.

Meena caught a quick wink from Sophie before they all left the room once more.

Meena walked slowly to match her pace with Sol's as they moved down the street. With their keepers in front of them, she looked up at Sol. The woman's words had been strangely appropriate. Meena hoped that there might be more than harmony in their future.

Sol held his arm out to her.

Meena slipped her hand inside his arm, turning her attention to the road ahead.

"What did she dedicate your union to?" she asked the couple in front of them.

"To love, of course!" Jules yelled over his shoulder.

CHAPTER 24

"*A*nother game of quugot?" Jules asked before they had even arrived back at the manse.

Sol smiled nervously. He would not be able to focus on anything other than the secret letter inside his doublet.

"That would be so fun!" Meena answered their host.

Sol clenched his jaw, trying to catch Meena's eye. After two days of constant company, he could not pretend to be pleasant in front of Jules and Ezra any longer.

"However," Meena continued, "I would feel terrible beating you so soundly so soon."

Sol exhaled. She was good at this.

Meena stepped closer to Sol, slipping her hand into his arm and leaning her head toward his shoulder. "The sun put me almost to sleep. I need a rest. I will challenge you to quugot as soon as we are rested."

"Let them be, Jules," Ezra said. "They didn't come all this way to spend time with us."

Jules's mouth formed a round shape. "Oh, you are quite

right, my love. Get some rest. We will see you for supper this evening."

Sol thanked the princess in his mind as they walked quickly down the hall. The tension in his shoulders relaxed as they left their over-present hosts behind. Excitement built in his fingertips; he hoped the letter held useful information.

"How did that happen?" Meena whispered, leaning her back against the closed door of their room. "Do you know who this Sophie is?"

"Robin said she was working on a contact here. I was hoping it would be someone more closely related to the fort, but I am not in a position to choose my allies." Sol slipped the letter out of his outer shirt. He quickly and carefully broke the wax seal.

"What does it say?" Meena asked, not even giving him a chance to read it. She leaned over his shoulder.

He tilted the sheet of parchment so that she could more easily see it. Something felt odd about the movement. He'd never shared a secret communication with anyone. In fact, he'd always taken great pains to ensure even his closest family members never knew he was still leading River's Thorn. But he'd tilted the letter to Meena without a second thought.

Was he growing lazy in his work here when it was most dangerous? Or did he instinctively trust Meena to carry this burden with him?

He did not like either thought.

The letter was written in coded symbols he had developed with Robin, so it was not legible at first glance. That was likely why he'd had no qualm showing the paper to Meena. It had nothing to do with laziness or trust—it was just common sense.

"What does it say?" Meena repeated, clearly unable to read the code.

"I don't know yet," Sol replied. He moved to the small table and set the letter down to decipher it.

He looked at the symbols, changing the ones he remembered in his head. He managed to make out a few words, but he would need to rewrite it in order to understand the full contents.

"Can I help you with that, *Rain?*" Meena asked. She was standing close to his side.

Sol looked up, confused. She was holding a fresh sheet of parchment and a feather pen. He took them from her and placed them on the table in front of him.

"What did you call me?" Sol asked, wondering if his ears had heard her correctly.

A quick look at her sparkling eyes told him she had called him a different name on purpose.

He closed his mouth, exhaling a long breath. "You were jesting," he said.

"Isn't your name supposed to mean 'sun'?" she asked, her voice still teasing. "You seem more morose, like rain. Not light and happy like the sun."

Sol momentarily forgot the letter in front of him. That was how she saw him?

Her mouth curved into a small smile that she tried to hide.

"Light and happy," he said, repeating her words thoughtfully. At least he hoped he sounded thoughtful. If she could jest, then so could he. "You perceive these traits as weaknesses, and therefore see the sun as weak?"

"Weak? No—" she started to respond, but Sol cut her off.

"The sun provides warmth, yes, but it also sends its rays

down in relentless heat. It guides the path of the moon, balancing the darkness of night. It gives power to the earth, causing plants to grow and people to survive." Sol found his voice growing louder as he convinced both himself and her of his point. "The sun is not weak. It is the anchor upon which all life is dependent." He paused.

Meena had stepped back, her mouth hanging open.

"So, yes. I suppose if that seems weak to you, there's nothing I could say to change your mind." He turned to look up at her, a smile of victory playing on his own lips.

"Sol." Meena looked thoroughly impressed. "Are you jesting with me?"

"Yes, rainy Meena mine," he said. He pushed his chair to the side, making room for her at the small table.

"I'm not yours," she said, sitting down on the corner of the bed and leaning forward. "I'm mine."

Sol smirked, appreciating her play on words.

"How do we read this?" she asked, her voice serious.

Sol leaned back over the table, explaining the code for the different symbols. Since he was more accustomed to deciphering, he found most of the letters, but she helped speed up the process by writing them down on the fresh sheet of parchment.

S,

New information. G is aware that a member of the Iseldan royal family is in Falqri. Watch your back. You are under suspicion. He expects treachery since he moved his special project there.

Sending N to aid you. He insisted.

Confirmed ally in Falqri whom I have been in contact with for some time. N will make contact first to confirm. Too risky to reveal your identity.

A and C send their love.

Stay well.

R.

"Who could 'N' be?" Sol asked Meena after skimming through the missive a second time. He recognized the rest of the names—G for Gareth, A for Aizel, C for Celesta. "None of your brothers have an 'N' name, right?"

Meena shook her head. "I have no idea. Robin seemed to think you would know. She said he insisted, which she assumed would mean something to you."

"Neven," Sol said. "Another Majis who was taken from Istroya with me. I helped him escape when Robin came for us."

"It will be good to have another person here whom we can trust," Meena said. "And he could be more useful on the ground than Sophie."

Sol pondered her words for a moment. He didn't *not* trust Neven. But he had just shared more secrets with Meena in a day than he had with anyone else his entire life. "I don't know how helpful he can actually be," Sol said slowly. "He is more of a follower than a leader."

"You give the orders then, and we will follow. We can use all the help we can get." Meena's inherent trust grounded him.

The letter was more concerning than helpful, especially the news about Gareth being suspicious. But as always, Meena naturally looked ahead.

That was strength. She was more like the sun, warm and bright and magnetic.

"What if you gave the orders and we followed?" Sol asked. "You seem particularly well suited for it."

Meena leaned back. A half smile played on her lips, but her eyes were squinted as though she were suspicious of him.

"I can't tell if you are trying to make me angry or if you are jesting with me again."

"I was trying to praise you," Sol responded.

"I seem particularly well suited for it?" Meena repeated his words. "And you meant it?"

"Yes," Sol said. "Why is that so hard to believe?"

"You keep trying to shield me, protect me. I got the impression that you don't think very highly of me."

Sol paused. Her words were not without merit. "Without you, I would be trekking across some wilderness trying to find this place. I am used to working alone. I have been shielding you out of habit as I tend to keep all the responsibility on myself."

"Oh." Meena did not seem convinced.

"Wherever you are, people gravitate to you," Sol continued, trying to find the right words to express his thoughts. "At first I thought it was because you were a princess, and I may have doubted your sincerity. But it seems to be far deeper than that."

Meena was uncharacteristically silent as he spoke. Her cheeks appeared slightly warmer than usual, but her eyes were wide and bright. She nodded slightly, as though encouraging him to continue.

Sol cleared his throat. "People listen to you," he said. He was not used to giving praise, but the sparkle in her eyes was intoxicating enough that he continued. "You know the right words to say. You make other people feel comfortable. Those are all skills I lack, and I am impressed by them in you."

"Thank you, Sol," she whispered. Her eyes fluttered down shyly, but her lips remained in a smile.

"Thank you," Sol whispered back, not sure if the words actually left his mouth or not.

CHAPTER 25

*M*eena's heart soared as they made their way
down the hall to supper.

Sol's kind words had seeped through her head and seared
themselves into her heart. Such praise from the silent and
brooding Majis was high praise indeed.

Her mind raced with the happiest of thoughts, finding joy
in everything she set her eyes on. She was surprised at how
effectively the temperature remained cool by utilizing the
additional depth underground. Though the sight of the
ground at the base of the window still made her laugh.

"Imagine if everyone were truly this short," Meena said,
pointing outside the window. "How strange would that be?"

"You were that short once," Sol responded.

Meena rolled her eyes. "Of course I was, as a child," she
replied. "But it was normal then. It was all I knew."

"And if you remained that short for your entire life, it
would be all you ever knew." Sol's voice was flat and logical.

"You are so dull," Meena responded playfully, overjoyed

that he was indulging her whimsical thoughts. "That's why I said 'imagine.'"

Sol instantly dropped to his knees and glanced over the base of the window, which his eyes could now barely reach. "Honestly, it would be quite nice down here," he said.

Meena threw back her head and laughed. Even when Sol jested, he did it so intensely.

"Princess," an oddly familiar voice said, startling her. "Prince."

Meena spun around to see Councilor Younn standing farther down the hall. She had no idea he was in Falqri, and she had no idea how long he had been watching their silly exchange in the hall.

Sol instantly jumped to his feet, straightening his back into his usual composed posture. His face also returned to its tense state.

Meena squeezed her fists for a brief moment, disappointment flowing over her. She loved to see Sol happy.

"Councilor," she said, forcing her voice to be airy and light. "How good to see you." She moved toward him gracefully, thankful she was dressed for dinner in one of her finer gowns. "How good of a surprise?" She turned the statement into a question with an inflection of her voice.

The councilor had said nothing about meeting them in Falqri.

Something was not right.

"A good surprise, indeed," Councilor Younn replied, bowing over her hand. "How are the two lovebirds enjoying their wedding trip?" He looked around her at Sol.

Meena turned and slipped her arm into Sol's elbow, pulling him into the conversation and closer to her.

Sol had tried to put a smile on his face but, as usual, it was making him appear far more uncomfortable than would his typical scowl.

"One of us is enjoying ourselves very much," Meena said pointedly in a sugary sweet voice. She squeezed Sol's arm. "And that is all that matters, isn't it?" She smiled warmly at the councilor, as though they were sharing an inside jest.

"Indeed, Princess." Younn smiled broadly in return, but his eyes flickered back to Sol. "It is good to see you so happy."

Meena laughed. It was an obnoxious sound in a ridiculously high register, and she instantly regretted it. But once she had started, she couldn't stop without sounding suspicious, so she finished it to the very end of its squeaking, scraping sound.

"What brings you to Falqri, Councilor?" Sol asked, his voice curt behind the stony smile still on his face.

"My king sent me on . . . an urgent mission," Younn responded.

"Oh?" Meena opened her eyes wide and leaned in. "Why so secretive?" she whispered.

Younn dropped his eyes to her. This time, the smile on his face felt a little forced, as though he were bored or annoyed by her cloying charm.

Good. That was how she wanted it.

"No secret," he replied. "Just urgent matters to attend to for our royal sovereign."

"Your royal sovereign," Meena said, straightening back up. "I am my own royal sovereign."

Younn's real smile returned. "If you say so, Princess," he indulged. "Though I believe the term 'sovereign' is reserved for the ruling king, not his entire family." He leaned forward as he patronizingly corrected her.

"Is it?" Meena responded with indignation. "How very rude. If I am ever king, I shall change that instantly."

Younn laughed.

Jules entered the hall, walking quickly toward the small group. Ezra was at his side, her long strides easily keeping up with his.

"Councilor," Jules said, coming to a respectful stop in front of his superior. "This is unexpected."

"Are you unprepared for me to see your progress at your new station?" Younn asked. His mouth was smiling, but he lifted an eyebrow.

"Of course not," Jules responded, the straight line of his back a far cry from his usually relaxed stance. "I mean, of course—you are always welcome."

"I have heard good reports," Younn said.

Jules relaxed slightly. "I hope your visit will exceed expectations, Councilor."

"I'm sure it shall." He turned to Ezra, who had stood silently by her husband's side. "My lady." He bowed.

"Younn," Ezra responded. "You are always welcome in our home."

Meena did not miss the way she addressed the councilor on a first-name basis. Not even her husband had done so.

"Thank you, Ezra," he responded.

"My dearest," Jules said, turning to his wife. "Shall we alert the kitchen that we will have our supper at the fort tonight?"

Ezra raised her eyebrows. Meena thought she did not agree with her husband.

"Perhaps call in the bards and have some dancing?" Jules continued convincingly. "What better way to welcome the councilor and entertain our royal guests?"

Ezra's hesitance turned into a smile. "That sounds like a wonderful evening, my dear," she said.

"That is not at all necessary," Younn cut in. His words sounded gracious, but Meena thought the pompous smile on his face said otherwise.

"Please Younn—some dancing would be good for all of us," Ezra responded.

"If you say so." Younn nodded his head to Ezra. "Captain, could you give me a review of your work here?"

"Of course, Councilor." Jules's back straightened, and he sent a quick look to his wife.

"I will take care of the rest," Ezra said reassuringly.

Meena noticed that Jules had not even asked a question, but Ezra had instantly known what his look meant. Despite her careful attention, Meena could not decipher the under-current of communication taking place beneath Jules and Ezra's conversation. Her mind kept forgetting that she couldn't trust them. They seemed so . . . trustworthy. At least Jules did.

As if sensing her thoughts, Ezra looked directly at Meena.

"Dancing sounds wonderful!" Meena said, clapping her hands together. She could talk to Sol later about the secretive behavior of their hosts. For now, though, she needed to ensure that Sol joined Jules and Younn in reviewing the fort. It would be the perfect time to finally get an inside look at their goal.

As Jules led the councilor down the hall, Meena looked up to find Sol's eyes on her.

He raised his eyebrows, tilting his head ever so slightly toward the departing men.

Meena couldn't stop the smile that came to her face. She did not have to be jealous of Jules and Ezra when she and Sol could communicate with just their eyes. She blinked twice and nodded.

Sol moved forward, quietly following just behind the men as though he had been invited to go with them.

Ezra noticed his movement, but before she could call out to him, Meena pounced forward. She grabbed the tall woman's arm, pulling her back toward the bedrooms. "Shall I change into something more suitable for dancing?" she asked.

With a final glance over her shoulder, Ezra turned her attention to Meena. "No, you are dressed as impeccably as always, Princess," she said.

Meena noted the forced politeness in the woman's voice. Clearly, Ezra would have preferred to go to the fort than discuss clothing options.

In any other circumstance, Ezra would have made a great friend.

Meena, too, wished to help Sol learn the lay of the fort. But this was the part she could play, so play it she would, even if Ezra hated her for it.

"Are you quite sure?" Meena asked. "Come see the other dress I brought."

CHAPTER 26

"Solano!" Meena cried when she spotted her husband in the main bailey of the fort. He was still in the company of Jules and Younn, so she remembered to use the fake name she'd given him. But the excitement in her voice was real. She was genuinely glad to trade Ezra's terse company for Sol's. Keeping Ezra distracted with silly nothings was exhausting.

Hearing her greeting, Sol made his way through the busy outdoor space, a fake smile plastered on his face.

Meena hoped that under the smile was at least a little relief to see her as well.

"Rainy Meena who isn't mine." Sol bowed over her hand as he approached.

Meena's frustration with Ezra instantly disappeared.

"Princess." Jules, who had followed Sol, bowed when he reached her. "You look as beautiful as ever."

"Thank you, Captain," she replied. She was tired of pleasantries. She wanted to speak with Sol and learn what he had gathered.

"Councilor," Jules said to Younn, who had also followed them. "Let us leave the two lovebirds to themselves for a moment. Surely they have much to say after their long separation."

Jules led Younn back into the crowd of soldiers and townsfolk.

"Anything?" Meena whispered as soon as they were out of earshot.

"Nothing," Sol responded.

"Nothing?" Meena repeated, her heart falling. "Nothing at all?"

"Some small things. I know where the prison cells are. Those would be an ideal location for security, but I don't think Gareth would want his precious cargo in close proximity to prisoners he doesn't trust. I still don't have any idea where it could be. Our dear general and captain were quite close-lipped and annoyed that I had followed them." He smirked a little at that.

Meena slipped her hand inside his arm. "That is not nothing," she said. "Every little bit of information gets us closer."

"It's not enough." Sol's face went back to its stoic mask.

"The night is not over yet," Meena replied.

"The Goldenreign Feast is tomorrow," Sol said.

"We can do it on a different night, then," Meena replied. "The Goldenreign Feast is an ideal time, but it is not the only time."

"I am concerned about Younn's presence," Sol whispered.

Meena stood on tiptoe, bringing her ear closer to Sol's mouth to hear him better.

"He and Jules have not yet spoken about why he is here," Sol continued.

"Then follow them," Meena said.

Sol nodded, his eyes watching the two men they spoke of.

Meena followed his gaze to see Jules, goblet in hand, introducing the councilor to several of his high-ranking soldiers on the other side of a table of food.

"I'll follow them if they leave to speak in private." Sol stepped backward, hiding in the shadow of the thick sandstone wall surrounding the city.

Disappointed to see him go, Meena reached out and grabbed his wrist. Touching his hand still felt too intimate. "Try not to think about it," she whispered.

"Think about what?" he whispered back down at her.

"The eyes. So many eyes." Meena grinned at her own jest, recalling Sol's comment at their wedding.

Sol smirked the tiniest smile. "Well, now I'm thinking about it," he muttered.

As Sol melted into the shadows, Meena turned her attention to the lively bailey.

Tables of food lined the sandy ground. Lit torches along the wall shed a pleasant glow on smiling faces. The center of the space was left empty, Meena assumed for dancing or festivities as the night grew on.

She wiggled her toes in her satin slippers. The room was filled with so many people. People she had never met, or communicated with, or danced with. Sol might be overwhelmed, but she felt a part of her heart sing with excitement. This, she could do. And enjoy.

And by keeping the attention off of her husband, she could give him a chance to observe what he needed to.

"Princess," an older man called as he approached her. His

well-tailored doublet was decorated with embroidered symbols denoting his impressive rank. "I have not seen you since you were a little girl."

Meena smiled warmly. She had no memory of meeting the Falqri soldier, but she'd spent her life meeting important people. "My father sends his regards." King Frederich had done no such thing, but mentioning her father was the easiest way to appease important people whom she did not remember.

The soldier held out his hand. "Dance with me and tell me the news from Iseldis?" he asked.

Meena smiled, dropping her hand into his. Sol was on her mind, but she had to remember he was naturally quiet and sneaky, like a real cypher. He would do better without her drawing attention to them. Laughing, she let herself be carried away into the dance.

After chatting with the older soldier, Meena took a moment to herself, searching the room for Sol.

Younn and Jules were still standing by the food and draining their goblets.

Sol was standing just outside the perimeter of the dance floor. Another soldier was speaking to him. Sol seemed to be listening intently, but Meena could catch the way his eyes scanned the room. He was waiting for Jules and Younn to make their move.

"My lady?" A young man bowed in front of her. "Are you lacking a partner?" He held his hand out hopefully.

With a final glance at Sol, Meena accepted the young man's hand. Sol seemed to have the situation under hand.

Her young partner spun her around dizzily, and she basked in the lights and movement and music.

"Thank you," she said at the end of the dance, dropping

the young man's hand. She glanced around the room, looking for Sol, hoping he had made progress. She could not find him immediately, which bode well. She also could not find Jules or Younn.

Her heart beat rapidly from the exercise. She hoped Sol would remain hidden and not put himself in danger.

"Another?" The young man held out his hand again, and Meena smiled up at him. He, too, was breathless and clearly enjoying the night. She had reached out to place her hand in his when a floppy mess of dark curls caught the corner of her eye. She stood up on her toes to peer over the crowd.

Sol was standing near a table, nodding along as another old soldier talked his ear off.

Meena dropped back down on her feet. "Thank you. That was delightfully fun, but I must see to my husband before your old superiors bore him to death." She squeezed the young soldier's hand.

He laughed as she dropped their contact. "Between you and me, that is highly possible."

Meena wound her way through the crowd, using the tired but courteous smile she'd perfected when she needed to get past people who wanted to speak with her.

Approaching Sol, Meena could hear the desperation in his voice. "I really must find my wife," he said.

"Of course, my boy," the soldier—also highly ranked—responded. "You must introduce me to the princess."

Sol had no response for that, but Meena slipped her hand into his arm, letting him know she was present.

Sol started slightly at the contact but dropped his head, smiling down at her with true relief.

The smile Meena gave back to him was not fake.

"I was just looking for a dance partner," she said, smiling

at the soldier. Though, upon closer inspection, she had no desire to spend time in physical contact with him. His eyes were dull and his smile flat.

"I would be happy to dance with you," Sol said, missing her meaning.

"Thank you, my dear." She patted his hand, emphasizing the term of endearment that Jules and Ezra frequently used for each other. "I was hoping you could introduce me to your friend here."

"Oh, yes, of course."

Before Sol could actually make the introduction, Meena held out her hand to the soldier. "A dance?"

"Yes, Princess." The soldier took her hand, his bland eyes opening wide.

Meena used her free hand to subtly push Sol away.

She did give herself the liberty of a satisfying eye roll behind the soldier's back as they walked to the dancing area.

SOL WOUND through the inner halls of the thick wall, moving in the direction he had seen Jules and Younn go.

With the number of people flowing in and out of the area —word about welcoming the councilor had spread fast—Sol did not feel conspicuous exploring the fort.

Hopefully, the night of the feast would be even more crowded.

Assuming that the two men had gone to speak somewhere in private, Sol tended toward the less populated areas. The luxury of the furnishings also made it easier to guess which part of the fort the superiors would inhabit.

Sol caught a glimpse of a door closing and instinctively rolled under a bench right outside it.

"You asked to see me, Councilor?" Jules's voice sounded through the door. "I apologize that your welcome was not what it should have been. We received no word of your coming and, to be honest, it took us by surprise." Jules's voice sounded strained.

"Do not worry, Captain," Younn replied, his voice big without being loud. "You've only been at your post here a few months. My aim is not to criticize you."

Sol could feel the tension disperse in the other room during the comfortable silence that followed.

"What can I do for you, Councilor?" Jules asked, his voice far more relaxed.

"I would like my presence to be attributed to the Festival of Goldenreign, as my real purpose here is more . . . delicate."

Sol stopped breathing. He needed to hear every word that was about to be said.

The latch on the door squeaked, and Sol's heart skipped a beat as the door shook. Did they know he had followed them?

"You trust your men, here?" Younn asked in a very quiet voice.

"Yes, Councilor," Jules responded, keeping his own voice quiet. "Should I not? Have you discovered a traitor in our ranks?"

"I meant your men guarding the door," Younn responded. He paused. "My information is not for anyone's hearing."

"Oh," Jules said. "I did not post a guard. One moment."

Sol heard the door open, and Jules called loudly down the hall.

Moments later, two soldiers flanked the door. The one on Sol's side sat down on the bench right above him.

Sol froze, listening as intently as he could.

"Should I be concerned about a traitor in your ranks?" Younn questioned. "Why would you ask such a question unless you were concerned about it?"

Sol could imagine the intimidating glare Younn was likely directing at Jules.

"No," Jules responded, his voice sounding strained once again. "The fort transitioned to my care more smoothly than I could have hoped. It is the greatest honor and best assignment I have ever received. Please, tell me how I can serve you."

Sol wanted to take back his wasted pity. Jules was a servant of the enemy, no matter how charming he seemed otherwise.

"You received a special shipment from Chendas a few weeks ago, did you not?" Younn asked after another evaluating pause.

"Yes, Councilor," Jules responded quickly and emphatically. "The greatest care has been seen to it, and all of His Majesty's orders regarding it have been dutifully followed. Would you care to see it?"

Sol felt his skin prickle in anticipation.

"Yes, but quickly. I have other matters to attend to," Younn replied. Sol had a feeling that he was the other matter Younn was referring to. "I would urge you to increase the defensive measures you have taken."

That was going to make Sol's task more difficult.

"Increase the defensive measures?" Jules asked. "Do you

have reason to believe it is unsafe, here in the strongest fort of the five kingdoms?" His voice may have held a touch of a challenge in it.

"Captain," Younn responded. "I will speak with you frankly. Iseldis has chosen not to align itself with our king—you may not have heard this news. The royal family is currently confined to their palace while our forces control every entry and exit into Iseldis from the Chendas border to the sea."

"That is grave news indeed," Jules responded. "They have made a poor choice. Except, their Princess Philomena is here in Falqri as we speak. She is staying as a guest in my home. I did not realize the situation had turned so dire."

"It would be an unanswerable crime if His Majesty's possession fell to the enemy's hand while Princess Philomena is here in *your* fort, Captain."

Even Sol could hear the veiled threat in the man's words.

"My men and I have committed to guarding it with our lives, Councilor."

Sol shrank deeper into his hiding place, instinctively shying away from the tension and also expecting the two men to walk through the door at any second.

As expected, the latch of the door squeaked again and, this time, Sol saw the door press open.

The general stepped through first.

"Councilor," Jules said as he followed him through the door. "Was it not you who permitted the princess and her husband to come to Falqri?"

The general's foot faltered for a moment. "You must be mistaken," he said.

Sol tilted his head at the blatant lie.

"Woe indeed, should anything befall our king's possession

should it fall into enemy hands while the princess is here." Jules's voice held a hint of satisfaction, even though his words merely echoed what Younn had already said. "Fortunately for *me*, Princess Meena is hardly one to be intimidated by."

"Never underestimate the power of a pretty face," Younn said over his shoulder as they continued down the hall.

Sol bristled at the man's callous words about Meena.

"You misunderstand me, Councilor," Jules replied. "Anyone who has met the princess would know she is as bright as she is beautiful. But it is also clear that she has not a bone of guile in her at all. No—fortunately for us, I believe she and her prince are truly and disgustingly in love."

Sol smiled, pleased that their ruse was working so well.

"I am not here to discuss the specifics of Philomena's romantic entanglements," Younn said. "Lead me to where you are keeping it while the festivities are in full swing."

"This way, Councilor." Jules took the lead. "Though, I don't believe you can call their relationship a romantic entanglement if they are married."

Sol remained under the bench until the two guards left as well. Then he silently crept from his hiding place and followed them through the dim halls.

~

~

~

MEENA SMILED in surprise when Sol stepped between her and her dance partner.

He held out his hands, taking the place of her partner, and she happily accepted his wordless invitation.

Her heart pounded wildly from the exertion of the dance —and from the spark of excitement she could see behind Sol's eyes. He had something to tell her.

The music was playful and loud, laying down an infectious rhythm.

Sol spun them around, dexterously moving them away from the center of the dance floor.

Meena relished the feeling of his hands holding hers, guiding her and swaying with her to the music.

She knew he was pulling her away to discuss what he'd learned. And she was anxious to hear it.

But a small, selfish part of her wanted to remain in the dance with him. She wanted to see him throw back his head and laugh with the intoxicating cadence of the rhythm.

She wanted an excuse to hold on to his hands for a moment longer.

As Sol spun them to a stop, leading them away from the dance and into the crowd of bystanders, Meena felt a stab of guilt for her thoughts.

She'd lived her life protected from harm. Protected even from the more cruel truths of the world. She wasn't here for her own satisfaction. This wasn't about her. She needed to do everything in her power to help her family protect the people of Iseldis from Gareth's cruelty.

Sol still held her hand, leading her to a shadowed staircase she hadn't noticed.

She gripped his hand appreciatively. This wasn't about her, but she was here.

And Sol was here. Ruse or not, they had developed a

friendship that was important to her, even if it was not important to him.

"What did you learn?" she asked.

"Younn knows we are here for the receptacle," Sol replied, his voice low. "We have to move quickly."

Meena squeezed his hand reassuringly, looking up the stairs at their destination. As they were moving away from the bright celebration below, Meena noticed the stars overhead for the first time since they'd arrived in Falqri. She threw her head back in awe, trusting Sol to lead her safely. "They're so beautiful!" she whispered, her jaw hanging open.

"The stars?" Sol asked. "Have you never seen stars before?"

"Of course I have," she responded. "But there're trees and torches in Iseldis—or maybe I just forget to look up."

Sol stopped at the top of the staircase, tilting his head back as well.

"They are just so much brighter here. More intense," Meena whispered in awe.

"Wait till I show you the stars from the western shore of Istroya," Sol said.

Meena dropped her gaze from the stars overhead to the sparkle in Sol's eyes. Had he just promised to show her the stars from his home?

"Meena, look ahead," Sol whispered, his voice tickling her ear as he pointed to the edge of the wall.

Meena dropped her head. They were standing atop the outer wall of the fortress. Directly in front of them, she could see the endless horizon of the sea. Dropping Sol's arm, Meena ran forward to get an unobstructed view. Leaning over the stone wall, she instantly wanted to fly over the edge and become part of the sparkling blue in front of her.

"It's so close but so far away." The wall was built straight out of the cliff. Looking over the edge of it was dizzyingly beautiful. An entire cliffside below her, the sandy beach stretched out, eventually swallowed by foaming white waves.

A bright moon in the cloudless sky reflected its light in the vast expanse of water, bouncing off the glossy surface as bright as daylight.

"There are stars," Meena breathed, "in the water!" She turned quickly to find Sol.

He was standing next to her, the bright moon also reflecting in his open eyes as a very small smile graced his face.

It was the sweetest smile Meena had ever seen.

She turned back to the sea, her eyes dancing over the sparkling blue stars that erupted by the thousands whenever a wave hit the sand. Like tiny pinpricks of bright blue light, they shimmered over the surface of the sand and along the line of the crashing waves. Unlike the stars, however, the sparkling lights faded after a few moments, giving their brightness to the next wave of explosive blue.

Footsteps sounded behind her, and another couple walked by on the lonely wall.

Sol stepped behind her, placing his arms around her with his hands on the railing at her side.

"What is it?" Meena asked, relishing the gift of his closeness and happy to speak of the waves until they were alone once more.

"No one knows exactly what causes it. Something in the water reacts to pressure, creating the burst of light." His voice rumbling over her ear made the moment more magical than she could have imagined.

"Is it always here in Falqri?" Meena asked. "Have you seen

it before? Does the sea do this on—" Meena caught herself in time, though the other couple was likely out of earshot. "On the shores of Allys?"

"No, not in Allys," Sol responded, his hands nudging closer to hers on the railing, his arms brushing down her shoulders. "But I've seen it in other places. It only takes place during goldenreign."

Meena wanted to ask him if it was a product of magic, but she remembered to keep that question for later. Instead, she relaxed, letting her back close the small distance between them as she leaned into his chest. "I love it," Meena said.

"I think it has something to do with the warmer weather," Sol said. "The changing temperature of the water allows for new organisms to grow." He stood back, removing his closeness. "They're gone."

Meena instantly stood up straight, twisting around to face Sol.

He had merely been doing his part to keep up their ruse. He had not leaned closer to her to be, well, closer to her. She needed to stop getting so distracted. "What else did you learn?" she asked, her voice serious.

Sol glanced around as if to ensure they were truly alone before he spoke. "It's in the cellar."

"The cellar? Below the kitchens?"

"Yes," Sol said.

"But wouldn't that bring too much attention to it?" Meena asked. "I'm assuming the kitchen is very busy."

"That was my exact thought." Sol sounded impressed with her reasoning. "There's a separate entrance up one of the canyons in the cliff."

"Oh," Meena made a sound with her mouth to let Sol

know he had been heard. She just did not know what his revelation meant.

"I'll go out again tonight and scour the northern cliffside. We can still carry out the plan tomorrow night."

Meena's hands suddenly felt clammy. "Sol, we don't even have a plan. There will be guards, and locks, and more guards." Meena's voice trailed off. She didn't want to think of Sol being hurt. This adventure was suddenly getting too real.

"We will have made contact with Neven by tomorrow night, hopefully," Sol added. "A secret entrance from the side should not be heavily guarded and, between the two of us, with our magic unleashed, Neven and I should be able to take them down and empty the magic receptacle."

"You know how to do that?" Meena asked, her fears not assuaged by his confidence.

"You displace the chaos magic with harmony magic. I've practiced on small items when I've had the chance."

"Won't that require an awful lot of harmony magic?"

"Yes, but harmony is the natural antidote to chaos," Sol explained. "The more chaos you displace, the more effective the present harmony is."

Meena nodded. "And what is my part in it?"

Sol paused, a little of his confidence leaving him. "I need you to keep Jules and Younn busy so they don't notice anything amiss."

"Are you sure you won't need more help than that?" Meena asked, slightly disappointed in her role, though she wasn't surprised.

"If anything goes wrong," Sol said, leaning down a touch closer to her, "I don't want you anywhere near."

"I'm not here to remain safe," Meena said. She wanted to

feel touched by his words, but she didn't. She felt protected, but not in a good way.

"It's not because I don't trust you," Sol said. "It's just that . . . if you are there, I will protect you."

Meena could no longer see the moon reflected in his eyes. "I am not another one of your responsibilities," Meena whispered. He did not want to create ties. "I will keep Jules and Younn busy or whatever else you need me to do."

She swallowed, hoping the darkness was enough to cover her face.

CHAPTER 27

Sol stopped at the window of the bedroom before he climbed out of it. He had changed his elegant princely clothes for his own comfortable trousers and basic shirt. Under cover of darkness, he was ready to find the secret entrance to the fortress cellar.

But something held him back.

Meena sat on the edge of the bed, holding a lit candle, watching him leave.

Sol glanced at the door, triple checking it was bolted closed. Perhaps it would be safer if he and Meena stuck together, now that Younn was on to them.

"Do you want to come with me?" Sol whispered. This had nothing to do with the way her face had transformed when she was looking at the sparkling blue effect of the waves. Or the fact that he was going to be walking along the shore for a good part of his search.

She stood instantly. "Yes."

His chest inflated with a strange light feeling when she

readily agreed. "You're sure? It might involve a little scrambling down some steep paths." She probably hadn't meant it, and he didn't want to get disappointed.

"I'm very good at scrambling," she responded. "Let me change my clothes for something more fitting. Or, less fitting, actually. Something loose."

Sol opened the window, inspecting their escape route as she quickly got ready. He smiled. They were getting close to their goal—he could feel it.

"I don't think I could sleep anyway, after everything that happened tonight," Meena whispered at his side.

Sol nodded in understanding. "Let's go."

She jumped nimbly up onto the window ledge. She'd changed into a loose pair of trousers, a shirt, and an overshirt held in place with a tied belt.

It looked suspiciously similar to the clothing Robin had worn in the forest. Sol thought she looked beautiful. The Majis women wore clothing that was suited to work and movement. This Meena felt like someone he knew.

"Oh, the candle," she said, pointing back to the lit candle on the desk.

"I got it," Sol responded. He'd been waiting for her to get out of the window before extinguishing their light source.

With a nod, she slipped over the ledge, clinging to it with her hands as she found a steady foothold for her feet. Their particular window was situated in the wall of the fort.

"They probably put us in this room thinking the window would be too difficult to climb out of," Meena whispered as he followed her.

"Little did they know, our keepers were actually making our task easier," Sol responded lightly.

Meena smiled. Somehow, despite the darkness, he could hear it.

Climbing carefully around her on the outer ledge, he led the way over the wall and showed Meena the steep path to the shoreline.

It took quite some time to get all the way down the path, even after their eyes adjusted to the bright light of the moon and the stars.

"What do we do now?" Meena asked as they stumbled onto the sandy shore.

He was not tired from exhaustion, but his body was ready to stop moving for a moment. "Now, we look at the stars in the sea," he replied.

"Sol, we don't have all night," she replied. "Literally. We need to get back before the sun is up."

"Our search will be better served if we rest for a moment. That was a long climb, and it was only the downward one." He wanted to see the enchantment on her face again as she looked at the sparkling blue waves. It was a selfish desire, and he knew it. But his words were also true. They would spend the rest of the night climbing up canyons. They both needed to catch their breath.

Meena had already turned from him. A smile lit her face, and she didn't even know that she hadn't seen the best part yet.

"Go," Sol whispered, "step on the wet sand." He stood back, not wanting to spoil the surprise.

Meena tentatively stepped forward, slipping off her leather shoes and carrying them in her hand. As her foot pressed into the wet sand at the edge of the incoming waves, blue light shot through the sand she'd displaced.

She gasped, lifting her foot up. The face she turned to him was pure jaw-dropping joy.

Sol smiled, stepping forward to join her as she traced her toe in the sand, creating a stream of blue light wherever she touched.

She ran down to the water itself, watching her footsteps shimmer and fade in the sand behind her. The moonlight was bright enough that Sol could see the way her hair danced over her shoulders.

Dropping his own shoes in the sand, he ran after her.

"You've seen this before?" she asked.

"Yes," he said, drawing to a stop next to her. "It happens in Istroya every few goldenreign seasons."

"I love it," she said, throwing her arms wide open as if to embrace the sea.

Sol understood the feeling well. The sea had always represented something bigger to him. Something beautiful and different and beyond himself, but something that made him feel more whole.

He was looking at Meena, though, and not at the sea.

He could feel the radiant delight on her face.

He could not take her with him, but he could leave her with the one thing that always brought him joy.

Stepping behind her, he placed his hands on her shoulders. "Close your eyes," he whispered.

He could not see her face, but he assumed she'd done as he had asked. He could feel her shoulders rising and falling gently with each breath she took.

"The joy you feel right now, that's the magic."

He could tell she was smiling from the way she exhaled a little more loudly through her nose.

"It can't be that simple," she replied, laughing a little.

He loved her. He loved that her mind always went to joy. He wanted to see the world through her eyes.

"Oh, you are being serious," she said, breaking the comfortable silence. He could feel her twist her shoulders as she moved to face him.

He squeezed her gently, asking her with his hands to stay in place.

He would lose the battle he was fighting if he could see her face.

"Sol, the magic is special to you, to your people," Meena said, her laughter gone. "I am fascinated by it and in awe of it, and I love it, but I cannot take it."

"You cannot take something when it is a gift," Sol replied. "The magic has shaped my people, and we have shaped it. But it is not ours to hoard. Everyone can access the beauty of it. I want to give you this small part of me. It's all I have that is free to give."

She placed her hand over his. "Sol." Her voice was sweet and sorrowful at the same time.

"I can't teach you how to use magic in a single night. I just want you to experience the feeling of it," Sol whispered, suddenly afraid that he had oversold his gift.

"I would love to experience that," she replied.

"Look out at the waves," Sol instructed, talking her through his own actions.

A small wave lazily crashed a short distance from the shore. Glowing blue light emanated from every drop that splashed.

"Breathe in, deeply." Sol could feel her shoulders rise under her hands. "Let that breath fill every part of your body." He waited for a moment. "Do you feel it?"

"I feel . . . happy. Calm. My mind knows that tomorrow

might be difficult or scary. But right now, I'm here." Her shoulders sank with her next exhale. "I don't feel the magic, though."

"No, you felt it," Sol reassured her. "That is the harmony."

"That's it?" Meena turned around. "Everyone can do that! Why was this such a secret?"

Sol laughed at her surprise. "It's a little more complicated than that. You have to learn how to channel that harmony and spread it around you, which . . . takes a little longer."

"Oh, that makes sense." She turned back to face the blue waves. "Thank you for sharing that with me, Sol."

"You're welcome."

Sol's eyes lingered on her hair long after her face had turned away. Simply being in her presence made him happy.

His wife.

He had never imagined a life for himself in which he had a comrade purely for the sake of companionship.

He was a Majis. He was leading a rebellion in the footsteps of his father, a hero. He loved his family, of course. But he couldn't allow himself to be close to them because he knew he would lose them.

He'd been close to his father. He'd loved his father. He'd idolized his father. And then his father had been chosen. And Sol had vowed to himself that he would never make the mistake of loving someone too closely ever again.

She turned back around, her soft eyes looking up at him tenderly. She lifted her hand slowly toward his face.

Sol knew he should stop her action, but he did not want to.

Before she touched him, however, she tensed, pointing over his shoulder. "What is that?"

288

Sol spun around, letting his eyes adjust from the brightness of the luminescent water.

"I thought I saw a torch up that canyon," she added, still peering up the dark cliffside. "It's gone now."

"This canyon should be impassible. I tried to get to the fort from every place on the shoreline last night. Could you seen have anything else?"

"It looked like the torch illuminated a man in a soldier's uniform, but he disappeared into the stone cliffside before I could fully get a glimpse of him. And everything was so far away, it was hard to see anything clearly."

"This must be it," Sol said, his body tensing in preparation for activity.

"Can you use magic in any way to find the path?" Meena asked.

"It's a good thought, but that's not how it usually . . . Actually, the wind did guide me once before." Sol closed his eyes for a moment. It was easy to find the harmony inside him after having just shared it with Meena.

He exhaled with a wordless sound, letting it rumble in his throat in harmony with the crashing waves.

The breeze from the sea picked up its pace, swirling around him like an old friend.

Reaching for Meena's hand, he let the wind guide him.

CHAPTER 28

"We did it," Meena whispered triumphantly as they climbed back along the hidden path. "We actually found it."

"And only two guards on duty," Sol said, his voice as excited as hers. "We don't know how many soldiers guard the kitchen entrance, but if Neven and I can get back here after dark tomorrow, we can take the guards out quickly and quietly. We don't want to give them a chance to sound the alarm."

Meena forced her tired legs to follow after Sol. They had climbed so much already, but the end was in sight. "How deep inside do you think the tunnel goes?" she asked. "And do you think it will be hard to find the right tunnel or cave or door once we are inside?"

"It might go fairly deep," Sol replied. "But thanks to the wind, which was partially your idea—at least, I wouldn't have thought about it if you hadn't asked since I'd never used the magic like that before—we should be able to get through whatever maze is inside."

"I hope this works," Meena said. Her hands were tingling strangely from a mixture of excitement and fear. "We are so close."

"Speaking of close," Sol said, his spirits still high, "we are close to home as well."

Meena looked up from her feet to stare at the outer wall of the fortress directly above them. The wall looked far more ominous in the dark of night, blocking out the bright stars above.

"This part might be difficult," Sol said, stepping to the side so she could pass by him. "But I've no doubt you can make it up. You have likely scaled something similar."

Meena smiled at his confidence in her.

He stepped behind her, his body cutting off the cool ocean breeze and instantly warming her. "And if you do need help, I'll be right here behind you."

Meena turned around. She wasn't quite ready to return to the stifling bedroom and dangers of the fortress.

"Actually, I was more concerned about you," she whispered. "Perhaps you should go first and I can catch you, since you are more likely to fall."

Even in the darkness, Meena could see the broad smile that split across his face.

He was laughing at her jest.

Meena's heart felt so light she thought it might float right out of her chest and into the sky. Unable to contain the feeling by herself, she reached up and placed her palm against his cheek.

His skin was rough but warm.

"Sol," she whispered. "May I?" She stood on tiptoe,

bringing her face closer to his as she looked from his eyes to his mouth.

His smile slowly relaxed into something more. She could hear him inhale. The intensity of the breathy sound tickled over her ears like an unexpected breeze.

She felt a shiver run down her spine, but she was not cold.

He dropped his head closer to hers, stopping when their noses gently touched. He slowly closed his eyes, letting out a breathy sigh. His hand came up to cover hers, cradling it against his cheek.

She moved her thumb, stroking the soft spot above the rough stubble on his chin. She wanted to feel his lips on hers. She wanted to share this moment with him, to express the excitement, anxiety, and absolute craziness of their ridiculously hopeless mission in a way that words could not.

"Meena," he whispered. His voice was full of longing, but she could feel the tenseness in his jaw below her hand.

"I'm not asking for forever," she said before he could deny her. "I just want to share this moment with you. Right here. Right now. Whatever tomorrow may bring. No ties." She moved her face back and forth, gently rubbing the end of his nose with her own.

"I would like nothing more." He opened his eyes as he spoke.

She smiled and slowly closed her eyes as he slipped his face even closer to hers.

His lips brushed against hers and gently remained.

She tilted her head back to meet his face better and inhaled through her nose.

He slipped one hand around her waist, holding her steady but not possessively.

His lips were soft, featherlight, dry, and warm.

Her whole body relaxed into his touch. Her mind relaxed, losing track of every other worry. All of her was exactly where she wanted to be.

The pressure in her toes brought her back to reality, and she inhaled shakily as she dropped back down to her heels, breaking off the softest of kisses.

"Thank you," she whispered.

Sol nodded. As he slowly slid his hand from her waist, he pressed her side gently, turning her around toward their destination.

She turned away, her eyes filled with unbidden tears.

She wanted forever.

She could not ask him for what he couldn't give.

But he had given her this one moment, and she would cherish it in her heart forever.

SOL WATCHED the woman in front of him deftly climb her way back up to their window.

Even if he could think of the words he wanted to say, he was too afraid to move his mouth. His lips remembered the feeling of her so perfectly, and he didn't want to lose that memory.

He wanted to grab her waist, twist her back to face him, and kiss her properly. Kiss her with the promise of tomorrow, not the regret of yesterday.

He reminded himself that he couldn't afford to love her. Loving her meant losing her. The ironclad excuse, which had always protected him, felt like a sheet of parchment in a storm. But as excited as he was about the discovery they had just made, his doubts about successfully completing the mission were greater.

With every step toward the manse, his body grew more tense. Something was bound to go wrong when they put the plan into action.

But all looked well as they approached their window. Everything was dark and quiet. Meena climbed through the window first, soundlessly landing on her feet on the other side.

Sol followed her just as silently.

"We made progress, Sol. We can celebrate that." The tone of her voice sounded like she needed something to celebrate.

Sol, still unable to speak, nodded as he quietly closed the window covering, locking it in place.

The sun had not yet started to rise, but it would make its appearance soon.

When he turned around, Meena was stifling a yawn.

"Go to bed, Princess," he whispered, his voice barely more than a breath. "We did make progress."

She nodded. "Goodnight, Sol." She turned away from him, making her way toward the bed.

He knew it would be useless to try to sleep. "I'm going to light a candle in the corner and draw out a map of the interior of the fort, at least what I remember of the cellars. Will that bother you?" he asked.

"Not at all. I could sleep through anything," she replied in the darkness.

Sol smiled despite the pain in his heart. He knew she could sleep through anything.

He found his way through the room and pulled the tinderbox from the corner of the desk, intending to strike a spark so he could light the candle.

His hand stilled. This was a noisy task.

Stepping silently to the door, he ensured the latch was locked closed.

He was being overly cautious, but something felt wrong.

Kissing Meena had awakened desires he sought to avoid. Like the desire to survive this mission, even if that meant failing it.

He walked back over to the small table. He could use his magic to light the candle.

He needed to refocus his mind on what was truly important.

Holding his hands in front of him, he began to draw on the dwindling harmony within him to create a small glowing orb of light. Placing it gently over the wick of a tall candle, he waited for the flame to catch.

It sparked with a hiss that sounded obnoxiously loud in the quiet room. He jumped.

"Get some sleep, too, Sol," Meena whispered. "We need you well rested for tomorrow night."

"I will," Sol replied automatically, even though he intended to do no such thing. He straightened a piece of parchment on the table and pulled out the chair to sit down.

Suddenly, the door to their room burst open with enough force to break the lock and the latch.

Meena screamed.

Sol swung toward the intruder, instantly funneling his

magic into the small orb of light he already carried so that it glowed brighter.

The light illuminated the terrifying sight of several Falqri soldiers pouring into the room. Sol pushed the orb of light into their faces, hoping to blind them as it was the only thing he had access to.

Reaching behind him, he grabbed the lit candle and moved into the defensive stance that was more natural to him than walking.

Multiple soldiers were already upon him.

He tipped the candle forward, brandishing the flame in the face of the soldier nearest him.

The man flinched but pushed forward, swiping the candle out of the way and simultaneously putting out the flame.

As the soldiers grabbed his arms, he twisted them out of the way, responding quickly and effectively against their attack.

But there was only so much one man could do in a crowded room filled with enemies.

Within moments, he found himself forced to his knees while his arms were bound behind his back and a familiar weight settled around his neck.

They had locked his magic.

"Unhand the Prince of Iseldis!" Meena shouted.

Sol could not see her through the crowd of soldiers, especially from his position on the floor. He struggled against the binding on his wrists.

He had always known they would come for him, but he had never imagined they would come for Meena.

Not the cheerful, loyal, self-giving seeker of justice who had been the best companion these last few blissful days.

"Unhand the Princess of Iseldis!" a new voice called out.

It took Sol a moment to recognize the voice as Jules's. His commanding tenor was far more powerful than his flattering host voice. Even Sol paused for a moment at his order.

The soldiers must have also listened because after a short scuffle, he could see Meena's head pop up over the crowded room. She was standing on the bed, and her eyes sought his.

"Release him immediately! You will answer to my father for this!" she yelled.

"You do not make the orders here, Princess," Councilor Younn said from the doorway.

"What goes on here, Councilor?" Jules asked. His voice sounded confused, but Sol guessed he had been in on the entire plan.

"I have reason to believe that *Solano* is a dangerous Majis," Younn said. "He will be taken to Chendas for the Council to deal with him."

"No!" Meena screamed. "My husband can't be a Majis! You've made a mistake!"

Sol fought against the rope at his hands, though he knew it was useless.

"If a mistake has been made, then King Gareth will send him back to his irritatingly stupid little wife." Younn's voice was filled with disdain as he looked at Meena. "You will be on board the next ship sailing north."

"No!" Meena's scream filled the room, piercing Sol's ears and his heart.

As Sol was led out the door, Meena tried to catch his eye.

He twisted his head as they pushed him forward and managed to blink twice.

He couldn't tell if she saw it because when he opened his eyes she was hidden from view.

He hoped she would keep fighting. He would, until the very end.

A sharp stinging pain on his left hand momentarily distracted him. He shuffled his wrists together to try and reach the awkward spot between his thumb and pointer finger. He could feel a hard substance stuck there.

When he rubbed against it, the small spot burned with pain and the substance refused to move.

It was a drop of wax.

He'd been burned with a drop of wax. It had probably happened when he was brandishing the candle, but he had not noticed the pain in the moment.

Meena still screamed at the soldiers behind him.

He rubbed the spot again, despite the additional pain it caused. It irked him that one tiny thing could hurt so badly.

CHAPTER 29

*M*eena shook her head frantically as Sol closed his eyes, breaking the only contact they had left. "Don't leave me," she whispered.

The soldiers pressed him forward, quickly moving him through the crowded room. Sol opened his eyes, somehow still staring directly at her even though he had moved.

He deliberately closed his eyes again.

Before he could open them, the soldiers had forced him through the doorway.

He was blinking at her. Twice.

"No!" Meena screamed at the soldiers flooding from the room. "You can't do this!"

She jumped from the bed after them.

Jules caught her, holding her back. "Stop them, Jules." She fought his hold on her. "I thought you were the captain here."

"Princess," Jules tried to speak over her. "There's nothing we can do. Calm yourself."

The last of the soldiers disappeared down the hall.

Meena spun to face Jules. "Calm myself? What kind of monster are you? You expect me to not be upset? What would you do if someone wrested your perfect Ezra from you?" She pushed away on his chest, still trying to escape his grip.

"I'm sorry," Jules responded, still holding her tightly. "The councilor does have superiority here."

"Sorry?" Meena clasped her hands together between them. Throwing her whole weight to one side, she swung her hands around in a tight arc.

The unexpected central force caught Jules off guard, and he was forced to let go of her.

Meena jumped back out of his reach, running to the open doorway.

They were gone.

She turned back to Jules. "Don't apologize when you knew about this from the start."

Jules shook his head. "Princess, I promise, I had no idea he was planning this." The look on his face was more anguish than triumph.

Meena did not believe him, but she had no more words to yell. She climbed onto the bed, curling her knees up to her chin.

She was alone.

Except for Jules, who was still in her room.

"Get out," Meena said, not having the energy to raise her voice above a whisper.

Instead of leaving, he walked across the room, his brow furrowed.

Meena watched, annoyed and confused.

He reached down to the floor and picked up the candle,

which had fallen during the fight. He set it back on the table, laying it on its side and waiting for it to stop rolling.

Then he lifted the tinderbox from the back corner of the table. Pulling it open, he felt the iron plate, the place where a spark was created when one was lighting a fire.

Meena hugged her knees closer, unsure what he was looking for. Maybe just a burnt finger.

Except the plate would be cold because Sol had used his magic to light the candle, not the tinderbox.

Meena tried to swallow, but her mouth was dry.

Jules also picked up the brimstone—a thin slice of wood that was supposed to catch the spark. He felt the flammable sulfur-tipped end on either side and smelled them as well.

"How did your husband light this candle?" he asked.

"I'm sorry?" Meena's heart had been racing since the soldiers broke into their room, and it was not slowing down.

"The candle. How did Sol light the candle?" Jules asked again.

"With the brimstone," Meena responded, acting as though it was the stupidest question she'd ever heard. "My beloved husband has just been taken into custody, and that is all you have to say to me?"

Younn had somehow guessed that Sol was a Majis, but Meena did not want to give Jules any opportunity to prove it.

"Get. Out." She pointed at the door.

"This is my home, Princess," Jules said, but he moved toward the door.

"It is not your home," Meena spat, raising her voice further with every word she spoke. "It's the house of some person who was forced to leave it so you could live here. Out!"

"Goodnight, Princess." Jules bowed his head and left the room.

"Badmorning, Captain," she muttered as he closed the door. The morning light had started to seep through the cracks of the window covering, and so it was no longer night. Nor was it good.

Falling to her side on the rumpled bed, Meena hugged her knees to her chin and wished tears would come.

They had failed.

She had failed.

King Gareth would launch his attack on Iseldis with the ships from Istroya. He would destroy them in a matter of hours using the chaos magic he'd tortured from innocent Majis.

The Majis would continue to suffer.

Her people would suffer.

Her family would suffer.

Sol would suffer.

Her eyes remained dry, but her stomach turned.

She buried her eyes in her knees, pressing until it hurt.

It had been a hopeless mission from the start, and she had done nothing but treat it like some grand adventure. She'd smiled and talked and asked clever questions, thinking she had been making a difference.

But she had done nothing.

Sol, their only chance at finding and destroying the magic receptacle, was gone. She was nothing. Her part in the ruse had been a ruse in and of itself. She was the jest.

What was it Sol had said? That she should be the leader because people would listen to her?

A sob finally escaped Meena's throat. Of course Sol would say that. The man who had been little more than a slave his entire life, treated as powerless, had been kind enough to tell her she was not powerless.

The tears came. Fast and hard and ugly, blinding her eyes and swamping her cheeks.

How wrong he had been.

No one would listen to her. She was a spoiled princess who used smiles and fluttering eyelashes to get what she wanted.

Younn thought so little of her, he did not even suspect her. It had not seemed to cross his mind that she was a part of Sol's plan, or even aware of his identity. He just saw her as a lovesick princess because that was all she had shown him.

Meena relaxed her body. The sobs had clogged her throat, and she struggled to breathe.

She loosened her knees, opening up her chest and shakily inhaling.

Sol was the only one who believed in her. He had blinked twice. He had consoled her when he was being taken.

There was no more plan to hide. No more blinks to share. No more Sol to destroy the chaos magic. She certainly couldn't do it. No one would believe her.

Meena rolled onto her back.

No one would believe her. No one would even notice her. No one saw her as a threat.

She sat up.

She couldn't drain the magic receptacle, but she could still find Neven. He was a Majis, too.

She knew where they needed to go. Mostly.

She still had Sophie, even if she didn't know how the woman could help her.

Meena stood from the bed.

She was still in the brown trousers she'd worn to look at

the blue waves. That beautiful evening already felt like a distant memory from another life.

Sitting at the table, she found a pen and ink in the drawer and stared at the blank parchment in front of her.

It was time to make a plan.

CHAPTER 30

"*Y*ou've overestimated my abilities, Younn." Ezra's quiet voice was unmistakable, even in the dark fortress room where Sol was being held.

"I have all faith in you," Younn replied, opening the door and letting Ezra into the room before him.

Sol kept his face forward.

Once again, he was on his knees, cut off from his magic, powerless against the cruelty of chaos.

"You are too good to me, friend," Ezra continued. "But this time I must decline. What you ask is too important to approach without perfect control."

"I can respect that," Younn replied. "Here he is. He was under your roof for days, and you suspected nothing?"

"I thought you had all faith in me?" Ezra did not hide the hurt in her voice. "Of course I suspected something. I asked my maid to keep a close watch on him."

Sol was glad he'd never spoken in front of Laila when she came to assist Meena. Not that it mattered in the end.

"Why else would she have let you into my home in the middle of the night instead of raising the alarm?"

"Because I paid her off," Younn replied.

"So you don't trust me?" Ezra replied. "All you had to do was ask, my friend."

"You are taking offense at nothing, Ezra. If I didn't trust you, would I offer to let you siphon him?"

"I'm not siphoning him. Not because you don't trust me, but because I don't trust myself. Though, now I'm having second thoughts."

"Let us put this behind us," Younn said, his voice ever the friendly diplomat. "I clearly trust you. It's your turn—do what you do. Work your magic, if you will."

"Thank you," she replied, sounding somewhat placated. "I'll make sure the gem is full. That should prove *our* theory is correct."

"And if our theory is wrong, leave the gem on, and Gareth will accept him regardless." Younn chucked at his own cleverness.

Ezra did not respond.

Sol saw her feet step closer to him.

They could crush him all they wanted, but they would never break him. That was the only power he had left.

Raising his face, Sol looked directly into the eyes of the woman who had entertained, fed, and laughed with them over the last few days.

She met his gaze without remorse as she approached him, hands held forward.

His body tensed in preparation for the all too familiar pain.

As she began to speak in a high, dissonant voice—which

sounded imperial with her icy tones—the small wax burn on Sol's hand began to rage like an inferno.

The feeling of the burn spread through his hand and up his arm, trapping his throat and cutting off his ability to breathe.

Sol felt the wave of pain wash over him, but he didn't fight it. He felt it. He knew it was cruel and unjust. And he hated it.

Ezra was not only a Quotidian, she was trained in using chaos magic.

Sol let her work her pain through his body, almost relishing the chance to feel an anger and desperation he could not express.

Out of habit, he bit his tongue so as not to yell out in pain. He knew he needn't have bothered, because the gem would have silenced him anyway.

But he refused to let them see him break.

The moments passed surprisingly quickly, and Sol felt her magic loosen its hold on his body.

He slumped forward over his knees, dropping his head to the ground with a dull thump since his hands were not free to catch him.

The external pain in his head was not worth noticing. It was expected, even. No one ever caught him when he fell.

Another stab of pain flowed through his chest, but this one was not physical. Meena had literally made a jest earlier that morning about carrying his weight so he didn't have to.

"He is a Majis," Ezra said, her voice emotionless. "Though I imagine he does not feel close to harmony right now."

"So, Solano is the missing Sol." Younn sounded quite pleased with himself.

Grasping the last bit of defiance he still held, Sol lifted his shoulders, stretching his neck up to meet her gaze once more.

He wanted her to see his hatred. He wanted her to think she had not broken him, even though he knew otherwise.

Only something whole could be broken, and he had never considered himself whole.

Until Meena.

Until Meena had offered him something whole.

And what was whole could be broken.

Ezra's cold eyes held his for longer than necessary. Her gaze flickered once, as though she would tell him something, but she blinked and the look passed.

Sol spat, his saliva landing on the ground at her feet.

"Are you sure you don't want to do the siphoning?" Younn asked.

"Don't tempt me," Ezra responded, taking a step back. "We are finished here. Send him north. Our king will be pleased with you."

"Pleased with me?" Younn's voice was slightly uncomfortable.

"I helped you clean up the mess you made, Councilor. I trust you won't forget it."

CHAPTER 31

*D*ressed in her second-finest gown, Meena waited
for Laila to come help with her hair. The maid
never arrived, so Meena did it herself. It was not quite fancy
enough for the evening's festivities, but perhaps she could
get Laila to redo it before then.

She didn't have time to wait around now—there was too
much to be done.

She sailed out of her room, pinching her face in concentration.

"Ezra!" she called as her host entered the front door of
the manse. "Exactly whom I wanted to see!"

"Princess?" Ezra froze for a moment, still holding the
door latch. "I did not expect to see you looking so . . . put
together."

"I have cried all my tears, my dear friend," Meena said
dramatically. "I was hoping you could help to cheer me up
before the festivities this evening."

"Oh, you do not have to attend the feast tonight," Ezra

replied, stepping inside, seemingly recovered from her reticence a moment earlier.

"Not you, too!" Meena wailed. "What do you expect me to do all evening? Stay in my room, our room . . . alone?" She stifled a sob. "No. I am going to the feast tonight to distract myself."

"Of course you are, Princess." Ezra's voice dripped with condescension. She reached out and patted Meena on the shoulder like a child.

"I knew you would understand." Meena dried her tears and held up a silk slipper. A large rip ran along the heel of it. "Can we go to the seamstress to get this fixed? It's my best pair for dancing."

"Oh, no." Ezra's sympathy was as fake as Sol's forced smile. "One of my maids can surely sew it up for you. There is no need to go out."

Meena turned the slipper over in her hand, fingering the rip. "Please?" Meena blinked up at Ezra, forcing tears to her eyes. "I don't trust just anyone. It must be done by the best. This is my favorite pair."

"Alright." Ezra sighed.

"Thank you." Meena dashed to the door and threw it open.

"Oh, right now?" Ezra asked.

Meena walked out into the street without looking back.

"I FORGOT SOMETHING," Meena said to Ezra a short while later. "I'll be right back."

"You can't just leave me here!" Ezra protested. She was standing in front of a floor-length mirror at the seamstress's shop. The seamstress in question was kneeling on the floor at her feet, meticulously pinning up the hem of the extravagant yellow gown Ezra now wore.

"I'm not *leaving* you," Meena protested, backing away slowly. "I'll be right back."

Ezra sent Meena a sharp glare through the mirror.

Meena frowned. Yellow was not Ezra's color.

"I thought we were here for *your* slipper?" Ezra said, her voice dangerously flat.

"We are, and the dear seamstress will take care of it in time for tonight. But I just had to see you in that yellow dress. It suits you."

It had taken some convincing to get Ezra to slip into the large evening dress the seamstress had on display.

After that, Meena simply had to ask the dressmaker to measure out the necessary fittings. If Meena had learned anything from Ashlin, it was that a seamstress held complete power over her client while making adjustments to garments.

"In fact, I'll even purchase it for you as a gift of gratitude for your hospitality," Meena said. Then she turned and ran from the shop before Ezra could respond.

Purchasing the bright yellow dress for Ezra, who clearly hated it, would make an excellent jest. And it would be a delightful payback for the woman's annoying cold-heartedness.

Free from the sewing shop and her keeper for a few moments, Meena dashed across the street into a familiar open courtyard. "Mistress Sophie?" she whispered, not bothering to knock as she slipped inside the sunken door to the wise woman's home.

"My dear princess . . ." The older woman held a hand over her heart. Her eyes were wide with shock. "You frightened me."

"I'm so sorry," Meena said quietly, flinching just a little in apology.

The wall covering behind Sophie fluttered closed, as though she had just stepped out of it.

"What can I do for you, my dear?" Sophie asked, adjusting her head covering, which was tilted to the side.

Meena took a step further into the room, glancing to ensure no one else could hear her. "I came to ask for your help," she whispered.

"I presumed as much," Sophie replied blandly. "That is usually why people seek me out."

Meena was confused. She had expected Sophie to know exactly why she was here. Sophie had given Sol the letter in front of Meena—and mentioned harmony.

Meena's eyes went wide, glancing back to the wall covering that hid the door Sophie had used previously.

Perhaps Sophie had not just exited the room—perhaps she had pushed someone into it. "Is it safe to speak?" Meena asked, whispering as quietly as she could.

Sophie's face relaxed. "You can come out now, Neven. It's safe."

Meena smiled in double satisfaction when an older man pushed back the curtain and stepped into the room. "You are exactly who I was looking for." She smiled.

CHAPTER 32

"But what shall I say if they ask about Solano?" Meena said, clutching Jules's arm tightly. "I can't say he's been seized for being a *Majis*." She whispered the last word as quietly as she could, pretending to be ashamed of it. "That would be so embarrassing."

Meena could practically hear Ezra roll her eyes. The woman was walking a full arm's length away even though Jules had offered her his other elbow. She was, however, wearing the yellow dress Meena had insisted on.

Meena delighted in the fact that she had literally come between the adoring couple. She knew it was petty, but if she couldn't be spending this evening with Sol, they did not deserve to spend the evening together either. Especially since Meena was sure they'd had something to do with Sol's arrest.

"Perhaps you could just say he has fallen ill and needed to rest tonight," Jules responded to her earlier question. "Are you sure you should be coming tonight?"

Meena could hear both concern and suspicion in his

voice. She planned to be extra careful around her keepers tonight so they would suspect nothing.

"I'm not sure what I would cry for more if I stayed home," Meena replied. "Missing out on the fun of the festivities or missing Sol." She squeezed Jules's arm as she said the last word, letting her voice break the tiniest bit.

Jules patted her hand.

Ezra sped up her pace, moving slightly in front of Meena and Jules as though she wanted to remove herself from their company.

Meena did not blame her. She would be annoyed with herself as well if she weren't having so much fun annoying them.

She reminded herself that the night was not about having fun.

Her stomach fell, and she clutched Jules's arm for real.

"Are you alright?" he asked. "Perhaps we should turn around."

Meena shook her head. "I will not go back," she said, easily lining her voice with the conviction she felt.

Jules gave her an odd look, but she smiled up at him obliviously and then turned her chin forward.

Perhaps it was better to focus on the fun. If it helped her to move through the evening, it was surely the better choice.

Just then, she caught a glimpse of the sea as they crested the bailey into the main area of the fort.

She inhaled at the beautiful sight. The breath calmed her stomach and reminded her of Sol.

She couldn't use the magic in the same way he did, but she could rely on its harmony to get her through the night.

She would do this for Sol.

The bailey was decorated with flowing fabric and

glowing lanterns. She could smell the delectable flavors of roasting meat and sweet sauces.

The outdoor space was already overflowing with townsfolk. They were dressed for a feast, in bright colors and flowing fabrics. It was the most beautiful sight she had ever seen.

With a smile of encouragement to herself, she followed Jules into the midst of the chaos.

"I did not expect to see *you* here this evening, Princess," Councilor Younn said, stepping forward and blocking Meena's path with a bow.

"I did not expect to see *you* here, Councilor!" Meena replied. "I thought you had important business in Chendas?" She narrowed her eyes, hoping her loud voice did not betray her. "Yet here you are, at a feast." Surely Younn would not stray far from his prisoner, which meant that Sol was somewhere near. Maybe she could discover where.

The councilor looked around, his face turning red. "Quiet, girl," he snapped. "Being at this feast *is* my business."

"That's not what you said this morning, though, Councilor—when you were speaking to my husband?" Realizing that she held the upper hand as long as she could pressure him, Meena kept her voice loud.

"Perhaps we should find you some food or drink, Princess?" Jules cut in, still escorting her with his arm.

"I did tell your husband I was returning to Chendas, my dear," the councilor replied, ignoring Jules and raising his voice to be heard as well as hers. "But I said I was leaving *tomorrow*, on the ship which just arrived *today*. Where is your husband, Princess? Surely he remembers the conversation?" Younn twisted his head around as though he might see Sol somewhere in the crowd.

"Unfortunately," Meena hissed through a forced smile, "he was feeling unwell this afternoon and decided to rest. He is sad to have missed the festivities." Meena glanced around the space again. "I assume he is somewhere near, though?" she whispered so only Younn and Jules could hear.

"Perhaps you can give him my regards when you see him next?" Younn said loudly. He raised his eyebrows, the concern on his face barely disguising his glee. "And no, Princess," he whispered, leaning forward. "He's nowhere near. I placed him far outside of your reach. As if *you* could do anything about it anyway."

Meena knew she had lost the upper hand, but she wouldn't let him have the last word. "I would love to, Councilor," she said loudly. "Have a wonderful evening. May this goldenreign season bring you everything you deserve." She couldn't resist getting one more barb in.

"I think it shall, Princess." Younn bowed low. As he stood, he moved closer to Meena, whispering in her ear. "For I will be graced with your presence tomorrow morning at first light on board the Sapphire. I will escort you home, where you should have been all this time."

Meena opened her mouth, gasping at the rudeness of his words. But he had turned away and pushed through the crowd.

Meena closed her mouth.

"Did you hear that?" she asked Jules, raising her voice again to be heard above the chatter.

Jules shook his head. "No, it's too loud." He leaned closer to her. "I know you are angry at the councilor, but he is leaving first thing tomorrow morning to escort your husband to Chendas himself."

Meena tensed, leaning closer to hear every word.

"And I will send one of my best men to plead for him before King Gareth," Jules continued.

"I know." Meena smiled up at him. "You've mentioned that multiple times today." Her heart was pounding. "Captain, perhaps this evening was a little ambitious."

"Shall I escort you home?" Jules asked quickly, concern on his face.

"No, I'm sure I shall be fine." She didn't have time for that. "I shall just find a quiet spot to sit down for a moment. You should go attend to your wife."

"Of course." Jules kept her hand tucked into his arm and pulled her through the crowd. "You can rest in my personal study. No one will disturb you there."

"Thank you," Meena replied.

He led her through the halls of the fort, dropping her off in a spacious room with a view of the sea.

Meena instantly caught sight of a familiar ship anchored far below. It looked so lonely, anchored past the waves.

Jules lit a candle on his desk as the light was fading. "Stay here as long as you need, Meena," he said. "And come find me as soon as you are ready to join everyone, or if you would like to go home. I can't go losing a princess on my watch." He stopped at the door. "And if you can't find me, surely Ezra will be close."

Meena forced herself to meet his smile. He was being very accommodating, which made it much more difficult for her to hate him.

"Thank you, Captain. I'm sure I'll feel better momentarily." She sank back into the chair with a satisfied sigh.

Jules left, closing the door quietly behind him.

Meena waited a moment, then sprang from her seat. She

went to the window, looking down at the ship below. *I placed him far outside your reach.*

Sol could be on that ship.

She didn't have much time. Neven was likely already on the beach, waiting for the sun to fully set before they put their meager plan into action.

If she was not back in time, she would jeopardize their mission.

But if she succeeded, she could increase their chance of survival. If she could rescue Sol, they would have two Majis instead of one.

Her palms grew sweaty, and she breathed through the lightness in her head.

Meena slipped out of the captain's room and hurried through the halls, looking for the nearest exit.

CHAPTER 33

*M*eena crept through the busy crowd. Fortunately, the townsfolk were too engaged in merriment to even notice her. She kept her head down and stayed close to the shadows. The one time she caught sight of Jules and Ezra, they were dancing with their heads bent close as though deep in conversation.

Meena slipped outside the bailey and made her way toward the gates, walking quickly through the marketplace at the entrance of the city. The vendors were packing their wares, but the area was still quite busy. Everyone was probably making their way to the festival for a free feast.

Soldiers flanked the gate, talking to everyone that entered through it. Meena had forgotten about that.

She slipped into a shadowed alleyway to avoid being seen while deciding what to do.

The soldiers probably didn't know who she was on sight; this wasn't Iseldis. But could she risk leaving the safety of the fort if there were gatekeepers stopping her re-entry? Or would they even let her in if they didn't know who she was?

She exhaled in desperation.

She knew in her heart that she would do anything to reach Sol. She would dive into the ocean and swim across it. She would run up a mountain if that were required to save him.

But there was one thing she could not do.

She would not sacrifice the fate of her kingdom and his people.

She grabbed the rough sandstone on the wall beside her, staring past the soldiers, letting herself imagine for a single moment what it would feel like to see Sol once more.

She could not even rely on Jules's generous offer. No—once she was done with destroying the magic receptacle, Jules would no longer be willing to help her.

Meena exhaled. Despite the pain in her heart, her body felt strangely calm. She had made the right decision.

As she gazed at the open gate one final time, two familiar faces sauntered through it.

Her feet tingled with excitement.

Or perhaps that was just the sifting sand she could feel through her silk slippers.

Either way, luck was handing her another chance. Perhaps it wasn't luck. Perhaps it was the harmony.

Leaning into her own decision before she could second-guess herself, Meena reached out from her place in the shadows and grabbed the arm of the passing sailor.

"Tillon!" she whispered, pulling against him with all her weight until he stumbled off the main road and into the shadowy alleyway with her. "It's me!"

"Curses," the sailor muttered as he struggled to regain his balance.

Meena could see the silhouette of his frame outlined by the torchlit street behind him. He raised his arm, swinging it back to defend himself against the attack.

Perhaps dragging him off the street had not been her finest idea.

"Tillon," she hissed. "It's me. Meena."

His fist remained raised, but the sailor reached toward her in the darkness, deftly grabbing her throat with his free hand. "Who's me?"

Meena threw her head back, instinctively struggling against his grip.

"The princess," she whispered with the last of her breath.

Tillon's hand instantly left her throat. "Princess? Why didn't you say your name?" He put his hands on her shoulders, leaning his face close as if it would help him to see better in the darkness.

"I did. Twice," she replied, rubbing her throat. "It's Meena."

"Right, I guess I just wasn't listening." Tillon sounded embarrassed, and he leaned back to give her some space. "I guess I've been a little jumpy recently."

"Do you have him?" Meena asked, cutting to the heart of her mission. She knew this was a bargain. Just because Tillon had been friendly with her on board the ship did not mean he would be willing to defy those in power to aid her and Sol. But she had to at least try, especially when he'd literally walked right past her.

"Yes," Tillon replied, the embarrassment still in his voice. He seemed to instantly know who she was referring to. "We didn't want to do it, Princess, I promise. But the councilor . . .

we couldn't say no. And we were supposed to lift anchor this afternoon, but then the wind picked up even though the sky was clear, and we couldn't risk another freak storm like last time, especially with that councilor's precious cargo on board."

"I need your help," Meena cut in as soon as her breath returned. "Would you and your crew help me save Sol from Gareth's clutches?" Meena hoped her words conveyed the urgency she was feeling. "I don't have much to offer you, except for the protection of Iseldis. It's a weak offer at the moment, but if you help me bring Sol back to the cove, he can deal a deadly blow to Gareth's power that would tip the scales against him." Meena paused for breath. "And I promise Iseldis will shelter you for as long as we stand against Gareth."

Tillon said nothing.

Meena swallowed nervously, realizing he could reach back out and destroy her here in the dark alleyway. No one knew she was here. He was blocking her exit. And she had just asked him to become a traitor against his king, kingdom, and their most powerful leading ally. "And we'll need you to sail us out to safety later this evening, wind or no wind." Her voice seemed to both squeak and croak. Why was she still speaking? "I understand it's a lot to ask, so if you're not interested, I'll just take my leave." She stepped sideways back against the wall, toward the light of the street.

Tillon's hand on the wall at her shoulder stopped her movement.

She inhaled sharply.

"Princess," Tillon finally whispered. "You don't have to ask twice."

It took a moment before her lungs cooperated enough to

breathe again. And another moment for her mind to realize he was accepting her offer. She exhaled.

"You are sure?" she whispered.

"I've been trying to think up a way to drop Sol off somewhere safe without raising the ire of the king. I was even thinking we could go out as far as the Isle of Exile. As horrible as that would be, surely living there would be better than living as a prisoner of Gareth. But His Highness refuses to speak to me. Which I can't fault, since he is a prisoner on my ship."

"You have to remove the necklace," Meena said, realizing instantly what the issue was. "It's a magic necklace, and it's muting him. He can't remove it himself. Go back to the ship immediately. Remove the necklace. Tell him the plan is still on and take him to the inlet where he directs you. Oh, and let him know that you are the escape route as well. This is a lot to remember—maybe I should come with you." Meena wanted to see Sol so badly it hurt. "No, I still need to play my part. Do you have all this? Can you do it?"

"Free Sol. Remove the necklace. Tell him you love him. Yes, I got it."

Meena lightly slapped the sailor's arm. "Now is not the time for jesting."

"I wasn't jesting," Tillon responded indignantly. "You clearly love him, or you wouldn't be endangering your life to save his."

"Go." Meena pushed him back into the open street, where collided unceremoniously with Esven.

"There you are," Tillon growled. "I just got yanked into a dark alleyway and you walked off without me. It took you this long to even notice I was gone?!"

"Well, you turned out just fine," Esven said, peering over

Tillon's shoulder into the alleyway.

"Come on." Tillon pushed his friend back into the street. "Let's get back to the ship."

"But we just got here," Esven complained. "We haven't even got the food yet."

Meena rearranged her gown around her, listening to the two sailors banter as they went back through the gate.

It felt good to see them again, like they were old friends.

She waited a few more moments before exiting the safety of the dark alleyway.

She wrinkled her nose, blinking away the stinging sensation in her eyes. Sol would want her to protect his people— and hers—before him. She had to trust Tillon and Esven to do their part.

But someone needed to distract the guard on the inside of the tunnel.

And someone needed to make sure Jules and Ezra did not destroy all their hard work. They had been acting especially suspicious all day.

Together, they would stop Gareth before he wrested control of all the kingdoms and wreaked chaos on those who stood in his way.

Slipping out onto the street, she made her way quickly back to the fort.

CHAPTER 34

$\mathcal{B}$ ack at the bailey, Meena slipped through a side entrance, hoping to continue avoiding detection. The sun was almost completely down.

Neven would begin his ascent up the cliffside canyon any moment. Meena had given him very specific instructions on how to find the hidden path up the hill. She had also tried to explain how Sol had used the wind for navigational aid.

Neven had said he would try it.

He would then need to get past the two guards outside the cave entrance and still navigate whatever was inside the caves to find the magic receptacle.

They had been fools to even attempt this. So much could go wrong. But Meena's heart still beat with excitement. This was something she couldn't *not* do.

For her part, she had to get past the kitchen and into the cellars. Then she had to distract the guards on the interior side of the tunnel system. In the most successful scenario, she would distract them, somehow ascertain whether there was a key and acquire it, get through whatever door led into the tunnels, then meet up with Neven and help him find the receptacle.

The most likely scenario was that she would simply distract the guards so they would not notice any sounds behind the door, stalling for time in case anyone—such as Jules or Younn—tried to get to the magic receptacle.

Hopefully Neven could handle finding and draining it. Or better yet, Sol might be with him to help.

Meena knew it was foolish to hope, but she had promised to focus her thoughts on the fun of tonight's adventure. It was the only way fear wouldn't freeze her.

"Princess, you're awake." Ezra's voice sounded from beside her in the dim archway. "Jules said you were resting. Are you feeling alright?"

Confused, Meena couldn't answer immediately. Ezra sounded . . . genuinely concerned about her. "Yes, I am feeling much better," Meena lied. Or, at least, she had been feeling better before Ezra had appeared.

"Would you like to go back to the house?" Ezra asked. "I can have a soldier escort you."

"No—I am feeling fine, really," Meena responded. She couldn't let Ezra send her home.

"Come, grab a drink with me?" Ezra asked. "I feel like we have not gotten to know each other very well. And I was just feeling like we might become great friends." A broad smile filled her face.

Meena leaned closer to the other woman. She knew exactly how this game went. She'd been playing it since she'd arrived in this stifling kingdom. "What game are you play-ing?" she whispered, trying to be as menacing as she could from her shorter height. "I can tell when someone is trying to steer me to their will—it's my own specialty. I play it best. Did your husband send you to distract me? Where is Jules?" She glanced out toward the crowd.

"What's game have I been playing?" Ezra shot back, dropping her sweet facade. "You have the audacity to show up at my house, demanding to be treated like a princess."

"I didn't show up. It's not your house. You stole it. And Councilor Younn set it all up."

"I know it's not, and do you think that doesn't bother me? We couldn't say no to Younn. He wields Gareth's wrath."

"What are you doing here? And where is Jules?" Meena felt more uncomfortable the longer this conversation went on. Somehow, she knew Jules's absence was the key piece to solving the puzzle.

"What are you doing here, Princess?" Ezra shot back.

"I didn't come all this way with a man I didn't know just to be stopped in the end by a power-hungry woman who pretends to love her own husband!" Meena didn't hear the harshness of her words until they were out of her mouth. They had been spoken in anger and frustration, not in jest.

But to Meena's complete surprise, Ezra's face relaxed into an amused smile.

"You've been playing it this whole time, too? Come." Turning on her heel, Ezra beckoned Meena inside the fort itself.

Not even stopping to consider running in the opposite direction, Meena followed Ezra into a more private room.

"Jules and I instantly noticed that you were both suspicious," the woman explained without actually explaining anything. "But you were directly from the royal family, so of course we couldn't trust you."

Meena was still not following. She didn't have time to play games. "Where is Jules?"

"He's on his way to the ship to free your husband Solano —or is it just Sol?"

Meena relaxed, the tension in her body turning to excitement. "To free Sol?"

"We've been waiting for word from our contact in Chendas. We knew a Majis was supposed to arrive soon. And then you showed up and started poking your noses everywhere, and we had to do our best to keep you occupied so you wouldn't interfere at the fort at the same time as the mystery Majis. But this whole time *you* were the Majis. Or your husband was."

"You mean this whole time we could have been helping each other instead of getting in each other's way?" Meena snickered in laughter. "Do you want to do that right now?"

"Get in each other's way?"

"Help each other."

Ezra stared at Meena. Her demeanor no longer looked cold; rather, Meena realized it was thoughtful and focused. Rather like Sol's.

"What did you have in mind?" Ezra asked, smiling conspiratorially.

MEENA FOLLOWED the captain's wife into the fort's kitchen. "Can I have a flagon or two for the princess and myself?"

Two people instantly dropped their current tasks in the busy kitchen to answer their lady's imperious demand.

"Or three!" Meena added.

Ezra smirked, nodding in approval of Meena's request.

Moments later, one of the kitchen boys handed two bottles of wine to Ezra and one to Meena.

"Our thanks," Ezra said, leading Meena through the kitchen. "We are not to be disturbed!" she called over her shoulder as they descended another flight of stairs.

Meena pushed open the heavy wooden door at the bottom, since she had the extra hand.

It opened into a long, low-ceilinged cellar. A few more kitchen hands dashed through the space, carrying cold cuts of meat, dried herbs, and more wine bottles.

Ezra ignored them as she confidently walked through the empty aisle at the center of the room.

Meena matched Ezra's pace and tilted her nose up just a little more than usual to emulate the taller woman's stately grace.

The kitchen hands melted out of their path without a word.

Meena smiled, letting her hips sway as she walked. She felt like a powerful combination of her older brother Ian with his purposeful stride and her new best friend Ezra, who seemed confident in herself.

At the end of the cellar, hidden behind a long stack of barrels, four soldiers sat around a small table. They were engrossed in a game that involved small carved figures on a checkered board.

They looked up instantly as the women walked toward them, but they did not appear intimidated.

Rather, their interest seemed to be piqued by the two women approaching them with arms full of bottles.

"Dalir," Ezra said, nodding to one of the men. "Faithful guards." She nodded to the other three men.

"Lady Levek," Dalir responded.

"It's a pity the four of you are stuck down here while everyone else gets to enjoy the festivities," Meena said.

"Someone has to stay on duty," Dalir said. His eyes were still entirely focused on them, flicking from Meena's face to the bottle in her hands.

"The princess and I would like a few moments to ourselves," Ezra said. "Go grab yourselves something to drink from the feast upstairs."

Four pairs of eyes opened wider. The soldiers glanced between each other. It looked like each one wanted to take Ezra up on her offer, but no one wanted to be the first to say it.

"Please?" Meena said, her voice soft and sweet.

"She is the captain's wife," one of them whispered. "Her word is basically his, right?"

"Precisely," Ezra said, smiling conspiratorially. "Give us an hour—"

"Or two," Meena cut in.

"And no one ever needs to find out," Ezra finished.

"If you insist, Lady Levek." Dalir stood up, and his companions hurried after him.

Meena met Ezra's eyes with a wide-open stare of her own. She wanted to burst out laughing. "That was easier than expected," she whispered instead.

Ezra smiled back at her. A real, genuine smile.

"Let's keep going," Meena said. She pulled at the latch on the door. To her relief, it opened instantly. "I was expecting it to be locked."

"The next one definitely will be," Ezra responded.

"I thought you said you hadn't been down here before?" Meena stepped through the door, pulling it closed behind them.

"I haven't." Ezra had exchanged her bottles of wine for a lantern. "But Jules was here for two days straight when the shipment arrived. There were very specific instructions about securing it."

"How specific?" Meena asked nervously.

"Lots of guards. Definitely locks."

"That's not very specific," Meena replied, disappointed.

Ezra held up the lantern, illuminating a meticulously carved sandstone tunnel.

Meena felt like a child exploring the tunnels under the old castle in Iseldis for the first time. A tingly feeling of anticipation sparked across her skin. She didn't have a map, but she was not afraid to be under the ground. Perhaps it helped that she knew the cliff face was not far away, so it did not truly feel like she was underground.

"If I had known it would be important, I would have paid more attention," Ezra said. "At the time I was rather busy studying how to write in coded symbols."

Meena wanted to ask how Ezra and Jules had been recruited by Robin, but that would have to be a story for another time. "You don't happen to have keys for the locks, do you?"

"No."

"Unfortunate." Meena stepped fearlessly down the tunnel.

"But I might be able to pick the lock," Ezra added.

"Oh!" Meena spun around as she walked to catch Ezra's face behind her. "You'll have to teach me sometime. I never could figure out lock picking."

"Let's see if it works first," Ezra said.

"Which way should we go?" Meena asked, indicating a split in the tunnel ahead.

"There are likely guards at the door itself, so it shouldn't be too hard to find. Let's start with this side."

The chosen branch of the tunnel turned out to be fairly short. It had multiple smaller side rooms filled with additional chests and barrels of storage, as well as a cache of swords, spears, and arrows.

They returned to check the other branch, both remaining as silent as possible.

As they rounded the corner, they could see a faint light up ahead.

Ezra quickly extinguished her lantern. The light was coming around another corner a good distance away.

In complete silence, Meena and Ezra crept down the tunnel. Meena carefully glanced around the corner, then stepped aside so Ezra could do the same.

Two guards sat on a bench at the end of the tunnel. A solid wood door filled the space behind them. Meena could hear the faint sound of their voices echoing down the symmetrical walls of the square tunnel, but she could not hear their specific words.

Remaining out of sight, Meena and Ezra stared at each other for a long moment, not daring to speak and reveal their presence.

Meena's toe silently tapped the ground as she tried to come up with a plan. The ground was rough under her feet.

Leaning down, she used her fingertips to find a few small chunks of rock. That was a start.

Holding the rocks in her fist, she silently mimed her plan to Ezra.

The dim light reflecting off the side of the tunnel was just enough to see each other by.

Ezra nodded and held up a hand, asking Meena to wait for a moment.

She appeared to be deep in thought. Then she looked down at the yellow dress she was wearing. Sending Meena an apologetic grimace, she grabbed at the decorative ribbons that fluttered around her waist creating the illusion of a belt.

With a few gentle tugs, she broke some of them free from their stitching.

Meena nodded, not entirely sure what Ezra was planning.

Ezra nodded at Meena. She was ready.

Spreading her palm wide, Meena positioned a rock on her open palm. Putting her other hand into position, she prepared her fingers and leaned around the corner.

She flicked the rock from her hand. It flew in a beautiful arc, bouncing off the far stone flagstones with multiple resounding echoes.

The two guards instantly jumped to their feet, staring at the wooden door where the sound had originated.

Meena barely held in a scream as her finger instantly stung with pain. She ignored it. Taking advantage of the soldiers' surprise—and turned backs—Meena stepped into the tunnel and threw the larger chunk of rock as hard as she could at the soldier on the left.

The soldiers were turning around, but not fast enough. Meena's rock hit her target on the side of his head, and he fell to the ground stunned.

She flinched, but immediately turned her attention to the other soldier. He was standing completely still, his eyes wide open with shock as he stared at Ezra.

Turning to her companion, Meena heard Ezra let out a low, pained groan. Her hands were held in front of her, palms facing forward, and her head was curled down toward her chest.

"Bind his hands," she said. "Quickly."

The ribbons Ezra had been holding were scattered along the ground.

Meena picked up the longest she could see and ran down the tunnel.

The soldier stood there immobile as she approached.

Within moments, she had his hands bound behind his back. "He's secured," she called.

Ezra dropped her arms, letting out a deep bellow of pain. She sank to her knees, her hands clasping her stomach.

Meena ran back to her friend. "That was magic," she said. "Are you alright?" She reached out to touch Ezra, but the woman held up her hand and shook her head.

"I will be," Ezra said. "I need a moment."

Meena grabbed some more ribbons from the ground at her feet. "I'm going to secure the other before he wakes up."

That had been chaos magic. Ezra didn't have to say it for Meena to recognize it.

Slightly ashamed of herself, Meena felt relieved to be putting space between her and the chaos Quotidian.

She didn't think she was afraid of the woman—Ezra could have taken multiple opportunities to harm Meena, if she had wanted to—but this new knowledge did make Meena uncomfortable.

She kept her eyes on her task while consciously waiting for Ezra to recover.

"Are you alright?" Meena asked again, after the moments had stretched out too long.

Ezra finally sat up. "Getting there, thank you."

Without turning her back fully on the other woman, Meena tested the wooden door. "It's locked."

"I can use chaos magic," Ezra responded.

"I noticed," Meena said.

"That was how I planned on unlocking the door," Ezra explained. She got to her feet and slowly walked the length of the tunnel, keeping her hand on the wall for balance. "I just need a few more moments."

"You drew the magic from chaos inside you," Meena said, watching her approach.

Meena's finger still ached. Rocks were much more painful to flick than acorns. She put her finger in her mouth to dull the pain.

Ezra nodded. "The pain—or fear—can come from anywhere," she explained. "I just no longer draw it from others."

"That's very noble of you?" Meena implicitly believed what Ezra was telling her, and she felt a little angry at herself for accepting it so readily.

"It hurts," Ezra responded.

"I'm sorry." Meena took her finger out of her mouth. Hopefully, that was the only flicking she would have to do tonight. She didn't think her poor finger could take another hit. "But we got past the guards without harming them too badly. I hope."

"Let's finish this." Ezra held her hands in front of her, and a grimace appeared on her face.

Meena stepped away from the door.

Ezra inhaled and closed her eyes, bracing herself against the wall.

The lock on the door clicked.

As the door swung open of its own accord, Meena realized that Ezra had not yet exerted any power.

Someone was pushing through the other side!

Jumping in front of her vulnerable friend, Meena raised her hands to protect them from more soldiers.

CHAPTER 35

*F*ully expecting another pair of guards, Sol swung the door open and readied his magic to sing them to sleep.

Meena stood facing him in the doorway, her hands also held defensively in front of her.

Time froze for a single second while he stared into her shocked brown eyes. They sparkled with joy as she registered his face. She threw her raised fists into the air above her head and opened her mouth as she inhaled.

"Sol!" she shrieked, throwing herself at him and wrapping her arms around his neck.

He caught her instinctively. But as soon as she moved, he saw Ezra standing behind her.

Sol swung Meena around to his side, holding her slightly behind him with one arm. "She's a chaos Quotidian," he alerted Neven and Jules, the other two members of his party.

Ezra raised her hands above her head in a show of surrender. "Wait—Sol, I'm on your side."

Jules pushed around Sol and Meena, standing in front of his wife and also holding out his hands in peaceful defense. "She's right," Jules said. "She was trained in chaos magic, but she no longer uses it. We are both working with River's Talon like I said. I promise."

Sol did not relax his stance. "She used it on me this morning," he corrected Jules. "Although she didn't use it very well, since the silencing gem turned out to be empty . . . Oh." Sol dropped his defensive gaze. "That was you?"

"I'm sorry I drew upon your pain," Ezra said. "It was the best way to disperse the magic in the gem as quickly as possible."

Sol nodded his thanks. He was grateful for her help, but she used pain to take control. She was his enemy.

"Ezra, you guard the outer entrance." He pointed behind him to a door on the other side of the room. "Jules, go with her." He needed Ezra as far away from the room full of chaos magic as he could get her, and he didn't trust her on her own.

"You can trust her, Sol," Jules replied as if he could read Sol's mind.

Sol shook his head. "Maybe one day, but not right now."

Ezra nodded. "I understand." She walked through the room to the open door, and Jules followed her.

"Neven?" Sol asked.

"I'm still fairly depleted," the older man responded. Neven had spent a large portion of his magic navigating the trail and singing the four guards to sleep. He had also spent a significant portion of his energy climbing the steep terrain.

"Guard the inner door." Sol pointed to the door Meena and Ezra had come from. "We are most likely to be discovered from that side. Go far enough that you'll have time to warn us if someone is coming, but not so far that we can't hear you."

Neven nodded.

"Rest. Refill," Sol said as Neven left the room. "I may need your help soon."

Sol turned back to Meena, who had not left his side. Her eyes traveled the length of the small storage room in awe.

Every part of the man-hewn cavern was completely covered in strings of glass beads. They were in a multitude of colors, mostly shades of blue, and fairly uniform in size. Almost as large as his thumbnail.

Sol had lit the room with a stationary glowing orb, and the glass beads sparkled enticingly in its light.

Meena brought her eyes back to him. "Each of these beads is filled with chaos magic?" she asked.

Sol nodded.

"I thought it would be one large object, like a jewel-encrusted goblet or something. These look so small and insignificant. And beautiful."

Sol had not slept in hours, and he was facing the most dangerous and important task he had ever undertaken. But Meena's unfiltered thoughts filled the aching in his muscles and his mind. He inhaled, soothed by the harmony her presence offered him.

"We don't have much time," he said, reaching for the closest string of beads.

"An hour," Meena said. "Maybe two, but probably less than one."

Sol untied the leather knot at the end of the strand and unstrung a single bead. He did not know how much magic each bead contained. Despite the urgency he felt, he knew better than to attempt draining an entire strand at once.

Holding the bead in his palm, Sol curled both hands loosely around it. He closed his eyes, breathing in deeply to calm himself and access his magic.

With a low hum in his throat, he pushed his own harmony magic into the small bead in his hand.

The magic in the bead pushed back against him, more fiercely than he'd expected.

Sol took another breath, surprised. There was so much pain in this one tiny bead. So much pain that had been channeled through an innocent victim.

Sol felt his eyes sting with tears.

His father had been one of those victims. A part of his father was in this room, perhaps in the very bead he held.

He clenched the bead in his hand.

The part of his father still contained here was filled with pain. His father was a hero. A tall, quiet man who listened carefully and thought strategically. Who had sacrificed his life in the hope that his children might have a better future.

Sol unclenched his fist.

Meena touched his shoulder. "Can I do anything for you?" She must have sensed his sadness.

Sol shook his head. "No." Her calming presence was more important to him than she knew. "Yes," he contradicted himself. "Keep your hand on my shoulder."

Inhaling once again, Sol continued to force his own magic into the bead. Very, very slowly, his magic made a dent in the store of chaos magic.

A crackle of lightning snapped out of the bead as a small portion of the chaos magic left it.

Sol jumped, opening his eyes to see the surprise mirrored on Meena's face.

"That would be the chaos magic dissipating," Sol

explained. He had to take a few more breaths to steady himself before he could channel his own magic again. This time, with each flash of energy that left the bead, Sol felt the tightness around his heart loosen.

He would cleanse this place of his father's pain, of his people's pain.

By the time the bead was empty, Sol was damp with sweat.

He handed the single bead to Meena and drew another off the string. It had taken far more energy and time than he cared to admit to remove the evil magic from the tiny object.

Without his bidding, his eyes swept over the uncountable number of beads strung throughout the room. This would take days.

He had no time to waste. Lifting the second bead, he began the process again, hoping it would be faster as he grew accustomed to it.

He was able to replace the magic in this particular bead at a better pace, but he was breathing heavily by the time he was done. He could also feel his magic store depleting quickly.

He held out the second bead to Meena.

She took it from his hand. "Sol?" Her voice was hesitant. "Will all of them take this long?"

Sol shrugged, wishing he had a positive answer. He picked up the string to slide another bead off it. "It takes a bit of time to get started since each bead is separate. So I don't think I can do it any faster. I'll get through as many as I can, though. Perhaps you should go relieve Neven?"

"What if we ask Ezra for help?" Meena suggested. She squeezed his shoulder with her hand.

Sol looked up quickly.

"She drained the silencing gem of chaos magic, and she said she did it quickly."

Sol shook his head. "She is a Quotidian. We can't hand her a string of chaos magic." He held up the string of beads in his hand.

Meena nodded, but her hand on his shoulder remained firm. "She freed you."

Sol shook his head. His entire body felt tense and exhausted.

"She helped me take out the soldiers."

"She caused me pain," Sol whispered. He was not speaking about the few moments earlier that day, but rather on behalf of every Majis prisoner who had been forced to endure another person's chaos.

"You don't have to do this," Meena responded. "But she did cause herself pain to spare it from the guard." Her hand massaged his shoulder.

"I want to hold her responsible," Sol said, untangling his thoughts from his feelings. "For all of it."

"That is not her burden to bear," Meena said. "And neither is it yours."

Sol exhaled.

"Would you trust me if I could wield chaos magic?" Meena asked.

Sol looked back up, realizing with surprise that he did trust her. Completely.

"I think she's our only chance," Meena continued. "Alone, you can get through maybe thirty or forty beads before they find us. With her, you could potentially empty half this room."

Sol nodded. She was right, but he didn't trust himself to say it.

"The worst will happen either way," Meena continued. "This is far more magic than either of us was prepared for. I don't want to force you into this decision, but if you choose so, she can help us take this power from Gareth forever."

"Yes." He clenched the string of beads in his fist, releasing the tension in his muscles, or at least the tension in one hand. The rest of his body still felt an invisible pressure. "It is a big risk, but it's worth it."

With a quick step forward, he dropped a soft kiss on Meena's forehead. If this was the end, he wished he had a moment to take her in his arms and kiss her for real. But their task came first.

"This wouldn't be an adventure if it wasn't exciting," he whispered, feeling a little reckless despite the logic in their decision.

CHAPTER 36

*A*s Sol brought Ezra back into the cavern, Meena hoped she had not pushed him too hard. He did not have to befriend Ezra, but together they could accomplish far more.

Sol handed a string of the beads to the chaos magic user.

"I can draw the chaos out," Ezra said. "But it still has to go somewhere."

"The small flashes of lightning from the two I did were harmless," Sol responded.

"That was two beads," Ezra responded. She gestured to the rest of the room. "To do the same with the rest at a faster speed would collapse the entire cliffside."

Sol nodded.

Meena bumped her fist against her forehead, recalling the little she knew about the magic.

"Let me siphon this out," Ezra said. "At the very least, we can see how much chaos there is." As she spoke, Ezra held the string of beads in one hand and dropped it slowly into the other. She moved the string in a circular motion until it sat in a comfortable spiral in the palm of her hand.

Tensing her fingers around it without fully closing her hand, she inhaled and dropped her head forward.

Meena could see Ezra's hand start to tremble, the tendons on her forearm standing in stark relief to the rest of her arm.

Ezra then held out her empty hand, opening the palm out flat. A purple orb began to gather in the space above her palm.

Meena instinctively shrank away from it. The glowing sphere reminded her of the curse the mage had used to attack Aden.

Ezra opened her eyes. Her face was calm, but her closed fist and opened palm still trembled slightly. "That's all of it." Her voice was tense but not strained. Since she had drawn the chaos from the orb, she did not have to put herself through pain, only concentration.

"Now what?" Meena asked.

"We have to channel it into something to disburse it," Sol replied.

Aden's curse had been cured when Isa kissed him, offering him a lifegiving love. She'd unknowingly used the power of harmony to cancel the chaos.

"Can you use your harmony magic to cancel the chaos magic?" Meena asked Sol.

"I don't have enough magic to replace," he replied. "I'm already almost out."

"And there's no way we could just carry it out of here?" Meena asked. "And disperse it in the middle of the sea?"

Sol shook his head. "We wouldn't make it halfway to the boat before they captured us all."

"We have to do something with it," Ezra replied.

"And quickly," Meena added.

"Maybe the wind could carry it away?" Sol said.

"How?" Ezra asked.

Keeping his eyes on the purple orb of power, Sol intoned a note in his throat. His face looked both purposeful and peaceful.

A fluttering wind whispered through the enclosed cavern. It circled around Meena, picking up speed.

The hanging glass beads around her clinked lightly as the wind swept by them. As it passed Ezra's outstretched hand, the wind picked up strands of the purple orb, carrying them with it out the open door.

Within moments, the orb was entirely depleted.

The wind left the room.

"That was incredible," Meena said. "I'll handle the beads, Ezra can withdraw the magic, and Sol can summon the wind."

She didn't wait for confirmation before she scooped up an armful of beaded strands.

Handing a new one to Ezra, she swapped it for the magic-depleted strand. Ezra began her process again, and Sol closed his eyes to access his harmony magic.

Meena dropped the empty beads in a specific spot so she could organize them as they went.

The wind rushed through the room around them, playing an ever-constant melody with the hanging glass beads.

Ezra did her part as quickly as possible, keeping Meena on her toes—literally, as she twisted around the small space —passing the strands back and forth.

At first, Meena felt cold as the wind rushed around her, but her body soon warmed from the constant movement.

After a short while, it became clear that the floor would be difficult to navigate if she kept dropping the empty beads. She started re-hanging the empty strands back on their wall hooks. She kept a broad space between the two sets of beads so she would not lose track.

Despite the never-ending strands of beads, they made quick progress through the room.

They were perhaps halfway finished when Jules stumbled in, pressing with all his might against the outgoing wind.

"A storm rolled in," he said. He was dripping wet from head to foot. "It's getting pretty bad."

Sol looked at Meena.

Her watery eyes blinked, so she smiled and blinked a second time.

Sol smiled.

It was a tired, small smile, but she could tell he was laughing at her.

"We can't leave it half finished," he told Jules. "You can wait in here if you want. It's unlikely anyone will be able to scale the cliff if it's as bad as it looks."

Jules nodded and stepped across the room to stay out of their way. Within moments, he was standing next to Meena, helping her pass and organize the strands of beads.

They increased their speed.

Meena worked without thinking until something wet and cold soaked through her slippers. She looked down to see water pouring into the room from the outer tunnel.

"Oh no," Jules said as he noticed the same thing. "It's getting bad out there. That's a lot of rain to have traveled this far inside."

Meena looked up at the final wall. They only had a

quarter of the beads left to drain. They needed to finish quickly.

"Do you think we are causing the storm?" Ezra yelled above the wind and water.

Meena froze. That made sense.

"You're right," Sol said. "The chaos needs to be dispersed somewhere."

"If we keep going, it will only get worse," Meena said. She looked around the room at the flooding floor and remaining beads. "We might be able to carry the rest," she suggested.

Neven burst through the door at the other end of the room. "They're coming," he said, breathless.

Meena ran to the wall of remaining beads and began filling her arms with as many as possible. "Jules, help me. Neven, here too."

Sol and Ezra had already turned toward the door, hands ready in defensive positions.

Councilor Younn burst through the door with a squadron of soldiers behind him.

"Go!" Meena pushed Neven and Jules out the opposite door. They had managed to gather most of the remaining beads. Meena could get the final handfuls herself.

"Stop them!" Younn yelled, his face enraged. He held up his hands to protect himself from the harsh wind.

Meena had the remaining strands in her hands. "Let's go!" She stepped back into the getaway tunnel.

Ezra and Sol kept their bodies facing Younn, but they began to back toward Meena.

"Ezra." Younn sounded shocked. "Why am I not surprised?" He held his hands forward as he spoke, dropping his last word into a high-pitched note. "You cannot steal magic from a magic user, you fools!" he yelled into the wind.

He inhaled, his hands spread wide to the hanging beads.

After a few moments of nothing happening, he looked down at his hands as if expecting them to not be empty. "No!"

He quickly looked back up, seeming to panic as he realized what was happening. Drawing his hands back toward himself, Younn stood taller.

Meena guessed he was going to draw on his chaos—or someone else's, since the beads around him were empty.

Clutching the beads, and now wet and cold from the rain and wind, Meena was tempted to slam the door closed and run down the tunnel to safety. The inflowing water was now powerful enough to hold the door firmly in place. At the very least, it would be very difficult to open the door against the flow.

That was it. She glanced back up. Sol and Ezra were still standing inside the door.

"Now!" Sol yelled.

Clutching the strand of pearls that was already in her hand, Ezra yelled a powerful screech. The wind inside the room had settled since Sol had stopped controlling it. But that just made the thunderous storm outside all the louder. Ezra's high voice carried above the thunder.

Purple ribbons shot from her hands. They wrapped around Younn, immobilizing him. As they continued to stream from Ezra's hand, the ribbons wove through the squadron of soldiers, stopping their movement as well.

Younn breathed heavily despite being unable to move his limbs.

Though she couldn't hear it, Meena could see Younn shape his mouth, preparing to sing again.

He could still access his magic.

"Run!" Meena screamed. "Now!"

Sol had already noticed, but instead of running out the door, he leapt toward Younn while pulling a white ribbon from his pocket and wrapped it around the councilor's neck.

A small jewel dangled from it, but because of Sol's position, the jewel swung over the man's shoulder.

"Ezra," Sol called, tying the ribbon as quickly as he could. "Fill it."

Ezra shrieked again. Meena heard true pain in her loud voice. She was using her own chaos to fill the gem.

Ezra slumped against the wall, her fingers still held out toward Younn.

Meena rushed back into the room, throwing her free arm around Ezra's shoulders to support her.

Younn let out a low rumble, and purple power gathered at his fingertips.

The gem on his shoulder flickered briefly, stopping his voice before he'd finished.

But the purple magic had already gathered at his fingertips, and he shot it forward. It struck out as two bursts of lightning toward Ezra.

Without the time for thinking, Meena used all her weight to pull Ezra straight forward.

She landed on her back with a splash, still clutching the beads in both hands. Water splashed over her face, dripping down her nose and throat. Ezra, already slumped over, landed on top of her as the lightning attack struck the wall where her head had been.

Sol lifted Ezra and half carried, half dragged her to the getaway door.

Meena scrambled after them, pushing off the ground with her hands. Coughing the water out of her lungs, she stopped for a brief moment to slam the door shut behind her with one foot.

It closed with a slam, carried even faster by the momentum of the running water.

Tripping after Sol and Ezra, she dove headfirst into the heart of the storm.

CHAPTER 37

S ol looked back over his shoulder to ensure Meena had made it out of the room. He couldn't grab both of them, but he trusted her more than Ezra to get out on her own.

He was far too familiar with the pain Ezra had just put herself through. And he was also familiar with how fearlessly and energetically Meena always tackled whatever problem was in front of her.

Sure enough, she was right behind him, slamming the door closed with her foot.

A brilliant idea. The running water would buy them some precious minutes.

He had no idea how long it would take for the chaos ribbons to loosen their grip on the squadron of soldiers.

Younn would not be able to remove the silencing necklace by himself, but it would not take him long to get someone to take it off for him.

As they exited the tunnel, the full force of the wind and

rain hit Sol in the face. He bowed his head forward, trying to protect Ezra from the onslaught.

Thunder boomed overhead, and he flinched even though it was not unexpected. The explosive sound shook the earth below his feet and reverberated through his body.

Jules, with his arms full of beads, was waiting down the first bend of the trail. Even through the rain pouring down the man's face, Sol could see the concern in his eyes for his wife.

Sol reached out for the beads so Jules could support Ezra.

Fortunately, moving down the path was faster—even if it was more terrifying—than climbing up it. Even if they stumbled, they would still end up closer to their goal.

The storm whipping at their faces and drenching their clothing also ensured that it would be difficult for Younn and his men to pursue them.

Eventually, they caught up with Neven and then with Tillon, who was waiting near the bottom of the path closer to the beach.

Esven waited on the shore with the small rowboat.

Ezra appeared to be walking on her own again.

The blue shimmer in the waves looked strangely out of place in the chaos of the storm.

Tillon helped Neven load his armful of bead strands into the bottom of the boat. Sol added his to the pile and turned around to take Meena's final few handfuls.

Jules helped Ezra over the side of the boat and jumped in after her. Sol held his hands around Meena's waist as she swung her sopping-wet skirts over the side of the boat before climbing in herself.

Sol watched the cliff behind them, scanning it for any movement or light.

If their pursuers had escaped the tunnel, he could not see them through the pouring rain.

The small boat was full, but Sol swung himself over the edge and crouched next to Meena, huddling close to her for warmth.

He had spent every hour as Younn's prisoner wishing he could wrap his arms around this woman one more time.

She leaned into his touch.

Esven and Tillon pushed the boat into deeper water and jumped on board themselves. They sat precariously near the edge, using their oars to maneuver the small bouncing boat through the choppy waves.

"Ezra," Sol called. "Can we start emptying these beads now?"

"If this storm can get any worse, I don't want to see what it looks like," she replied. Despite her negative response, she leaned forward and picked up a strand of beads.

"Release it directly into the cliffside," Sol said.

Ezra drew the power out of the beads and flung her hand forward, releasing the purple orb into the night.

It flashed through the air, touching down like lightning on the other side of the canyon, away from the fort.

The bright flash illuminated every drop of water in the sky, temporarily blinding him. The blue light glowing from the waves erupted explosively in the tumultuous water.

Ezra handed the empty beads to Meena.

Undoing the knot, Meena tossed the glass beads into the ocean, one by one.

Ezra continued, sending the chaos magic straight into the land around the fort. She never hit it directly, but the strikes caused an astonishing amount of damage around the structure.

Each flash of light revealed tumbling rocks bouncing down the cliffside, landing in flurries of sand, and splashing into the sea.

This, in turn, caused the sea to flare brightly with blue light just in time for another lightning strike to hit.

Sol clung to Meena, watching in awe as the world exploded around them in chaos and beauty combined.

CHAPTER 38

*M*eena held on to the knotted rope ladder as she climbed from the boat to the ship.

Ezra had emptied all the beads.

They had made it safely back to the ship.

Gareth's secret source of power had been destroyed.

And best of all, she had her arms wrapped around Sol, her husband. At least for the moment.

The sea tossed and turned underneath the ship, pitching it in every direction and throwing them around the slippery deck.

The sailors helped everyone get safely to the lower deck, but Meena nudged Sol toward their small cabin.

Just as they stepped through the door, the ship tossed them forward. They stumbled onto the small bed, laughing and crying and clinging to each other.

Straightening up in the darkness, Meena kept one hand on Sol and used the other to search the dark cabin wall for the handhold that had kept her steady during the last storm.

This time, however, she managed to laugh at the strange sensations in her stomach as the ship rose and fell beneath her. She'd been through a storm before, and Sol would ensure they got through this one as well.

Sol.

At the moment, he was sitting at her side, one arm around her back to keep his hand on the wooden support as well.

"I knew you could do it," he said, his voice tickling her ear.

"Do what?" Meena asked, knowing exactly what he referred to.

"Lead." Sol kissed the side of her head.

"Then why didn't you give me more responsibility in the beginning?" Meena asked, half jesting but also half serious.

"I didn't know you wanted it," Sol replied.

Meena twisted to the side so she could face him in the darkness. "On the second day I knew you, I literally dragged you around the castle grounds with a hand-drawn treasure map. I think it should have been very clear from the beginning that I would make the best cypher."

"I guess I will just have to spend the future paying better attention."

Meena inhaled, trying to find his eyes. "It's too dark," she whispered.

She felt Sol move his arm. He stilled for a moment, then exhaled. "My magic store is completely depleted," he said.

"Oh." Meena shifted her wet skirts around her legs. Now that she was no longer moving, the water was making her cold. "Oh!" she repeated. "I still have these." She pulled two beads from her pocket and transferred them to Sol's hand in the darkness. "These are the first two you did, that you put harmony into. Can you use that?"

Her answer was a soft orb of light, floating in the air between them.

Meena looked back up at his face. His wet hair was plastered to his forehead, and his face looked tired. Exhausted, really. But his eyes were still and green in the warm light of the magic orb. There was no storm in them.

"What was that you were saying about the future?" Meena asked. Her words were not flirtatious but honest. Coy but not shy. They had just faced death together and survived.

"I was just looking forward to spending it with you," he said. "If you'll have me."

Meena smiled, letting his words wash over her.

She put her hand on his chest, feeling the warmth of his skin through the wet layers of clothing. She wanted nothing more.

Or, rather, she wanted one thing more.

"Sol," she whispered. "Our task is done. Against all odds, we have succeeded. This marriage was a ruse from the beginning." She inhaled as tears stung her eyes.

She blinked them away.

"I will not hold you to it for the rest of your life." Her hand slid up to his cheek. "I could never hold you down."

Sol's eyes melted, and he looked at her with an intensity that awed every muscle in her body and set her heart on fire.

"Will you marry me?" he asked. The intensity in his eyes was exactly what she had always dreamed to see. It was direct and powerful and all-consuming. And it was entirely focused on her. But it was also different. More peaceful. Calm.

"We're already married," she replied, tilting her face closer to his. Wanting to be closer to him.

She was no longer cold. They had spent the last several days in close company with each other, but this time it was different.

This time, Meena's heart was racing just like the other times. But her breath was normal. Her arms were warm and comfortable, not tingling with nervousness. She wanted to step into this moment he was offering her. It felt right.

"No—we had a wedding before," Sol replied. "A marriage only happens when two people choose to give themselves to each other, in love." His arms pulled her closer to him, holding her steady as the boat rocked ferociously beneath them.

Meena smiled, relaxing into his touch. "I meant the words I said at our wedding," she said, looking up at him through her eyelashes. "I gave myself to you in love then."

"Don't jest with me, Meena mine. You didn't know me well enough to love me then." He nudged her forehead with his own, tilting her face up toward him.

"I knew you well enough to like you." Meena turned her face to the side, cheekily avoiding his incoming kiss.

"Do you love me now?"

There it was. The shivering sensation ran up her neck as her stomach filled with butterflies. She turned back to face him. "Yes." She wasn't whispering. Her voice came out loud and clear.

Sol smiled, transforming his face.

"You are stronger than sunshine, Meena," he replied. "I love you."

Meena eagerly accepted his kiss. "I love you. So much." It

felt so wonderful to say the words that had long been in her heart. "I've loved you for days."

"Days?" Sol replied.

Meena nodded. "I loved you first."

"Is this a competition?" Sol asked.

"Yes." Meena smiled.

Sol woke from his sleep to find a head of sleek, dark hair tangled over his arm.

The ship rocked calmly in peaceful waters, and sunlight streamed through the cracks under the door.

He didn't want to move, though, because he didn't want to disturb Meena.

His Meena.

He inhaled, nestling her closer as he shifted to a more comfortable position. They had fallen asleep while the storm still raged.

His hand tingled numbly, looped as it still was through the bar of wood to hold them steady through the night.

He slipped his hand free, flexing his wrist as sensation returned to his fingertips.

Meena sighed in her sleep, pressing her face close to his chest as if to block out the light. But she did not wake up.

Sol smiled.

Here he was, literally held down by the woman he'd chosen to be his family. And he felt more free than ever.

The future loomed dangerously overhead—their actions had just catapulted the long-brewing tension into an actual war.

But he felt free to move into the future. He didn't want to waste it by cutting himself off from the people around him.

If he and Meena had decided to part ways, it would have crushed his heart. But it also would have been worth it.

The brief time he had spent with her made him feel like a whole person. And he was thankful for that.

He was thankful for a future in which he had something to hold on to.

LADY OR MAID

 *en Years Earlier:*

ROBIN UNSTOPPED HER FLASK, shaking the final splash of water into her mouth. She would need to refill at their next stop.

"I hate donkeys," Lind muttered behind her for the seventeenth time.

Robin did not respond to her lady's maid. Instead, she leaned forward, patting the thick neck of her stocky mount. "She does not mean that," Robin whispered to the plodding animal.

The donkey shook its head happily in response to Robin's soothing touch. Humphrey might not have the elegant features of a horse, but he did have the sweetest disposition of any animal—or person—Robin had ever encountered.

"Just imagine . . ." Lind's tone instantly switched from

complaining to excited. "You get to spend Silverfest at the palace of Iseldis! Surely the venison pies they serve to the king himself will be bursting!"

"Mhhh," Robin replied, her tongue sticking to the top of her mouth. Not even the thought of a savory meat pie could lift her spirits. She swallowed drily, willing away the tears that nipped at her eyelids.

"Will you save me some?" Lind asked, pressing her mount closer to Robin's.

"What?" Robin blinked, forcing a quick smile.

"Will you save me something from the feast?" Lind asked again.

"Have I ever failed you?" Robin teased, this time with a genuine smile. "But if the king can afford the kind of feast you've been describing for the last twelve miles, surely he'll also be providing something sumptuous for the palace staff?"

Lind's eyes clouded over as her mount slowed, falling behind. "Perhaps. But I do not know that every lord is as generous as your dear father was, my lady."

Robin's smile faded. Her parents had been exceptional in most ways before a sudden sickness claimed them both. At fourteen years of age and with no other relatives, Robin had found herself quite alone in the world.

"You are ever so lucky, my lady," Lind continued, "to be the ward of King Frederich himself. I'm sure many others would kill to be in such a position."

Her maid was only trying to cheer her, but lucky was not the word Robin would have chosen. She was lucky to have spent her childhood roaming Lockwood forest with her herbalist mother. She was lucky to have had a father who allowed—and even encouraged—her to ride and hunt, to learn swordplay and archery. Robin twitched her nose as it suddenly burned.

"Oh, Robin." Lind dug her heels into the side of her lagging donkey, urging it forward. "I did not mean to make you sad again. Things are changing for the better now. Think of all the new velvet gowns and furnishings and delicious foods you'll get to have! Your father did his best, but you won't have to worry about harvestreign taxes draining the holdings or re-dying old dresses to mark you as a lady instead of a mere farmer's daughter like me."

Robin forced another smile, though the weight on her chest was still heavy. "I won't be missing turnip root mash, that's for sure."

Lind grimaced. "Neither will I. Ugh." She scrunched her nose, abruptly changing the subject. "Why does Lumpy always smell so foul?"

"It's Humphrey." Robin sighed. Personally, she found the warm, earthy aroma rather comforting. She preferred Humphrey's mild temperament, steady plodding, and low profile. Donkeys were less expensive to care for than horses and worked twice as hard, so her father had sold their best horses some years ago when early frosts were decimating their crops. It was one of many small sacrifices he'd made for his people.

"I do hope the crown prince isn't there to welcome us immediately. I imagine if he saw you riding in on a donkey, he would never even consider a betrothal with you!" Lind giggled.

Robin inhaled, turning toward her maid. "I'm the king's ward, Lind, nothing more." She kept her tone both firm and gentle.

"Ah, my lady, I was only teasing," Lind replied. "You know

what they've always said since your fathers were such close friends. Imagine how happy Lockwood would be if one of their own was on the throne."

Robin shook her head. As much as she appreciated Lind's cheerful presence, she would prefer to live with her parents in their poor forested holding than marry the crown prince.

The two men traveling as her escort pulled their mounts to a stop up ahead near a stream.

Robin gratefully reined Humphrey in as well. Her whole body was stiff from riding all day and despite Humphrey's short height, she did not relish the thought of having to remount him if she dismounted.

Lind had slid off her mount the second they stopped moving.

"Could you refill my flask?" Robin asked her maidservant.

"Oh, Robin," Lind sighed, sinking into the frosted grass at the side of the road. "I don't think my legs will be the same again."

Robin had spent many days traveling beside her father to visit their rural tenants, and she was more accustomed to the saddle than her maidservant. "I'll get it then," she said, sliding off Humphrey. "Does yours need to be refilled?"

"You are too kind, my lady," Lind responded, handing over her own flask.

When she remounted Humphrey some moments later, Robin groaned silently. Surely King Frederich would hardly let his ward out of the castle, much less ride through the forests upon a donkey.

"My lady," Lind said as they continued down the worn dirt road, "I've been trying to cheer you up all day, and I know you are nervous that the palace life won't suit you. I'm sure it will when you give it the chance, but, in the meanwhile, I just might have an idea."

Robin turned toward her.

"What if . . ." Lind lowered her voice conspiratorially, pressing her mount even closer until the poor donkeys were nearly tripping over each other. "What if we led them to believe that I am Lady Robin Lockwood?"

Robin froze, unsure what her maid was implying. "What are you saying?"

Lind exhaled quickly. "I'm saying . . ." Her voice had risen in exasperation.

"Hush!" Robin warned, glancing ahead at their escorts. "Keep your voice down."

"If you pretend to be me," the maid continued, bringing her voice back to a whisper, "you could enjoy some freedom in Iseldis before locking yourself into this new life."

"That's impossible." Robin immediately shook her head. "How would that even work? I've never been a lady's maid before, and we could not keep up such a deception indefinitely. How would we switch back? What would the king do?"

Despite her resistance, Robin felt a small flicker of hope in her lonely heart. What if she could be free for just a little while longer? Free to do whatever she liked, just as she had always done.

"I would cover for you, of course," Lind responded to the first of her questions. "You've always been so kind to me. Once you feel comfortable with the royal family and have had a chance to explore the city freely, we could explain everything. Call it a safety measure that your mother requested on her deathbed to ensure you were treated properly, and not shunned or forgotten."

Robin slowly nodded, her mind suddenly filled with all the ways in which this tantalizing dream could become a possibility. "But . . . but your hair?"

As was most common in Iseldis, Lind's thick hair was a glistening raven black.

"I was presented to the king and queen when I was a child," Robin continued. "My father said they continually marveled over my golden hair. If they remember anything about me, it would be that."

Lind shrugged. "I'll say I dyed it so as not to outshine Princess Meena." She looked at Robin's fair locks. "And we'd better coat yours with coal dust so you do not stand out."

Robin pinched her lips. She had not yet consented to this wild plan, but she let her maid's words lie uncontested.

WALKING down the hall to his castle room, Ian reenacted a dramatic lunge with his wooden sword. "You didn't even see that one coming, did you?" he said, gleefully referring to a recent sparring session with his younger brother.

"No, no. I did see it," Onric protested. "I was just trying to block with it a clever parry instead of head-on as the captain showed us. It almost worked, too."

Ian heard the frustration in his little brother's voice. "That would have been a smart defense," Ian responded. As the crown prince of Iseldis, he had been taught to always be gracious—at least out loud. The confident swagger of his walk remained even as he praised Onric's attempt at defense.

"She's here!" Princess Meena crept out of her room, whispering in a loud hiss as the older boys walked by.

Ian stopped abruptly. "Already? Why are you hiding from her?"

Meena scrunched her small nose. "She said I was cute."

"What's wrong with that? It's true," Onric blurted out, not seeming to notice that their only sister was quite upset.

Ian chose not to point out that the six-year-old girl was wearing an airy purple dress with an enormous ribbon tied atop her loose dark curls.

"It was the way she said it," Meena defended, still whispering as her eyes glanced toward the door at the end of the hall. "I don't like her."

"She can't be all that bad," Ian responded, hoping Meena was wrong. The Sirilian siblings were a close-knit family, but as children of the king, they rarely found friends who would treat them as equals. They were all excited to welcome a fresh new face into their inner circle—especially since it was a girl. Although, Ian knew better than to mention that last part in front of his younger brother. He would never hear the end of it if he did.

"She squeals," Meena declared before twirling around and slipping back into her room, slamming the door behind her.

"Shall we go meet her?" Ian asked his brother.

Twelve-year-old Onric had his eyes warily glued to the far door. "I don't like girls. And I especially don't like girls who squeal."

Ian nodded, pretending to agree with his brother's assessment. He was not sure he had ever met a girl who squealed, but he guessed he wouldn't like it too much. Secretly, he hoped she was pretty.

"Come on," he repeated. "Let's go meet her."

"Ooh!" The girl's squeal was so loud when the two brothers opened the door to the family salon that Ian visibly flinched.

At least he hadn't covered his ears as Onric had done.

"You must be Prince Ian and Prince Onric," she said, dropping into a dramatic curtsy. "It's so good to see you again after all these years!"

"Lady Lockwood," Ian responded, bowing his head lightly. "Welcome to your new home. I am so sorry to hear about the loss of your parents."

"You are too kind, my prince," she said, smiling up at him.

She was not un-beautiful, Ian decided, though he felt that her smile was too . . . elated. Perhaps her parents had not been as kind as his own. "Please, call me Ian."

"Ooh! Thank you." She turned toward Onric expectantly.

Ian's younger brother was openly scowling when he dropped his hands from his ears after her second squeal. "Do we have to call you Lady Lockwood?" Onric asked. "That seems a bit . . . generous."

Ian jabbed Onric's side, a little harder than necessary. Since they were still wearing their padded sparring armor, Onric probably couldn't even feel it.

The new girl glanced between them, her broad smile still plastered to her face.

Ian felt his hopes begin to fade. "Let's go clean up before supper," he said to Onric.

"Could you escort me to dinner, my prince?" the girl asked, dropping her large eyes and blinking rapidly. "I'm afraid I'll get lost in this large castle."

"Ian, please," he repeated. Something about the way she said "my prince" irked him. Perhaps Meena was right. He did not want to make a snap judgment of this girl, but in less than a hand's length on the sundial she had come across as thoroughly annoying. "Of course, Lady Lockwood. Though I'm sure you'll find your way around soon enough."

No matter that they had several staff members who could have easily shown her the way to the dining hall. He knew when graciousness was expected of him. "I'll wait for you outside your room."

"Ooh! Thank you!" She nearly danced out the door.

"Meena was right," Onric said, hardly waiting until the girl was out of earshot. "I plan on never speaking to her again."

Ian nodded, envious of the fact that his younger brother did not have to act like a mature fourteen-year-old crown prince.

"Have fun escorting her—" Onric started to taunt, but Ian quickly cut him off.

"Who's that?" he said, distracting his brother as he gestured toward the window.

In the private courtyard just below the family room, a young girl stood next to a drowsy donkey. She was holding its reins in one hand, but her attention was fixed on the stone walls around her.

Ian squinted to get a better look at her upturned face. He did not recognize her, though he prided himself on knowing all the members of the palace staff. He wanted to be a kind and just ruler like his father.

The girl's expression was difficult to read. She seemed both uncomfortable with her surroundings and also unimpressed.

"How should I know?" Onric replied, peering out the window. "Probably a new servant or farmer's daughter dropping off vegetables for the kitchen."

"If she was from a farm, she wouldn't be in the private courtyard," Ian pointed out.

"It's just some girl." Onric shrugged.

If she was a new servant, she was not acting like it. All the servants Ian had ever seen were either rushing around with focused intensity or chatting in a corner with their friends. This girl was standing in the center of the courtyard, not seeming to mind that there were people busily traversing it and that she was blocking their way.

"Maybe I should go talk to her and see if she's lost," Ian said.

Onric snickered. "Look at Ian on the chase, can't resist a pretty face," he chanted.

Ian punched his little brother on the shoulder.

Onric punched him back.

Ian didn't feel a thing through his padded armor, though he suddenly felt quite warm. "I hadn't even noticed she's pretty. But now that you say it . . ."

Onric punched him again.

"Fine, fine. I'm sure she can find her own way through the castle, whoever she is. Let's go get out of this obnoxiously warm armor."

THE NOVELLA, *Lady or Maid,* is available as an ebook on Amazon.

ABOUT THE AUTHOR

Emily Deady grew up as an avid reader who hated writing. One day she realized that most authors loved cats and tea, her two favorite things. So, she stopped fighting the inevitable and she began to write. Her stories contain a generous helping of romance with a sprinkle of magic.

She loves growing things in dirt, brewing lightly roasted oolongs, chatting with her real-life hero who patiently listens to all her plotlines, and hitting the trails for a hike in sunny San Diego.

Visit her website to connect with her directly and sign up for her email newsletter list (where she has a tendency to give away free stories.)

~

www.emilydeady.com

CPSIA information can be obtained
at www.ICGtesting.com
Printed in the USA
BVHW031425140623
665887BV00007B/783

9 781734 986570